MW00892090

"Also by the Author"

THE BARRELMAN

A thirty-five year history of the Denver Bronco Football
Club, as seen through the eyes of the 12th man—
the fan. 1992, Kendall Hunt Publishing

A PINCH OF DRY MUSTARD, 2009, Trafford Publishing

Child of Dreams

*...a fictitious story of two women
with physical disabilities*

a journey of a
thousand miles begins
with the first step

Barbara Roose Cramer

Barbara Roose Cramer

Order this book online at www.trafford.com
or email orders@trafford.com

Most Trafford titles are also available at major online book retailers.

Printed in the United States of America.

ISBN: 978-1-4907-4185-7 (sc)
ISBN: 978-1-4907-4187-1 (hc)
ISBN: 978-1-4907-4186-4 (e)

Library of Congress Control Number: 2014912555

Trafford rev. 07/17/2014

 www.trafford.com

North America & international
toll-free: 1 888 232 4444 (USA & Canada)
fax: 812 355 4082

For my parents who inspired me to succeed

To dream the impossible dream,
To fight the unbeatable foe,
To bear with unbearable sorrow,
To run where the brave dare not go.

To right the unrightable wrong,
To love, pure and chaste from afar,
To try when your arms are too weary,
To reach the unreachable star,

Joe Darion, Mitch Leigh

CHILD OF DREAMS

A morning mist settles over the field
A fence surrounds it
Built of brick and stone
There's a lock on the steel gate, black and rusting with age
A child wants in
A child with steel and leather against flesh and bone
Flesh and bone, warm with life, unused, untouched for years
Beyond the fence, grass, weeds and
Yellow daisies
Magically, the gate opens
The child enters
This place where dreams come true
This place of beauty
Where there is no sickness, no disease
This is a place to run
To play
While catching raindrops in her mouth
She jumps over the puddles
Birds sing here
The child runs on legs of iron
No longer encased in steel
Her golden hair blows and she soars
The air fills her nostrils
And leaves her breathless
She skips over the daisies
The mist is gone
The child is free
There are no more locks on the gate

Introduction

After being strapped down to the steel plate in the ground, and as pouring rain beat down upon her, she readied herself for her first throw. She first closed her eyes and thanked God for allowing her to be at the Paralympics.

As she was handed the shot put and she looked straight ahead, she saw the small, orange flag flowing freely at the international record mark. She placed the implement in her right hand, grabbed the back of her wheelchair's push handle with the left, looked up to the sky and saw a small red bird flying high in the blackened, rain filled sky. She placed her eyes on the bird, and with a deep breath and then a grunt, she let the shot put fly as if to hit the free-flying bird. The shot put soared just like that red bird, and landed three inches past the record marker. She had done it. She had reached her goal. Jennifer Collins was a Paralympic gold medalist. Her dream had come true, and she thanked God.

Prologue

The eradication of **Polio** from the western hemisphere in the late 1970's was among the most significant public health achievements of all time. It was a crippling and potentially deadly infectious disease caused by a virus that spread from person to person, invading the brain and spinal cord. Vaccination is the best protection and keeps the disease from spreading. The disease, however, has never been completely eradicated in countries like Afghanistan, Nigeria and Pakistan and is once again spreading throughout Syria, Cameroon and the Horn of Africa, due in part to no vaccine available to those living there.

Barbara Roose Cramer, author of "**Child of Dreams**" contracted both spinal and bulbar polio, meaning that the virus invaded the motor neurons of the spinal column, infecting the muscles, and therefore causing paralysis of the right side of her body and from her waist down. Bulbar polio, which only affected about 2% of those with paralytic polio, is caused when the virus invades and destroys the nerves within the bulbar region of the brain stem, causing difficulty in breathing, speaking and swallowing. She currently suffers from post-polio-syndrome. PPS, as it is often called. It is a condition that comes with aging, overuse of the neuron units or serious illness, and causes fatigue and extensive muscle weakness.

Mrs. Cramer's story takes place, in part, in the early years of her life when polio was an epidemic across the United States, and she became a victim of the horrific disease. She attempts to share some of those challenges with the reader, i.e. when there was no vaccine, patients living in iron lungs and the many people who succumbed to the disease. Most of all, she shares her story of a successful career, a wife and a mother. As the story in "**Child of Dreams**" progresses, Mrs. Cramer has chosen to "fast-forward" to the Twenty-First Century to tell the rest of her story, part in fiction. Her disability and the challenges that come with a disability, her marriage, being pregnant and giving birth four times and the dream to win paralympic gold are true facts.

Chapter One

As Continental Airlines Flight #789 began it's descent over Buffalo Springs, Colorado, Jill Goodwell-Casey looked first at her husband of only a few hours, Tom, who was sleeping soundly in the seat next to her. She peered out of the window of the giant aircraft that carried her and Tom, and approximately 415 other passengers to their destination. The flight had departed from Portland International Jetport in a serious thunderstorm with severe lightning. Although the rain had subsided throughout the flight, the skies remained cloudy and overcast. The flight had been lengthy, and, although she tried to sleep, she could not make herself relax. As she watched the city taking shape below her, she closed her eyes for a moment to recall the last twenty-four hours.

She and Tom had boarded the plane in Portland, Maine at 6:30 a.m. after only a few hours of sleep. Their wedding had taken place in Booth Bay Harbor, Maine, at the beautiful Our Lady Queen of Peace Catholic church, at 3:00 p.m. the previous day. Jill's mother, Loren, dressed in a light blue organza knee length dress, had been her maid of honor, and Tom's friend, Darin Van Gordon, had stood beside him as best man. Both lieutenants in the Coast Guard, they had worn their dress white uniforms. Jill had been stunning—everyone said so—in her white organza strapless gown, with a sweetheart trumpet train. Her hair, which had grown much longer in the past year, had been set in an up-sweep with a beautiful headpiece of pearls and clear crystals, attached to an elbow length, three-layered beaded veil. She had felt like Cinderella and, after the reception at the Booth Bay Harbor Inn where 300 family members and friends had joined in the celebration, Tom had made her feel like a real queen as they made love over and over in the comfy king size bed at the Inn.

Tom had carried her across the threshold into the bridal suite, kissing her as he did so. She chuckled as he set her down on the bed and started to kiss her again, first on the cheek, then on the neck and then softly on the lips. She had stopped him from proceeding further, stating that she had a surprise for him and had immediately retreated into the bathroom.

There she had taken off her beautiful gown, hung it up carefully on a white satin-covered hangar, touching it gently before hanging it over the shower rod. She removed the rest of her white under garments and opened up her overnight case. She took out a sexy sheer black negligee, a black garter belt, black stockings and black high heels. Making love was not new to Jill and Tom. They had been intimate during most of their relationship, but this was her wedding night and she wanted it to be extra special. They had abstained from having sex for the past two months— much to Tom's dismay—so as to be much more desirable to one another on their wedding night. She had been planning this surprise for weeks.

Jill opened her eyes, realizing that instead of landing, the plane seemed to be circling the airport, and she wondered if there was trouble with the aircraft. She had been so busy reminiscing that she had not heard any messages from the captain. She glanced over at Tom, who hadn't stirred, and decided to wait for an announcement. Fifteen minutes went by, and finally the oft-spoken words of "this is your captain speaking" came over the intercom system of the aircraft.

"Ladies and gentleman", he said, "this is Captain Ray Waters. We don't want to alarm you, but there has been a minor mishap at the Buffalo Springs Airport, and we have been asked to circle for another fifteen minutes or so, after which time we should be able to land and get you all to your destinations safely. Please do not be alarmed, it is a minor incident, and the runway is being cleared as I speak, but please do keep your seat belts securely fastened. It's raining here, so hopefully you brought your rain gear."

He thanked everyone for their attention, and things seemingly returned to normal.

Jill closed her eyes once again and, smiling, thought back to the previous night.

She had vainly looked at herself in the full-length bathroom mirror and smiled at what she saw. She had taken the pins from her brownish blond hair, fluffed it up with her hands, letting it fall over her slim shoulders. She placed a small amount of her favorite perfume, Crystal Passion, in a couple of sexual hot spots, turned off the bathroom light, and walked into the bridal suite.

"Here I come, ready or not," she said in a sexy voice.

She walked across the room in a sexy strut and got onto the bed where Tom still lay fully clothed.

"Oh my gosh!" he exclaimed, eyes wide open, looking up at this full-bodied, sexy woman. "Is this the woman I just married or some call girl sent over by the Paris Point Escort Service? Wow Jill, you're gorgeous!"

"Just who would you **like** me to be Lieutenant?" She asked, kissing him on the cheek, then kissing his nose his lips, and, then, as she had so many times before she took his Lieutenant's cap off the end table and placed it atop her head.

"I can be either one", she said, batting her baby blues at him and pulling up the long black negligee to her waist. She got to a sitting position on top of him, placing her legs to either side of his chest. He touched her face, then her breasts, as she began to unbutton his white Coast Guard jacket, his shirt, and his pants. She kissed his chest, tongued his nipples and kissed him on the lips as she began helping him out of his clothes.

Jill jumped just slightly when the captain's voice again came over the aircraft's intercom. As she listened to the deep voice she felt a moment of disappointment for the interruption and that she wasn't able to finish the rest of her mental replay of the night before. She smiled and chuckled, as she looked over at Tom and gently shook him on the shoulder. As she awakened him, she was thinking about what surprises tonight's stay in the bridal suite might hold. She leaned over him and lightly kissed his cheek.

"We've been cleared to land," the captain said. "Please make sure your seat belts are securely fastened and your luggage is placed securely under your seats. I'm sorry for the delay. If any of you have connecting flights we will do our best to see that you make those flights on time. Once again, thank you for flying Continental Airlines."

Jill looked at her handsome husband, his dark black hair in disarray. She took his hand, leaned over and gave him another peck on his right cheek.

"We've arrived, Lieutenant Casey," she said smiling.

"What time is it, Jill?" he asked somewhat groggy. "How long have I been asleep?"

"It's honeymoon time, sleepyhead", she said kiddingly. "We were delayed a few minutes, but we're safely on the ground now. It's raining pretty hard so let's hope our rental car is available and we get our luggage quickly. The Sky City Hotel bridal suite is calling our names."

Tom unbuckled his seatbelt, stood up and, as he looked at his beautiful wife, he thought, "I have loved her from the very first time I saw her coming off that cruise ship in Portland, and I will love her for the rest of my life." He smiled as he assisted her to a standing position, then embraced her, kissing her lovingly.

"I love you, Mrs. Casey", he said to her, his eyes twinkling, oblivious to all the passengers around them, "are you ready for the next ten days?"

"I am Mr. Casey, sir!" she said saluting him. "I certainly am."

Chapter Two

The parking garage attendant at the Sky City Hotel waved the newly weds, Mic and Jennifer Collins through the parking gate, gave them a parking pass, and noticing the handicapped license plate directed them to an empty space close to the elevators. He also took down their license plate number and vehicle description.

'There is an empty and wide space right over to the left", he said cordially and added, "Nice Chevy". He chuckled as he read all of the gibberish written on the windows of their beautifully restored blue and white 1957 Chevrolet. "Love Forever", "Have a Hot Night In Buffalo Springs", "Jennifer loves Mic" and more. Jed Manning, the parking garage attendant, thought how sweet young love must be. He and Joyce had been married almost thirty years when she had passed on, and he remembered, yes, young love had been sweet for them once too, but that was a long time ago.

Jed Oliver Manning had been working at the Sky City Hotel for a little over two years. He had been just three years from early retirement as a mail carrier for the US postal service when his wife Joyce, had been killed in a freak car accident. She had died instantly from the impact, and he had gone in and out of consciousness while firefighters worked for two hours to unpin him from the wreckage. His left leg had been shattered; he had several broken ribs and severe cuts and bruises. He and Joyce had been coming home from a birthday party in Fountain, Colorado, and, while driving on Nevada Avenue just a few blocks from their Buffalo Springs home, a young man on a motorcycle had passed them at excessive speed. He had barely missed their front bumper as he passed, but clipped the rear bumper of the truck in front and to the right of them. The truck driver had lost control, spun around 360 degrees, hitting the Manning vehicle on the right side where Joyce was seated, killing her instantly. The motorcyclist was thrown from his bike and had suffered fatal injuries. The driver of the truck, a young woman in her early thirties, and who later on admitted to trying to dodge and get away from the motorcyclist, had suffered a broken arm and sustained severe head injuries. No charges had been filed against her, but the motorcyclist, although dead from his injuries, had complete insurance coverage, and his insurance company had paid well, but not nearly enough to cover all of Jed's medical expenses.

After Joyce's funeral, several surgeries to repair his shattered leg, a year of physical therapy and an immense number of medical bills, over and above what insurance policies covered, he was finally discharged. He had been placed on temporary disability leave. Later on, he tried working part time, but his busted-up leg just wouldn't allow him to walk his mail route any longer, and he had chosen to go on permanent disability. He would never again walk his postal service route—the one he had walked for over twenty-five years. He would never speak to the numerous friends/customers he had made over the years, and he found that being alone and without Joyce was more than he could handle. He needed a fix for both his pain and for the loneliness, and his only out, he found, was to use illegal drugs.

Soon he was addicted to drugs and alcohol and had started hanging out in low-life bars with low-life people. Finally, however, he had realized that he needed help and had willingly signed up for a weekly drug and alcohol abuse program. He had been going to therapy now for almost two years. During that time, his counselor had assisted in getting him the part time job at the Sky City Hotel. He found that sitting most of the time on the stool in the attendant's booth was something he could physically manage, and it also gave him a chance to meet a variety of nice folks, like the young couple he had just directed to a handicap parking space. The problem, however, was that in the past few months the pain in his leg had once again become almost unbearable.

"Oh, if only Joyce was here to straighten me out", he thought, but, sadly, he knew that was impossible. He wasn't sure at this point that anyone could straighten him out.

Mic Collins steered the car directly into the handicap parking space, making sure to give Jennifer enough space on the passenger side of the car to transfer herself into her wheelchair. He turned off the ignition, placed the car keys in his pocket, and leaned over to kiss his new bride.

"Happy Mrs. Collins?" he asked, touching her cheek.

"Very." Jennifer answered, her eyes sparkling," I'm very happy."

Jennifer Benson and Mic Collins had been married at 3:00 p.m. that afternoon in a small church in Billingham Colorado, seventy-five miles from Buffalo Springs. Jennifer had walked down the aisle on full leg braces, supported by one crutch while holding on to and balancing herself on her father's arm. Her father had held her small bouquet of purple and white roses so she could support herself on his arm, but no one noticed. Instead, all those gathered were in awe of this young woman who had always used a wheelchair due to a childhood disease and who was now **walking** down the isle on her wedding day.

Both she and Mic knew that she would tire readily and wouldn't be able to stand during the entire wedding and reception. After the ceremony, and after they had walked back up the aisle as man and wife, Jennifer sat back down in her wheelchair. She removed the sidearms, which enabled her to spread the skirt of her beautiful, white, satin gown across the entire framework of the wheelchair. Friends had assisted Mic in getting her down the stairs into the basement's fellowship hall where the reception had been held.

It had been a beautiful day despite the rain, and at 7:00 pm they had changed their clothes, Jennifer into a light lavender skirt and short-sleeved summer sweater, and Mic into beige slacks and a light blue shirt. Friends and family members helped lift Jennifer and her wheelchair back up the basement stairs and then down the front steps and out of the church. Through a barrage of birdseed and rice, family hugs and best wishes, they had gotten into their Chevy and sped away. Jennifer's mother, standing next to her husband and son, held tightly to her daughter's beautiful satin gown, and cried quietly as she watched her daughter drive away to begin her new life.

Jeannette Benson had always wanted a daughter, and she had been blessed with two daughters and a son. Sadly, however, the younger daughter, Lilly, had been diagnosed with leukemia when Jennifer was sixteen and her brother Karl, twelve. Lilly had only lived two years before succumbing to the disease. Friends and family commented often on how hard it must have been for the Bensons to cope with having one daughter with a debilitating disease and another die from cancer. Not only could the pain and suffering of losing a child and having a handicapped child be a hardship, but the financial obligations must have been devastating. Everyone asked how could one family have been so unlucky?

Jeannette never considered herself or her family unlucky. She knew that God was in charge of all things, and that He had been in control when He had blessed their family with precious little Lilly so late in Jeannette's life, and also when she had been taken away, way too soon. Lilly Marie had given their family so much joy in her three short years, and Jeannette had been so thankful for even that short period of time. Not that she didn't grieve, because she had, and often. Not just for Lilly and Jennifer, but for herself as well. She also believed that Jennifer had contracted poliomyelitis for a reason. In Jennifer's twenty-one years, she had watched her daughter touch more people's lives than most young women could have done in an entire lifetime. Jeannette believed whole-heartedly that Jen's disability was all a part of God's plan.

Jennifer was eight when she became ill with flu-like symptoms. It had been in early August. She had spent six months in Chamberville's Children's hospital, two of which were spent in the intensive care unit in an oxygen tent. But once again her family had given thanks to God, as Jennifer had not been placed in an iron lung—a certainty with children who had both spinal and bulbar types of the disease. In the early years of the devastating polio epidemic, children who were diagnosed with bulbar polio had immediately been placed in an iron lung. The spinal virus paralyzed the muscles, but the bulbar virus, affecting the bulbar part of the brain stem, caused the patient to stop breathing on his or her own, and they were immediately placed in the iron lung—a machine that breathed for them. Jennifer had fortunately not been placed in the iron lung, even though she had both of the viruses. The doctors had diagnosed the disease quickly, and although immediately paralyzed from the neck down with only the use of her left arm and hand, Jennifer had never complained. For over four months, she had been fed both intravenously and through a nasal tube that placed liquid nutrients directly into her stomach. She constantly lost weight, going from 90 pounds when she first contracted polio to only 40 pounds when she was released from the hospital six months later. Jeannette remembered the horrible heavy plaster casts—casts that had covered Jen's entire body, supposedly keeping her limbs from tightening up and deforming, but also causing serious open sores around her tailbone area. Jeannette remembered how Jennifer would scream from the pain when the nurses cleaned out those sores, but still, Jennifer never complained, always had a smile on her face, always encouraged the other little girls in her hospital ward, and, although she would cry at times, it would never be because of depression or fear but because of pain. Even at eight years of age, she shared with the young patients and the older visitors, the nurses, even with the cleaning crew, that Jesus loved her and had a plan for her life and for them not to be sad. Get well wishes, toys, flowers, even a dish of pet turtles and a bowl of goldfish, adorned her small bedside table for those many, many months in the hospital, and Jeannette smiled, reminded of the thoughtfulness shown to their daughter such a long time ago.

Now, as Jeannette watched her daughter driving away with Mic, she remembered how Jennifer had loved the Girl Scouts, learning to practice and play the piano and how much she had enjoyed writing poetry. She recalled how she had cheered at all the sporting events during her high school years, even though Jen could not participate. She remembered fondly how Jennifer had been asked to both the junior and senior class proms by boys who were just friends and the beautiful prom dresses she had sewn for her. She also remembered, somewhat painfully, how Jennifer had wished that certain boys would have become more than just friends, but it never happened. Jennifer had recovered two or three times from a broken heart. It was not just the teenage boys who had hurt her. Some of her high school teachers told her college was definitely off limits for a handicapped student. She should just learn to work from home or get a desk job somewhere, where she would be out of sight. Jeannette also recalled that neither her daughter's disability nor negative people had ever deterred her from her dreams or goals. When Jennifer Benson set her mind to do something, it usually happened. She hadn't had many boyfriends but now she had found that one special boy. She hadn't been accepted at a four-year college, but at a community college in the area, and now her beautiful daughter was married, had an accounting position in the local school systems and had reached at last two of her dreams. No, nothing had deterred her and most likely nothing ever would. Jeannette was very proud of her disabled daughter.

Jeannette once again looked down at the wedding dress she held in her arms and lightly caressed the jeweled neckline. She then looked over at her husband, lovingly took his hand in hers, and tearfully thought to herself, "We did everything we could to help Jennifer become an independent, successful woman. We taught her how to love and respect herself and others, always to be honest and happy, and never to forget her Christian beliefs and to always live by them." Now, she was married to a wonderful young man and Jeannette knew he would love and protect their daughter always. She and Jennifer's daddy had done their best in raising their handicapped daughter. Now it was up to Jennifer to do the rest. Their honeymoon in Buffalo Springs would consist of only a long weekend, as neither Jennifer nor Mic had accumulated many vacation days and money was tight. The one night stay at the famous Broodmoor hotel in Buffalo Springs had been a wedding gift from Mic's parents, and the other two nights would be spent in a less expensive hotel. They planned to spend their three days sleeping late, touring Colorado and Manitou Springs, taking long drives, and learning to get to know one another as man and wife.

The rain was coming down hard, and darkness was fast overtaking them when they left the church, and after only driving thirty miles out of Chamberville, Jennifer told Mic she was having an ice cream attack. Mic chuckled, realizing his wife's serious addiction to chocolate mint ice cream. After asking her kiddingly if she was sure it wouldn't spoil her appetite, he pulled off of the interstate at the nearest exit and into a convenience store parking lot. He asked her if she wished to get out of the car, and when she said no, Mic got out, walked into the store, bought two Eskimo pies, as they had no chocolate mint ice cream. They were back on the interstate within ten minutes.

A few miles outside of Crested City, the newlyweds came upon what looked to be a serious accident. Mic slowed the car down and soon came to a complete stop. He couldn't tell the nature of the accident, but there were several police cars and what looked to be a Swat Team vehicle on the side of the highway.

"Gee, this looks serious", Mic said, looking at his wife. "I hope no one was injured, and I hope we're not stopped here too long. Can you see that large van with Swat Team written on its side?"

Jen tried to look out of her side of the front windshield, but the rain was falling so hard and the wipers were moving so fast that she admitted she couldn't see anything except for a blur of flashing red and blue lights.

"I don't know, Mic," she said somewhat concerned. "I guess we'll just have to wait it out."

After only a few minutes, a Colorado Highway Patrol officer approached their car and signaled for Mic to roll down his window. With rain pouring into the car, the officer said hello, introduced himself as officer Lucas Lopez, and informed the newly married couple that there had been a robbery in Crested City, Colorado. The suspects were on the loose and a roadblock had been set up. He explained that he would need to check the inside of their car as well as the vehicle's trunk.

"No need to get out of your car," he said, noticing Jennifer's wheelchair in the back seat. "I just need your keys to check out your trunk. I won't keep you long." He then continued, "Have you two stopped anywhere in the past twenty miles, maybe gotten out of your car or left your car for a period of time?"

Mic turned off the car, took the keys from the ignition and handed them to Officer Lopez.

"We stopped just the other side of Crested City," he responded. "My wife stayed in the car, but I went into a convenience store for about five minutes."

"Thank you," the officer responded, taking Mic's car keys. "I'm sure there is no problem with your vehicle, just have to make sure. We don't need any surprises or anyone possibly hiding in your trunk."

A few minutes later, the officer returned, handed Mic back the car keys, and noticing the decorations on their windows, smiled, wished them well, and told them they could be on their way.

"Drive safely," the officer added, and then almost as an after thought, asked where they were headed.

"We're headed to Buffalo Springs, to the Sky City Hotel", Mic said proudly. "We were just married this afternoon."

"Good luck to you both," he said with a smile. "Drive safely."

An hour later, the newlyweds arrived at the Sky City Hotel. It was still raining hard, and being able to park in the underground parking garage was a godsend. The rain and the roadblock had slowed down their travel time, but having reservations, they were not concerned about their delay in arrival.

"Here you go, Jen," Mic said, bringing her wheelchair up to the passenger side of the car. "Hand me your back pack, and I'll put it on the back of your chair."

Jennifer handed Mic her backpack, then lifted her steel-braced legs one at a time out of the car, took a hold of one of the wheelchair's side arms and swung herself into her wheelchair. She placed her legs onto the footplates, and backed her wheelchair away from the car, as Mic closed and locked the car door. He retrieved two bags out of the trunk, and then thinking back to what the police officer had said, he took another quick glance at the inside of his trunk.

Thinking to himself that no one could have possibly gotten into such a small space, he chuckled to himself as he closed it, took Jen's hand in his, and together, as man and wife, they headed towards the elevator.

Once in the lobby, Mic approached the registration desk and was assisted by an older man whose gold lettered nametag read, Mr. P. Swenson. After a short check through the registration files, Mic was told that the bridal suite, number 706, which his parents had reserved, had been reserved by another couple. Mr. Swenson was very cordial and apologetic, but Mic, noticeably irritated, was not.

"Sir, er, Mr. Swenson," he said, "We've had these reservations for over six months. "How could this have happened?"

Looking over to where Jennifer sat silently watching him, the clerk once again spoke.

"I am sorry Mr. Collins, and, if you will allow us, we do have another suite available, number 726. It is not quite as large, but I believe it will work for you and your wife. Is Mrs. Collins able to walk or stand at all?"

"No!" Mic said adamantly. "She is **not** able to stand or walk. However, that has no bearing on this mix-up, but since we evidently have no choice in the matter, can I please have a key and I will check out the room before I agree to take it. I hope it's accessible to a wheelchair!"

The desk clerk smiled and gave him the key to suite 726, and Mic motioned for Jennifer to join him. They moved towards the elevator and, as Mic pushed the UP button, Jennifer noticed another young couple walking hand in hand over to the reservation desk. She could not help but notice them or help overhear them speaking to the same desk clerk.

"Hi, we're Lieutenant and Mrs. Tom Casey," Tom said, "and we have the bridal suite in the south building reserved for the next ten days."

"Certainly," the clerk said, still smiling while taking out another registration form and handing Tom a pen. "Please fill out these forms, and I will get you the keys; do you wish for one key or two?"

"Two keys, please," Jill quickly answered, and smiling up at Tom and putting her arm through his said, "although I doubt we will be apart much."

As she waited for Tom to fill out the forms, Jill turned away from the desk and noticed the young woman in the wheelchair entering the elevator. "What a pretty young woman," she thought to herself, "too bad she is disabled." With that, the elevator door closed and Jill turned back to where Tom was finishing up the forms.

Jennifer lovingly watched as Mic pushed the button for the 7th floor. She took Mic's hand, told him not to worry, assuring him that everything would be fine. She calmly waited for the elevator computer bell to ring, announcing the seventh floor. Mic leaned over, kissed her on the forehead, said how beautiful she looked seeming to have calmed down. As the elevator door opened, he helped push her wheelchair through the doorway, then took her hand once again and continued to hold it until they got to room 726.

Mic had always treated Jennifer like a "normal" woman—holding her hand when they walked together and only pushing her wheelchair if she asked him too. He always had her sit close to him in the car and together they went swimming, hiking or bowling; they even swung on the park swings together. Mic would give her a push, and with her braces locked and straight out in front of her, she could pump the swing and go as high as Mic.

Mic never treated her any differently than any of the other women he had dated. The two of them laughed a lot about what normal was or what normal wasn't. Jennifer couldn't walk, but there was no doubt she could do just about anything else, and if and when she did need assistance, she always kindly asked for help.

She and Mic had dated for over three years prior to their marriage having met in a bowling alley. She had been with another handicapped friend, and Mic had been bowling on a league with a handicapped friend himself. Introductions completed, Jennifer had run into Mic two or three times after that initial meeting and on one of those occasions he had asked for her telephone number. She gave it to him willingly, but it wasn't until six months later that he had called and asked her out on a date. They had clicked immediately.

Over the next several months, a serious relationship began, but they both agreed to take it slowly and make sure their love was real. Mic's parents were also not pleased that their son was dating and could possibly marry a woman who used a wheelchair. Jen worried, even now, that they might never accept her as their daughter-in-law.

"Who's going to clean the house, or do the laundry or take care of babies, if there are any?" they had asked. "Are you sure this is the right woman for you Mic? Mic, please don't rush into anything. Mic, take your time. You don't know if this is the right girl for you." Over and over they had questioned, no, harassed him about his disabled girlfriend.

Mic had stood his ground, stating that Jennifer was the right woman for him; he loved her and she loved him, and he was going to marry her.

Mic's brother, Carter, had been a difficult child, and an even more difficult teenager and Mic's parents unfortunately had had to bail him out of a serious financial/marital situation a few years earlier. They were bound and determined that Mic would be at least twenty-one years old, and no longer their responsibility when or if he married and screwed up his life, too. However, when Jennifer found out she needed a serious back operation and her rehabilitation would interfere with their wedding plans, the couple had asked both sets of parents if they could marry earlier. They wanted to be man and wife before Jennifer's surgery, and have the church wedding later on when she was able to walk down the aisle. His parents had had no choice but to give their blessing. After all, they wanted a nice church wedding for their second son, and they had a reputation to uphold. Having to explain the actions/problems of both their sons to their socialite friends would not have been in his parents' best interest.

Mic and Jennifer's church wedding had been previously planned for six weeks after Mic's twenty-first birthday. This way he would not have to ask for his parent's approval. With the upcoming surgery and rehabilitation the wedding would still have to be postponed to a later date, but at least they would be man and wife prior to her surgery.

On a blustery Saturday morning in January, the three couples drove to Charlton, Wyoming, and, after getting a marriage license at the Charlton courthouse and carrying Jennifer up the seven stairs to a private home on Cranberry Avenue, she and Mic were married by an eighty-four year old Methodist minister. His wife, Constance, and both sets of parents witnessed their marriage. Jennifer wore a lavender skirt and sweater and after a lovely dinner at a Syracuse, Colorado restaurant, which included champagne and roasted duck, she and Mic had taken off their wedding rings and returned to their individual homes.

"If you are going to wear a white wedding gown, and have a big church wedding in a few months, you must be a virgin," her mother had said, politely. Mic's parents had agreed.

"But we are legally married," they had pleaded… to no avail.

So, having had no sexual relations prior to or after their Wyoming wedding, they had agreed, mostly in respect of both of their parents, and they had committed to each other to not consummate their marriage until after their proper church wedding. There were no photos taken in Charlton, and both Jennifer and Mic promised their parents that they would never tell anyone that they had been married prior to their actual church wedding. At the "real" and "proper" church wedding in Billingham, there was no signing of the marriage license, no witnesses, as that had already taken place months prior. Only the parents and the pastor were aware of the "actual" wedding date.

After successful surgery and four months of rehabilitation, Mic and Jennifer had now begun their new life together and, with just a little apprehension, Jennifer would spend her honeymoon night with the man she loved desperately, but had never been with sexually. Sure, they had been intimate, but had not actually had sexual intercourse, and Jennifer wondered if, with her disability, she could be the full woman Mic wanted her to be. Could she be a complete woman where her sexuality was concerned? Was she really a "normal" woman? She was about to find out.

Chapter Three

The Sky City Hotel is noted for its five-star rating, and Tom Casey knew this when he booked their honeymoon suite months prior to their wedding. He knew that Jill would love it, so after checking in and taking the elevator up to the seventh floor, he unlocked the door to suite number 706 and carried Jill across the threshold for the second time in twenty-four hours. Upon entering the suite, she became utterly speechless as Tom put her down and she looked around at the exquisite room. The room was beautiful—no, it was breathtaking. There was a huge picture window overlooking Charlton Mountain, and directly below the window, the crystal clear Charlton Lake, where just as she peered out the window, two white-tailed deer bent down to take a drink. There was a basket of fresh fruit and a bucket with champagne chilling on the oak table, a lighted mirror above it, plush, white monogrammed bathrobes folded neatly on the dresser near the bathroom door, heavenly goose down pillows—she counted seven of them on the king size bed—and a gorgeous, white, silk coverlet turned slightly down, seemingly beckoning them to a night of lovemaking.

"Oh my goodness, Tom," she said turning around and putting her arms around his neck. "This is the most fabulous room I have ever been in. Check out this basket of fruit, and these gorgeous blue crystal champagne goblets. My goodness, I never imagined there could be such a beautiful place."

"We deserve it, Jill", Tom said, placing his hands on her shoulders. "I love you so much, and I want to spend the next week and a half showing you just how much."

As Tom began to unbutton her yellow silk blouse, kissing her softly, Jill mumbled something like, "don't we have dinner reservations soon?"

"Are you hungry Mrs. Casey?" he asked, nibbling on her ear and removing her blouse. "I know I am…hungry for you. Maybe you would rather join me in the shower first. I took a peek, there's also a hot tub for two and I think the champagne is chilled. The dinner reservations are for 9:00 p.m., we have forty-five minutes. How about dessert first?"

Kissing her hard and deeply now, Jill helped Tom unzip her beige pleated skirt, and, as it dropped to the plush white carpet, she took off her shoes and nylons as Tom undid her brassiere. Walking swiftly now to the bathroom, she helped Tom out of his clothes, scattering them as they walked and together they turned on the gold fixtures in the white tiled shower. Stepping gingerly into the shower, the warm water flowing over their naked bodies, they kissed, and caressed one another's bodies, and once again consummated their love for each other.

Mic and Jennifer looked for suite number 726, and, having found it with little or no trouble, Mic inserted the key, opened the door and took a peek. The room was beautiful, no doubt about it.

"Do you want me to check it out first, Jen?" he asked his bride, "Or do you want to take a chance that it will work out okay and I will carry you across the threshold."

Chuckling at her husband, Jen said yes, he could lift her out of her wheelchair, carry her across the threshold, and set her down either on the bed or in a chair in the room. Mic gently picked her up, as Jen placed her arms around his neck, and, as they crossed the threshold, Mic kissed her gently, told her how much he loved her, and before setting her down, carried her throughout the suite for her to see.

"It's beautiful, Mic," Jennifer said softly. "Set me down, and let's bring in my wheelchair and see if it'll go through the bathroom door."

As requested, Mic sat his wife down on the queen size bed, and as she rubbed her hands across the turquoise silk comforter, he brought her wheelchair in and set it next to the bed. She transferred into the wheelchair easily and wheeled over to the bathroom. Maneuvering herself towards the bathroom, she beamed as the wheelchair went through the doorway easily, with room to spare.

"It's great Mic", she said, thinking that this room would work out great. "It's beautiful in here, come look. It has a nice tub and shower, we'll have to ask for a shower chair and if they don't have one, I will manage. Look at these plush towels, whoa, and check out the gold fixtures!"

"It's nice out here too, Jen," he said, looking out the picture window. "This room overlooks the golf course. I guess it's not too bad in here; I just wish we could have seen the other suite. What do you think? Want to stay here? It's just for one night, and it's romantic don't you think?"

Jennifer rolled out of the bathroom, smiled at her husband of only a few hours and said yes, the room would work out great. She checked out the view, the small basket of fruit on the nightstand, and then looked at Mic."

"I love this room, Mic," she said, taking his hand in hers, "and I love you."

"Our dinner reservations are in twenty minutes, Jen," he said, "Let's go down, let the desk clerk know that the room is fine and have our bags sent up. Then we can go to the Penrose Room and have dinner."

With that said, he apologized to Jennifer for getting upset with the desk clerk earlier. He told her again how happy he was and that they should go down to dinner. Jennifer said she would like to freshen up a little first. She rolled into the bathroom, took her makeup case from her backpack, added a little lip color, fluffed up her hair and added a small dab of lavender perfume behind her left ear. She liked what she saw in the mirror—a happy, contented, normal woman—a bride of just a few hours, who was about to enjoy a lovely dinner with her handsome husband in this beautiful hotel. What could be better?

Tom and Jill took a quick hot tub, had a second glass of champagne and dressed for dinner. Jill dressed in an off-the-shoulder mini crème colored chiffon, knee length dress, with black Annie Bobbie pumps. She added a single strand of pearls and pearl earrings to her ensemble, pulled and tied her long hair back into a chignon and added a black flowing ribbon to cover the tieback. One look in the mirror and she knew she would have Tom ready to eat dinner and run directly back to their suite. She chuckled at the thought.

Chapter Four

$\mathcal{M}$ ic and Jennifer Collins took the elevator down to the first floor and, after confirming their reservation, went hand-in-hand towards the Penrose Dining Room. They were taken aback by the elegant surroundings.

"My goodness, Mic," Jen said to her husband. "Are you sure we can afford to have dinner here? This is unbelievable. Are you sure we're dressed appropriately?"

"I have on a sports coat, and you are beautifully dressed," he said, smiling at her. "As long as we are not dressed in our usual jeans and tee's we're fine."

"Just look at the tables," Jen commented, looking through the double doors into the restaurant, "the beautiful white linens and those gorgeous blue goblets and wine glasses. I have never in my life been in this fancy of a place. I won't know how to act!"

Upon entering this elegant restaurant, they were immediately directed by an older man in a tuxedo, who introduced himself as Jamison, to follow him to a table by the window. He asked Jennifer if she wished to stay in her wheelchair or if she wished to transfer to another chair, and Jen thanked him and said she wished to stay in her wheelchair. He pulled the chair from the table, and moved it to the other side of the room. After she rolled up to the table he asked her if she was comfortable, and when she said yes, she also smiled at him. Noticing his beautiful bride's discomfort at being treated so special, he too thanked Jamison for seating them, and that, indeed, they were very pleased with the seating arrangement.

Jamison asked if they would like to see a wine list, and once again Mic thanked him and ordered two glasses of champagne rather than wine.

"We're newlyweds," Mic said proudly. "We would love to celebrate with two glasses of chilled champagne."

Jamison thanked them and promised that a waiter would be with them shortly with menus and their champagne. Taking Jennifer's hand in his across the table, Mic asked her again if she was happy, was she having a good time, and was there anything at all she would have changed about their wedding earlier that afternoon.

"Oh, Mic," she said smiling. "I could not have asked for anything more special. Maybe less or no rain, but no, all of our family and friends were at the church. My mother did a great job getting all the food catered, our two ministers said just the right things, and I loved walking down the aisle with my dad. I was a little worried when I stood up so long to take pictures. I was getting very tired, and I thought I might fall over, but no, I would not have changed anything. How about you?"

Mic agreed that everything had been perfect. His brother, Carter, just out of the Navy, had been his best man, Jennifer's co-worker at the school had been her maid of honor, and two of their mutual friends—couples—had also stood up with them. One of Jennifer's young cousins had been the flower girl, and a mutual friend's three-year old son had been the ring bearer. The men had worn white tuxedo jackets with black pants, and the women had all been dressed in lavender knee-length dresses. They had all carried bouquets of white and lavender roses. The three-tiered wedding cake had also been decorated with white and lavender roses. The guests had been served a light catered supper in the basement of the church, and the newlyweds had opened all of their gifts before leaving on their honeymoon. Yes, Mic agreed, it had been a beautiful and memorable day.

"You looked spectacular, Jen." her new husband said. "I am so proud of you. You made a beautiful bride, and I couldn't help but notice the tears in your mom's eyes. She was proud too."

"I'm glad Jake and Tom didn't kidnap you like they planned," Mic said. "It might have been a fun gesture, but I don't think it would've been a good idea. After all, who knew when I would have gotten you back, and I want you all to myself."

Jennifer smiled, and agreed with everything he had said. She then began to recall how badly she had wanted to be married. She had not dated much during high school or her first and only year of college. Boys in college, or in her high school for that matter seemed to be afraid of her. She realized that they probably were not actually afraid, but more likely did not understand what it was like to be a wheelchair user. Sure, she went out with her girlfriends, and they would lift her wheelchair in and out of the trunk of their cars when they would go shopping or to a movie, but it seemed the boys were different, not as sure about being with someone with a disability. She had dated a few guys in wheelchairs, but they always ended up being more "friends" than potential boyfriends. She had gotten fairly serious about a guy in her neighborhood during her junior year of high school, but he too was uncomfortable or embarrassed when he took her places, so she had broken up with him after six months of dating. She had even been engaged for a short period of time directly after graduation from high school, but she had ended that relationship, too. Neither relationship had brought out the true love she was looking for.

Then she had met Mic through a mutual friend, and it had been so much fun dating him. Mic was not embarrassed to walk hand in hand with her, or take her to the movies or to high school football or basketball games, and from the beginning she was sure that this relationship was meant to be. She was enamored by his kisses and the way he treated her, and it had been difficult for the both of them to abstain from "going all the way".

After almost three years of dating, they were both so comfortable together and began to discuss their future. Mic admitted that it was no bother to have to place her wheelchair in and out of his car, or to lift her every once in awhile into a non-accessible place. They both agreed that they enjoyed each other's company and that they were sexually attracted to one another. Mic didn't mind that her legs were tiny and slightly deformed from the paralysis, or that her arms and shoulders were larger than other's women's due to having pushed a wheelchair for so many years. Most importantly, however, they agreed that they loved each other and wanted to spend their lives together.

There had been several times during their relationship that things had gotten very sensual and sexual. Their kissing and petting had gotten pretty far advanced on more than one occasion, but Jennifer was determined that she was going to wait for her wedding night to have sexual relations. Now that time had come. She was glad she had waited, but she was also afraid. She had questions, and no answers, and her mother had not been able to help her with questions about sexuality between an able-bodied and handicapped person. She had no married, handicapped girlfriends to whom she could discuss it with either. She would just have to find out for herself.

"You and Mic will have to communicate," her mother had told her, "maybe communicate more than most couples when it comes to love-making. With your disability, making love may be a little different for the two of you." Continuing, she said, "but knowing you, Jennifer, and Mic too, you two will make it happen."

The waiter brought their chilled champagne, presented them with their menus, and Mic asked him to return in twenty minutes to take their order. As they sipped their champagne, and talked about the day's activities, Jennifer noticed the newlyweds from earlier. She noticed how beautiful the woman was, and how well dressed. Jen felt just a tad bit envious—feelings not a usual part of her makeup. But the woman was striking, her outfit was gorgeous and she walked with such grace and style—the woman looked almost perfect.

"Stop this craziness!" Jen silently commanded herself, as she continued to watch the couple sit down a few tables away. "Remember," her thoughts continuing, "Mic thinks that you are beautiful and perfect, even with skinny legs and broad shoulders!"

Jen chuckled out loud, making Mic look up and take notice of her.

"Mic", she said discreetly. "The couple that I think took our bridal suite just came in and are sitting at a table to the left of us. They seem very happy, and by the way they are dressed, I would say they have a whole lot more money than we do. They look like they belong in here."

"Jen," Mic said sternly but lovingly, "It doesn't matter how much money they or we have; I'm sure we're just as happy as they are as newlyweds." Then, continuing, he said, "I know it's our wedding night but maybe we could say hello to them after dinner. I would have to make sure and count to ten, however, before I punched the guy in the face for taking our room."

They both laughed, and as the waiter came to take their orders, their thoughts turned to the excellent choices for dinner.

"I'll have the chicken-cordon-bleu," Jen said, looking up at the waiter. "I would also like a tossed salad with blue cheese dressing, and an iced tea with lemon."

The waiter continued taking their order. Mic chose a tenderloin steak with baked potato and vegetable and coffee and also asked if their champagne glasses could be refilled. The waiter assured them that he would be back directly, and left them once again to their private conversations.

Tom and Jill Casey had also ordered champagne. As Jill sipped on hers, she noticed the pretty young woman in the wheelchair once again. For some reason, she could not get her out of her mind. How could it be, she asked herself, that such a nice looking, seemingly vibrant woman, would have to use a wheelchair? She had noticed Jennifer looking at her when they were seated, and she had smiled back when she noticed her looking in her direction.

"Tom, see that couple seated over there by the window?" she asked.

"Yes, what about them?" Tom asked, glancing that direction.

"The woman is in a wheelchair, did you notice that earlier?"

"I caught a glance of her, I guess, when they were getting on the elevator. Why?"

"I just can't get over that she is so attractive and that the handsome man with her is so attentive to her. They seem very happy."

"I suppose a man could be attracted to a woman with a disability," Tom said. "I don't know though if I could've ever dated a disabled woman, plus sweetheart, I won't ever have to worry about dating again, will I?"

Then taking Jill's hand from across the table, he added. "You are the most complete, sexy and beautiful woman I have ever known, and I love you deeply."

Jill smiled at him, but Tom wondered to himself what the man saw in this disabled woman. Yes, she was attractive, but still, what could a man possibly see in a woman who had to use a wheelchair? He wondered if she could walk at all. He also wondered, looking across at the couple again, what sex might be like with a woman who could not use her legs, not stand up—he did admit to himself that this woman had aroused his curiosity.

Chapter Five

Lucas Jesus Lopez looked up at the living room clock—it was 10:15 a.m. He was working the late shift again today and wouldn't have to be at headquarters until 2:45 p.m. He had gotten up earlier than usual this Saturday morning, needing to tidy up the condo, clean his weapon and then pick up his uniforms at the dry cleaners before meeting Ken Porter, an ex-Marine and part time security guard, for a late lunch. Ken always had Saturdays off, and Lucas always worked the late shift on the weekends, so they made a point of seeing each other every second or third Saturday somewhere between Chamberville and Buffalo Springs. This Saturday, Ken was driving from Chamberville to meet up with Lucas. They would meet at the north end of Buffalo Springs at the Waffle House, that way, after lunch, Lucas could just hop on I-25 and head right to Highway Patrol Headquarters and be to work by 2:45. His police cruiser had been making some weird noises, and he wanted to check out his car at the police maintenance yard before his shift began.

Thirty minutes earlier, he had eaten a day-old blueberry muffin, left over from breakfast at Perkins two days earlier had made himself a cup of instant coffee, then added a little 2% milk that was definitely questionable. He thought about taking a sandwich for later in his shift, but decided instead to eat a bite in Crested City later that evening. The refrigerator was for the most part, empty, the three slices of sourdough bread looked and felt stale, and the sliced bologna definitely needed to be tossed.

"Man," he said out loud, "Do I ever need Erica here. I can't even fix a decent sandwich for myself."

Erica Jordaine and Lucas Lopez had been together for fifteen years, but had only been married for nine. They had gotten acquainted while she was on assignment with CNN and he was serving his country in the Middle East during Operation Desert Storm.

Erica had been privileged to report on many international news stories—several in Israel and Russia and some in Hong Kong. It was while reporting the news from Kuwait that she had met Lucas. She had been covering the news when Iraqi forces stormed a number of diplomatic missions in Kuwait City, and he had been there as a sergeant in the United States Marines Corp, protecting the US Embassy. They had seen each other several times during her months in Iraq, but not nearly as much as she would have liked, as their lives and their commitments didn't allow for much time together.

When Lucas was discharged, he moved back to Buffalo Springs, took classes and graduated from the Highway Patrol Academy. He had invited her on several occasions to visit him, and she had done so. He had gone to see her many times in Atlanta, and they had even met up several times in New York City. However, most of the time, Erica was taking off or landing in some far-away airport, or on an airplane somewhere in international air space. This on again, off again romance had gone on for almost six years; seeing each other maybe eight times a year. Then one day Lucas had asked her to marry him. Somewhere between Rome and New York City, on her way to god-only-knew-where and while on their cell phones, he had asked her to become his wife, and she had said yes.

"I thought you'd never ask!" She had told him, squealing.

"You were never in one place long enough for me to visit you or ask you," he responded. "I just hoped you loved me enough not to marry some other guy in one of those god-forsaken places."

"I didn't have time to fall in love with anyone else," she had replied. "I just hoped you would always wait for me to quit all of this traveling around the country and ask me to be your wife."

So, on a Saturday afternoon in her hometown of Atlanta, Georgia, with one hundred and thirty close friends and family members in attendance, they had shared their love for one another and repeated their vows. After honeymooning in Rome, Erica's favorite city, and after only eight months of marriage and moving back to Buffalo Springs, Erica had resigned from CNN. She had found the love of her life in a city thousands of miles away from US soil, was tired of flying and living out of suitcases and, furthermore, she wanted to start a family. It had taken years to finally marry the man she loved so intensely, and, she decided if she was going to keep him forever and make him a daddy, she would have to stay closer to home. The couple bought a condominium in

Buffalo Springs where she accepted an anchor position for CBS television and they had tried desperately to make a baby. Now almost nine years later, she still anchored a television station, Lucas was still a highway patrolman, but there had been no babies.

The Waffle House was within two miles of the Buffalo Springs headquarters of the Colorado Highway Patrol, so when Lucas left the Diamond Dry Cleaners, having picked up his uniforms and dropping off three more, he looked at his watch and told himself that he had two hours to have lunch with Ken Porter and make his shift on time. He was anxious to see Ken again. They had graduated high school together, gone through the Marine Academy together and Ken and Lucas had served in Desert Storm. Lucas had also been there for Ken when he had taken shrapnel in his left leg and upper left arm during the US bombing of Baghdad. Ken had been honorably discharged, spent several months in a DC veterans hospital and in rehabilitation before moving back to Colorado. His arm and leg had healed, but he was no longer the strong Marine he had been in Operation Desert Storm. He had a noticeable limp, weakness in his left arm, constant pain, and, although he tried desperately to find a decent position to support his family, couldn't find anything that suited him, and he had accepted permanent disability. He had worked at several part time positions for the past several years, but nothing really worked out for him. His wife of only five years had left him, taking their two young sons north to Montana. He knew it was totally his fault. He had a bad attitude, had taken up drinking, smoking pot, and had more or less given up on life. When Lucas had seen him over two years later, he had worked hard to get him out of his "funk" and into a controlled substance abuse rehabilitation center. Then with help from his supervisors and officers in the Patrol, he had gotten Ken on as a dispatcher working part-time during evenings and weekends. This position had lasted just a year when Ken met a lovely young woman from Chamberville. He had fallen in love again and married for the second time—this time to a woman with a four-year-old daughter, Taylor. He had given up his position as dispatcher for the Highway Patrol as the newlyweds had moved to Chamberville. Shortly after his marriage to Kimberly, and moving to Chamberville, he had gotten on at the United

American Bank as a part-time security guard. Now, with his pension, plus his part-time position at the bank, Lucas assumed that Ken and his family were doing okay.

Lucas pulled into the parking lot at the Waffle House and spotted Ken's Chevrolet pick-up truck in the handicap parking space. Lucas smiled as he recalled how guilty Ken had felt applying for and receiving a handicap license plate for his truck. "I'm not that handicapped," he had told Lucas. "I can easily walk to and from wherever I need to, and what if some other guy needs to park close, and needs it more than I do? Plus, no one is going to believe there is a disabled guy driving a pick-up truck!"

Lucas had disagreed, telling him he had a right to park close and upfront. "You served your country, got hurt, have a disability, and no one else deserves it more than you, man. If anyone questions you, tell them **I** said it was okay. Plus, your doctor at the VA said you needed it too and gave you the authorization letter."

As it was still raining hard, Lucas ran from the parking area into the restaurant. Lucas looked up towards the heavens, wondering if the entire rest of the day was going to be like this. Ken was already seated and drinking his third cup of coffee when Lucas entered the restaurant. Ken waved at him, signaled him to come on over, and Lucas removed his rain gear, shook Ken's outstretched hand and sat down in the booth across from him.

"Man, do you think this rain is ever going to stop? It poured all the way down here from Chamberville. Lots of water on the interstate, but thankfully, no accidents," and then added, "Good to see you again, Lucas. I wish we could see each other more often. How is Erica?"

The two close friends made small talk while they ate breakfast sandwiches and drank coffee. Ken talked about his security job at the bank, talked about his stepdaughter, Taylor, and asked Lucas about Erica and her job. Before they realized it, it was 2:15 p.m. and Lucas needed to report for his shift.

"Let's get together one night with the wives," Ken said to Lucas, as he painfully stood up to leave. "We always need to get a baby sitter, so if you and Erica could come up to Chamberville and come to our house, that would be easier for us. Plus, Kim and Taylor would love to see you again."

Lucas promised to do just that, knowing that Erica would love to see Kim and their daughter. He promised to call in the next week or so and set up a time for dinner. After paying the tab, they walked out of the restaurant and Lucas wondered if Ken and his family were really doing okay. Lucas knew Ken didn't make a lot of money as a security officer, and his wife only worked part-time, but there was something else strange about Ken's actions today. He couldn't help but wonder if Ken was going back to his old ways—drinking or doing drugs. He hoped not.

On the way in to headquarters, Lucas thought back to his days at the Highway Patrol Training Academy. He had gone into the Academy directly upon discharge from the service and had spent twenty-two weeks of demanding coursework and training at the center in Buffalo Springs. Lucas had always taken good care of himself and stayed in great physical shape, having played numerous sports in high school, but the three-a-week physical fitness programs had been very demanding. He knew, however, that being a patrol officer would be demanding as well. He had done well during the weeks of training and studies, and after graduation, had spent eight more weeks in the FTO – the Field Training Program, with one-on-one training with an experienced officer. He had also been required to take a 62-hour course in Arrest Control and Defensive Tactics Training. He was then ready to go out into the field. He had loved his job, covering the roads and highways between Manitou Springs, Buffalo Springs and Crested City, and having most weekends free to be with Erica. However, she had been in London and New York for the past two weeks on assignment and taking another class in news media communications. He had offered to work this weekend—work helped him forget how lonely he was without Erica.

He recalled how he and Ken Porter had both decided to sign up, become Marines and serve their country. Their lives had been so alike, until now, and Lucas wondered why he had been the lucky one—to come home from a war unscathed and have this great job as a patrol officer.

Lucas checked in, went directly to his locker, put on a clean uniform, put on his hat, took out his extra gun and holster, loaded the weapon and strapped them to his waist. He had cleaned this weapon earlier in the week and had left his second weapon, the one he cleaned this morning, at home, locked up in the gun cabinet. He walked over to his supervisor, Lieutenant Richard Bartell, asking if he could spend twenty minutes over at the maintenance garage checking out his vehicle before hitting the highways. Bartell gave him permission, and he left the area.

Checking out his police cruiser took longer than he expected, and after more than an hour, he was finally on the road. His schedule was to drive Highway 24 in and out of Buffalo Springs for the first three hours of his shift, then travel Interstate 25 between the Springs and Crested City until 11:00 p.m. During the first hours, he stopped one truck for speeding and ticketed the driver. He stopped and helped a woman change a flat tire and talked to two hitchhikers who said they didn't realize that hitchhiking on Highway 24 was forbidden. He gave them a warning. It was dark now, and he had been down I-25 twice already and was headed back for Crested City, when he got the call of a robbery and shooting in Crested City. A jewelry store had been held up and two robbery suspects were still in the area—possibly held up in a farmer's barn. A roadblock had been set up at I-25 and Highway 86, a Swat Team had been sent to that same area, and he was required to be at the roadblock immediately. Lucas turned on the car's sirens and flashing lights and headed for Crested City.

"Looks like this won't be such a boring night after all," he said to himself. "Good thing I had a huge lunch."

Chapter Six

$\mathcal{M}$ic and Jennifer finished their delicious meal, topped off with a delightful chocolate mousse and cups of steaming black coffee. At around 10:30 p.m. they decided to return to their suite.

"I am really getting tired," Jen thought to herself, but the best part of this day is yet to come. She smiled as she thought of the beautiful white silk negligee her coworkers at the school had given her, and she was anxious to get back to their room to change. She knew that Mic would love her in it. However, before they left the dining area and as they were getting up from the table, Jennifer suggested to Mic that they stop by the other couple's table just to say congratulations. Mic agreed and as they maneuvered through the tables all the while holding hands, Tom looked up from his meal and then stood up as they approached.

"We really don't mean to interrupt," Mic said, "but I believe we are both newlyweds, and we just wanted to say congratulations."

Looking at Jennifer, he proudly introduced her as his wife, introduced himself, and said they were from Chamberville.

"Hello", Tom said, introducing himself and then his wife. "We're from Maine, and, yes, we were just married Friday evening. When were you two married?"

Mic answered him and then Tom asked if they would like to join them, all the while hoping they would say no. Tom was more than relieved when Mic said, "Thank you, but no." The two couples shared room numbers and chuckled when they realized they were only a few doors down from one another. Mic told the couple that they would only be at the Sky City for one night and asked how long they planned to stay.

"Perhaps we will see you again before you check out," Jill said to Jennifer. "We hope to do some hiking and biking tomorrow, that is if the rain stops. Maybe you would like to join…us…?" Forgetting that she was talking to a disabled person who probably couldn't hike and for sure couldn't ride a bicycle. She immediately apologized to the both of them, but Jen, being Jen, put her at ease immediately.

"We appreciate the offer," Jennifer commented, "but we have a busy day tomorrow too. We just wish you all the best in your marriage, and we hope you enjoy your stay in Colorado."

"You are just too cool, my lovely wife," Mic whispered in her ear as they walked away from Tom and Jill's table and out of the dining room. "You certainly got Jill out of a ticklish situation, and Tom didn't even comment; I don't think he knew what to say."

Jen assured Mic that it was not a problem and that she was used to it and had been handling these types of situations her entire life. Her thoughts were not on Jill and Tom, or on hiking or biking, or anything she might or might not be able to do from a wheelchair. She was thinking only of this handsome man by her side and how she could make tonight one of the happiest nights of both of their lives.

Jill Casey bowed her head, placed her fingers over her temples, rubbing them as though she had a headache. She then looked up at Tom and commented on her stupidity.

"How could I have ever said anything so stupid? Jennifer probably thinks I have no sensitivity at all. Oh! I feel terrible."

"You weren't stupid, Jill", her husband replied. "It was very sweet of you to ask them to join us tomorrow. It was a courteous thing to do; you didn't think about her being disabled, except for that damn wheelchair, she doesn't even look disabled. Put it out of your mind, please? We have bigger and better things to think about tonight, and tomorrow, and tomorrow night, and the next night, and the next..."

Jill chuckled and thanked him for being so sweet, suggesting that they order dessert. But all through dessert she couldn't help but wonder what this beautiful young woman thought of her bungling, embarrassing words. Had she known Jennifer Benson Collins at all, she would have known that Jennifer hadn't given it more than a second thought.

The first thing Jennifer did upon entering their suite was to take off her leg braces. She had worn braces her entire life, or at least since the onset of polio, and they could become a real burden. The full-leg braces consisted of a steel band and leather straps around her waist and all the way down both sides of her legs. Steel clips at the waist and at her knees and ankles kept her legs perfectly straight. This way, she could stand up and, by holding on, she could walk around her kitchen cupboards, stand to put her wheelchair into the back seat of her car, and, she thought, beaming, could walk down the aisle in a dress with a long, satin train. She chuckled to herself as she recalled herself walking. She had never been very good at walking with her crutches, her balance was bad, but if she hung on to things, she could at least get to a standing position, stretch out some, and be tall, almost normal-looking if only for a short period of time. Smiling now, she unclipped her new white shoes from the bottom of the brace and thought of how long it had taken doctors and/or therapists, or some other genius, to finally figure out long-leg braces could be made with steel tunnels placed into the sole of a client's shoes. That way, the brace could fit tightly into the tunnel and the person wearing braces could have more than one pair of shoes! For almost fifteen years, she had worn the same old ugly brown shoes that were permanently attached into the soles of her shoes. Now, she had her new white wedding flats, and she had also gotten a pair of brown loafers. She had even put pennies in them. "Crazy", she thought to herself, giggling, "here I am twenty-one years old, and having penny loafers is a highlight in my life".

"Are you okay?" Mic asked, wondering why she was giggling. Can I help you, Jen?" Mic asked her, as she laid her braces on the floor.

"Nope. I got it, Mic." She said, still giggling. "Thanks for asking though. It sure was nice to have a new pair of white shoes for the wedding. I had nightmares of wearing those ugly brown shoes under my gown. Wonder what people would have thought when they watched you take off my garter, and saw those ugly nun-type shoes?"

Mic was laughing now, too. "Seeing those brown shoes under a wedding dress would have given anyone nightmares. How have you put up with those shoes for so long?"

Mrs. Mic Benson laughed some more and then said. "I'll be right back, Mic", she said heading for the bathroom. "Want to pour us another glass of champagne? I may need a little honeymoon courage!"

Still giggling, Jennifer went into the bathroom, changed out of her clothes and into the beautiful white negligee. It had three layers of silk and satin with a beautiful low-cut lace neckline. It was so long that it covered her feet hanging down over her footplates. She laughed to herself and said, "Wow, plunging neckline. The seamstress must have added the unused material from the neckline to the bottom of this thing!" After looking into the mirror, she liked what she saw and knew that Mic would like it too. She quickly brushed her teeth, used some mouthwash, ran a brush through her long blond hair, and then silently but reverently asked God if He would make this a beautiful night and to help her be a good wife and lover for Mic. She opened the bathroom door, turned out the light and went to be with her husband for the first time.

Mic and Jennifer had discussed birth control a lot in the last few months. Although they both wanted children, they realized that financially it would not be feasible to have children right away, plus they weren't sure how Jennifer would handle being pregnant. Her gynecologist, Dr. Jim Patterson, had assured them both that pregnancy for Jen should not be a problem but yet, she was concerned.

"If there's any problem at all," Dr. Patterson said after her back surgery, "it will be discomfort. Jennifer, the farther you get into your pregnancy and the larger your baby gets, the more uncomfortable you will get, and I am not sure you will be able to transfer readily. You could have to be bed-ridden for the last month or so. You'll have to be careful, but other than that, you are a fully normal, functioning woman with all the working parts you need to conceive and deliver a child."

"Normal!" Jen giggled again. "There's that word again."

She and Mic had agreed, with Dr. Patterson that she would start on a once-a-day birth control pill, and when they were ready to get pregnant, he would work with them to make sure all would go smoothly. Jen had started taking the pill shortly after their marriage in Charlton. It was hard abstaining from sex knowing that they were safe from getting pregnant. But they had promised their parents that they would abstain from sexual intercourse until after their church wedding. From the onset the pills had made her nauseous and she had also started growing short, stubby little blond hairs on her chin. "What the heck?" she had commented to Mic, but not knowing if the hairs were a side affect from the pills and wanting to make sure they were safe from getting pregnant, she had decided not to stop taking the pills until after she had seen the doctor again.

"I'm going to ask Santa for an electric razor for Christmas!" She had exclaimed.

Mic had changed out of his clothes and was lying in bed in his blue silk pajamas. He sat up, watched her maneuver her wheelchair to the side of the bed and wondered at this lovely wife of his.

"You look beautiful, Jen," he said as she transferred into bed and slipped under the covers. He kissed her gently, and said innocently, "Jen, this is new to me, too; I hope you will help me do the right things so that this first experience at lovemaking will be great for both of us?"

When their kissing became more intense, Mic touched her body in all the right places, helped her out of her beautiful nightgown, and took off his pajamas. Gently, he made love to his wife, and although he was satisfied much too soon, leaving her wondering what her satisfaction might have been, she knew that it would happen during their next lovemaking encounter. Mic apologized for not waiting longer, for not making love more slowly so she could be satisfied, but admitted that he was so in love with her and so enamored by her beauty that he couldn't hold back. At 4:00 a.m. Mic aroused again from her warmth and beauty and made love to her again. This time, with a little added help from extended foreplay and a little more time to work at their lovemaking, Jen was fulfilled, maybe not as intensely as it could have been, but with practice, she knew their love making would become perfect, and with Mic as her partner, she had no doubts. She fell sound asleep in her husband's arms, and when they awoke shortly after 8:00 a.m. they made love again; this time Jennifer had no doubts that she had married the perfect man.

Chapter Seven

*O*n Sunday morning Jill and Tom slept late. They made coffee in their suite, went for a twenty-minute swim in the beautiful hotel pool and, after showers and dressing in casual jogging clothes, enjoyed a light breakfast in the hotel's smaller, intimate coffee bar.

"It's still raining a little," Tom mentioned, as together they looked out of the restaurant window. "I think we should take the rental car for a drive, maybe over to the Garden of the Gods. The brochure I picked up when we arrived shows beautiful scenery. It should be a beautiful drive. What do you think, sweetheart?"

Without waiting for Jill to answer, he continued. "It's too rainy to do any jogging or hiking, and there are plenty of beautiful things and places to see in the Buffalo Springs area. Let's drive around today, find some quaint little place for lunch, and maybe come back here to the hotel for a little more playtime." He smiled at her like a man possessed and continued," We always have tomorrow or the next day to go hiking."

Smiling, Tom took Jill in his arms, kissed her passionately, and continued by saying there were a lot of hiking and jogging trails in the area, and that they could go biking one day, or hiking for a few days, or a little of both. What did she think?

"Let's drive the Garden of the God's this morning and check out some bike rental shops after lunch, okay?"

Jill agreed and, after another refill on their coffee, Tom paid the bill and they left to locate the valet. Tom had rented a new BMW at the airport, and as they waited for the sleek, black sports car, without saying a word, Tom kissed Jill lightly on the cheek. She looked up at him, and smiled.

Mic and Jennifer ordered room service at 9:30 a.m. Mic immediately jumped up and out of bed when he heard the knock on the door, quickly getting into his pajama bottoms he opened the door and asked the waiter in. After setting up their breakfast, Mic got back into bed and the young couple enjoyed their first breakfast together in the suite's huge, comfy bed. Shortly after beginning their meal, Jen spilled strawberry jam down the front of her white negligee. Mic picked up a napkin and lovingly started cleaning up the jam.

"Just what kind of a slob have I married?" he asked, licking the jam off her neck, then kissing her on the neck and nibbling on her left ear.

Jen, giggling now, kissed him back.

Not ten seconds later, Mic accidentally spilled an entire glass of orange juice over himself, Jen and the bed covers.

"Guess it takes one to know one!" Jen said, now laughing hysterically.

"Imagine what the maids are going to think. This bridal suite will never be the same!" Jen said, giggling.

Jen couldn't help but think what wonderful memories were being made and she shared her feelings with her new husband. She told Mic that she hoped there would be hundreds and hundreds of memories made in the next one hundred years.

"One hundred years!" Mic exclaimed. You have a great sense of humor, Mrs. Benson. Can't you see the two of us in a hundred years rolling around in antique, broken down wheelchairs spilling jam and orange juice all over ourselves?"

They both had a good laugh, and after only eighteen hours as man and wife, they agreed life was wonderful—messy, but wonderful.

After showers and packing up their suitcases, they called for the valet to bring their car around. After waiting for over fifteen minutes, the valet came up to Mic and informed him that their Chevy had a flat tire. He asked if Mic had a spare, and when Mic said yes and that he also had roadside service and would call immediately, the couple went to wait by their vehicle.

The AAA serviceman had gotten to the hotel in less than twenty minutes and changed the tire. After loading up their luggage and wheelchair, they were directed to a Mobil station for tire repair. Repairs complete, and in a softly falling rain, the young couple took a drive up Highway 24 to check out the Cave of the Winds—a popular underground cavern, discovered by two young boys in the late 1880's. Mic parked the car and went in without Jen to check how accessible the Caves were to a wheelchair user. The clerk assured him that part of the Caves were accessible but that there would be sections that Jen would not be able to maneuver in her wheelchair. He told Mic that they could go with a group and tour guide or go on their own. Mic purchased two tickets, deciding that they should go without a group, telling the receptionist that he would be back shortly to get their flashlights, explaining that he was going out to the car to assist his wife.

Having entered the caves and going only a fourth of the way through, a sign posting NO WHEELCHAIRS OR STROLLERS BEYOND THIS POINT could have impeded the rest of their tour. However, being the adventurous type, Jen suggested that Mic "spot" her, in case her wheelchair started tipping and challenged him to go a little further. They went another quarter of a mile before Jen admitted it was no longer safe. She insisted that Mic go the entire way. He was adamant about not going on without her, but finally, after kiddingly calling her a "nag" he completed the tour and met her back in the Caves gift shop thirty minutes later.

As they walked to the parking lot, Mic took Jen's hand in his, and they checked out the beautiful view of mountain ranges. They took a few photos, and then Mic and Jen back got back into their Chevy. As he was putting her wheelchair, this time into the trunk, he noticed a deep scratch in the car's paint. He touched it at first with his finger, and then tried to rub it out with the sleeve of his sweatshirt. After muttering a few choice words under his breath, he wondered where or when the scratch could have occurred and just how much it would cost to get it re-painted.

"It had to have happened in the hotel's parking garage", he said aloud. "I paid a lot of money for this paint job. Why can't people be more careful?" He promised himself to have it repaired when they returned to Chamberville.

By 3:00 p.m. on Sunday afternoon, the rain had completely stopped. After a beautiful drive through the Garden of the Gods and a tour of the Seven Falls area, Tom and Jill Casey had stopped for a late lunch at the Glen Eyre Castle and made reservations to take the Pikes Peak Cog Railway trip on Wednesday. The couple checked out a couple of bicycle rental shops and made plans to rent bicycles for the next two days. They planned to bike both the Monument Trail, which was a little over eight miles long, in the morning and bike and hike the trails up to

Cinnamon Ridge in the afternoon. Both being avid cyclists, they were used to biking the steeper and longer bike trails, and they looked forward to Monday's activities. On Tuesday, they planned to check out two more trails and drive through the Air Force Academy grounds, see the Air Force Academy Chapel and the museum, and then take in some of the nightlife in the area.

During their stay they also planned to see the world famous Pike's Peak, not only by rail on Wednesday, but by car later on. Friends back home in Portland had told them to make sure to drive the steep incline to the top of the mountain, and to also take the Pikes Peak Cog Railway. They planned to take a lot of pictures, eat the famous donuts that were deep fat fried at the 14,000-foot level, and buy several souvenirs.

Around 6:00 p.m, the couple returned to the hotel, showered and changed into more appropriate attire, and then took a taxi to downtown Buffalo Springs. After a delightful dinner, they saw a movie and at approximately midnight, returned to their hotel, had a glass of wine in the hotel bar and retired for the evening.

"This has been a beautiful couple of days," Jill said to her husband as they climbed under the silk sheets and comforters. "I am so very happy, and I'm looking forward to the next few days of hiking and biking with you. Let's get up early, stop at grocery store and pickup water and a few snack items to take along. We did pack our backpack's, didn't we?"

Tom assured her that he had brought their backpacks and that, yes, after a light breakfast at the hotel they would stop and pick up their bicycles.

"The weather is supposed to be perfect tomorrow," Tom replied. "No more rain, just sunshine and hiking and biking with the most beautiful woman in the world."

Tom turned off the bedside lamp, took his wife into his arms and kissed her gently before saying goodnight. What a wonderful life I have, he thought to himself. Nothing, absolutely nothing, could be better than what we have right now.

Chapter Eight

On Monday morning, even before the alarm clock rang out an annoying buzz, Jill and Tom were out of bed, showered, dressed and ready for a day of outdoor activities. They enjoyed coffee and bagels in the small hotel coffee shop and had driven to town where they purchased bottled water, fruit and granola bars. They drove to Mac's Bicycle Rental, had rented two bikes and purchased a map of riding trails in the area. They checked all their gear and headed out to ride the first trail. The shorter of the trails took them less than two hours, up and back. After finishing their first ride, they rested for a few minutes and then biked to the second trail less than one-half mile away. They agreed to bike until sunset as the second trail was quite long and would end at the top of Cinnamon Ridge, where the Rocky Mountain sunset, they were told, was one of the most beautiful sights around. They planned to head back down the trail before it got too dark, go back to the hotel, take a swim, and relax.

The newlyweds biked through several mud puddles the first two miles, stopped for water breaks a couple of times, and on more than one occasion had stopped to remove rocks that had tumbled down the mountain onto the trail. At the five-mile marker, they locked up their bikes at the Rocky Mountain Ranger Station, realizing from posted signs along the way, that the rest of the path was too steep for bicycles. They would have to hike the rest of the way to the top of the mountain and the trail's end. At this stop, they had also eaten their fruit and granola bars, drank more water and used the restrooms. Two other bikers had also stopped to rest and lock up their bikes, and the couples introduced themselves and chatted for about twenty minutes. The four decided that they would hike to the top of the Ridge together. Tom mentioned that the ranger had informed him earlier that the trail was well groomed and easy to hike, although steep. He told them to make sure to stop and take a few moments every now and again to take in the beautiful mountain views. The ranger had also assured Tom that their bicycles would be secure, that the station was open until 8:00 p.m. and that he would be there when they returned.

At the six-mile marker, there was a rock staircase up the mountain, where signage showed a waterfall and an overlook. Both couples agreed to take the staircase to the top. One by one, the four made it to the top. They marveled at the gorgeous mountain peaks, the magnificent waterfall that seemed to fall into oblivion, but in reality fell into a river several hundred yards below. They sat down at the edge of the falls to take it all in. Almost immediately after sitting down, there was a crashing sound and, as Tom and Jill turned around to look, a part of the rock ledge directly above and behind the two couples broke off the mountain— likely caused by all of the rain—and crashed down to where the four young people were sitting. A sizeable piece of the rock ledge missed their friends but hit Jill and Tom, knocking them both to the ground.

Only slightly dazed, Tom immediately sat up, looked around and called out Jill's name.

"Jill, Jill, honey are you alright?"

There was no response.

Tom crawled over to his lifeless wife, touched her gently on the arm and once again called out her name. Again, there was no response.

Finally, Jill opened her eyes and looked around. She tried focusing on those gathered around her, but couldn't immediately comprehend what had happened. She knew that she was lying on the ground, and she could hear someone calling her name, but she couldn't make any words come out of her mouth. She didn't feel any pain anywhere and she moved her arms, trying to reach out to whomever was calling her. When she tried to sit up, she couldn't. When she touched her hands to her stomach and her legs, she realized that her hand could feel her stomach and legs, but her legs and stomach could not feel her hand. Panicking now, she managed to call out Tom's name.

"Tom! Tom!"

"I'm right here, baby. I'm right here."

Tom, still kneeling by Jill's side, touched her cheek with his fingers, and assured her that he was right there with her.

"Tom! What happened?" Jill screamed.

"It's okay, Jill. It's okay, honey. I'm right here. Do you hurt anywhere?" Tom gently asked her.

By this time, their new friends had also knelt down beside the injured woman and her husband, and they asked Tom if he was okay. He said, yes, he was fine, but said calmly, "I really think that Jill might be seriously injured."

"She looks bad," he said softly so Jill could not hear. "We really need to get some help. We need to keep her warm and we shouldn't move her""

"Someone needs to call 911. Does anyone have a cell phone?" A stranger in the crowd of hikers that had now gathered asked, looking around.

A couple who had just hiked up the mountain behind the two couples, and had witnessed the rock ledge falling, said that yes, they had a cell phone but weren't sure there would be any reception this high up the mountain. They immediately promised to head down the staircase, and would keep calling 911 until they got an answer. They also suggested that someone also get down to the ranger station where they had left their bikes and report the accident. Another stranger also offered to go with them to try to get assistance.

Tom, still kneeling by his wife's side, took her right hand in his and when he began to squeeze it, Jill flinched.

"Does that hurt, Jill?"

"Yes, Tom, it hurts, please let go, Tom. It hurts."

Tom let go of her hand, noticed the severe abrasions, and then asked if she was cold. She nodded her head yes, and Tom knew that if he didn't keep her warm she might go into shock. There were no blankets to place over Jill, so he took off his backpack, took out his jacket and covered her with it. He knew that she too had a jacket in her pack, but did not want to turn her over to get to it. Another hiker hearing Tom's words, offered his jacket, and another hiker took off his sweatshirt and offered it to Tom. Tom went from kneeling over Jill to sitting down beside her. He lovingly brushed the dirt off her face and moved her hair away from her eyes. Tenderly, he told her that everything would be okay, and that help would be there soon.

"Does it hurt anywhere else, Jill?"

Without waiting for an answer he said. "Just hang tight. Help is on the way. Are you warmer now? Talk to me baby, what I can do for you?"

Jill started to cry, tears filling her eyes, and reaching out to him, she cried. "Tom, Tom, I can't feel my legs. Tom! I can't feel my legs!"

On Sunday night, Mic and Jennifer found another hotel, the Dream Lodge, just a few miles from the Sky City. They checked into their room, unpacked their luggage and went to a small diner down the street for dinner. Afterward, they took in the nightlights at the Seven Falls, took a drive through Buffalo Springs, and by 10:00 p.m. they were ready for a good night's sleep. Since she had spilled strawberry jam all over her white negligee, Jen slept in Mic's pajama top, and he slept in his pajama bottoms. Halfway through the night, the young lovers once again found each other. Although Jen was unable to move her legs they found out that each time they made love they would find a new position of love making that would work better. Satisfaction came easier and easier for Jen and she was thankful. Her fears had been put to rest. She could be a good lover and a good soul mate for Mic, and she thanked God for this wonderful blessing.

On Monday morning, just because it was driving him crazy, the newlyweds went back to the Sky City's parking garage as Mic wanted to see if the parking attendant, Jed Manning, was on duty. He desperately wanted to find out if anyone had been hanging around his classic car on Saturday evening, or if Jed had seen anyone that looked suspicious, perhaps had flattened his tire, or caused the deep scratch on his back fender. Unfortunately, Jed Manning was off on Mondays, but the attendant on duty would leave him a message and Jed would get it on Tuesday afternoon.

"Is there a problem?" the attendant asked.

"No problem. Thanks anyway. We will be leaving on Wednesday to return to Chamberville, but if I get a chance I will stop by and talk with him before we leave."

Mic thanked him again, and got back into his car figuring that he would just have to live with the scratch on his beautiful classic Chevy.

The stranger on the Ridge had found telephone reception just a mile down the trail and the call to 911 had gone through. He hiked back up the trail to give Tom and Jill the news. The dispatcher had assured him that the paramedics were on their way. He had also been told what Tom already knew, to keep his wife warm and as comfortable as possible, not to give her any food or water, and not to move her. He had also been told that there was no place for a medical helicopter to land on the Ridge, so the paramedics would be hiking up the trail, and they would have to bring Jill down on a stretcher or body board. It would most likely take a couple of hours to get her stabilized and back down the mountain and to a hospital. The dispatcher assured the stranger on the phone that the Buffalo Springs Fire Department and an ambulance were on their way, and asked the stranger to please stay on the line if he could, and if they did lose the connection, please, for him to try and call her back. The Park Ranger was also on a connection with dispatch and with the fire and police departments. Everyone was doing what could be done to get to where Jill was waiting and then down the mountain to a safe place.

As the stranger who had made the call to 911 was giving Tom the information from dispatch, Jill overheard almost the entire conversation and began to cry again.

"It's going to take them a long time to get up here, Tom," she cried, "What'll we do if it takes too long; it will be dark soon, what if they can't get me down the staircase?"

Tom assured her over and over that she would be just fine, that help was on the way, and for her to try and stay calm.

"I know this is difficult, Jill," he said, "But try to stay calm. We're all here for you. Everything will be okay sweetheart. I promise."

By this time the afternoon sun was low in the sky, and Tom, looking into the western horizon, realized that it would be getting dark soon, and getting Jill back down the mountain might be a challenge. He knew that with all of the rain the past few days and being high up in the Colorado mountains, it would also start turning much colder. Showing no emotion or fear so as not to upset Jill anymore, he once again promised her that they would be continuing their honeymoon in no time. She would be down the mountain soon and into a hospital where the doctors would fix her up good as new.

Tom, however, wasn't so sure. His thoughts went back to the woman he and Jill had met two days before, the woman in the wheelchair. Putting his hands to his forehead and closing his eyes, he thought to himself that Jill just had to be all right, that she could not possibly be paralyzed and have to use a wheelchair. Not his Jill!

"Not my beautiful Jill, not my beautiful Jill!" he repeated over and over again to himself. "It just can't happen to my beautiful Jill!"

Chapter Nine

Officer Lucas Lopez had just given a speeding ticket to a woman driving a 2006 bright red Corvette for going 25 miles over and above the 65 MPH speed limit. As he was getting back into his patrol car, he got the call from dispatch. There had been an incident just outside of Manitou Springs, up Highway 24. He was given few details, but was told there had been a rockslide with possible injuries, and he was to go directly to the base of Cinnamon Ridge Trailhead. He and two more officers who were already on their way to the site were needed to help control traffic, the fire department and the ambulance arrivals, and with whatever else was needed at the scene. He would be the investigating patrol officer at the scene.

Lucas knew the area well, had even hiked that exact trail before with Erica. It was a beautiful area with a gorgeous view—a very popular place and he imagined there would be a lot of hikers on the trail today. There would also be a lot of curiosity seekers once the fire trucks and ambulance arrived. He figured this to be a long afternoon and even longer evening. As he pulled onto Highway 24, he was once again thankful that he had eaten a late lunch because it looked like he just might miss tonight's dinner break.

At Buffalo Springs Fire Station, 19 the 911 dispatcher had just finished speaking with Vernon Mallard, the fireman who had taken the call. As he set off the fire alarm to prepare the rest of the team for departure, the dispatcher put in a second call to Fire Station 27 in Manitou Springs.

"We think there may be more than two people injured," the dispatcher said, "and we may need more than one ambulance and at least four to eight fireman to get the injured down that mountain."

As the alarm bells were going off throughout Station 27, Captain Eugene Simpson notified his men and women through the station's intercom system that there had been an accident.

Within three minutes, two fire trucks with seven firemen and an EMT on board, an ambulance with two paramedics, and the fire chief and his assistant were on the way to the trailhead. It would take approximately six minutes to get to the site. The second fire crew including two more trucks and another ambulance, were headed down the mountain from the opposite direction. Both crews would arrive within minutes of each other.

Every time Captain Simpson and his crew left the fire station on a call, they knew it was their chance to save lives, and help the sick or injured. He was proud of his crew, knew them all as well as he knew his own family. He had no doubt that they would all do their best at the scene of the rockslide. His paramedics, John Dawson and Jake Hudson, were two of the best. He had watched these two skilled men numerous times over the years, as they worked tirelessly time and again to help and care for the sick or injured. People's lives often depended on their quick reactions and their competent care; how fast they could get the patient stabilized and get him to a hospital. These two, he thought to himself, often checked up on their patients or their family members weeks after the original incidents. He was proud of all his team, but especially his two paramedics.

With sirens blaring, the fire trucks and ambulances, coming in from both the east and the west of Cinnamon Ridge, arrived at the scene within five and one half minutes. Ranger West Browning, one of the rangers from the Cinnamon Ridge Ranger Station, was waiting for them, as were three officers from the Highway Patrol and three Buffalo Springs police officers. Barricades had already been set up, blocking off one lane east and west on Highway 24, the two major streets going both north and south, and those going in and out of the Trailhead parking lots. Lucas moved the barricades to let both the fire department vehicles and the ambulances in, replaced the barricades and introduced himself to Captain Simpson as the captain stepped down from the fire engine.

"What's the full story here Lopez?" the Captain inquired.

"From what we understand, there is a young man, I believe the husband of the victim, with bumps and bruises, and his wife, who is conscious but unable to move. There were two others with them at the time, but they seem to be uninjured."

Captain Simpson took charge and gave orders to both teams. He needed two backboards, blankets, oxygen, neck braces and all other appropriate medications and medical items needed for a person with a severe injury. The emergency room doctors at Pike's Peak Medical Center were already on call and were standing by to assist the paramedics by telephone with proper medical procedures as soon as they arrived on the scene.

"I need six of you to go up the mountain," he said. "This is not the best of terrains to be bringing down the injured, and I want six of you standing by down here. We will take two backboards and a basket, just in case there are any more serious problems and just in case the husband needs assistance as well. You all know the drill, now let's get to it!"

Captain Simpson asked if Officer Lopez could get a police officer up ahead of his crew to clear away onlookers and anyone else who really didn't need to be on the scene, and asked another officer to keep the trailhead clear of anyone trying to still go up the mountain. He knew the media would be on the scene in a matter of minutes, and he wanted no one to get in the way of what his team needed to do. Speed was of the essence here, a life might be in jeopardy, and he wanted no one to impede his team while they did their jobs.

The fire team, which included one woman, grabbed their gear, including two backboards and the basket, and hurriedly began the trek up the trail. They were all in excellent physical condition. Even while carrying the heavy packs of gear and backboards, they hustled up the trail. In less than an hour, they had reached the ranger station. They continued at a fast pace the next two miles, and one by one the fire crew and paramedics climbed the staircase to the top.

Mic and Jennifer had driven up Highway 24, through Manitou Springs, past the Cave of the Winds and had taken the Pike's Peak Highway, planning to drive all the way to the top of the mountain. The road was only partially paved and, when they came to the unpaved, dirt area, Mic slowed down, not wanting to damage his Chevy in anyway. They slowly made it to the top of the mountain and were in awe at the number of cars and people who had also made it to the top.

"Wow, this must be a popular place, Jen," Mic said. "Do you want to get out? It's really a very clear afternoon, and I think we can see for miles up here. Look, the Cog Railway just made it up here too. Let's get out, okay? Grab your jacket."

Jen agreed, and even though the parking lot was unpaved and rocky and bumpy, with Mic pushing her entirely on her back wheels, on a wheelie, she made it into the gift shop and restaurant. After ordering two cold drinks, the young couple went out onto the balcony overlooking the incredible mountain ranges, saw several big-horn sheep and mountain goats, several large birds, either ravens or blackbirds, and once again were enthralled with the beauty of nature.

After spending time in the gift shop, and using the restrooms, the newlyweds got back into their car and headed back down to Highway 24. They turned right, heading back into Manitou Springs, and, as they got closer into town, noticed several police cars and fire trucks to the left of the Highway. A police officer was directing traffic, and as they slowly crept by the scene, Jen said aloud, "Mic, isn't that the officer who also stopped us on I-25 last Saturday? The one who is talking with the fireman?"

"I really can't look right now, Jen; I have to keep my eyes on the road. They've blocked off one lane in each direction." Continuing, he said, "but it could be him I guess. The Patrol covers this whole section of highway."

Jen kept watching as they drove slowly down the highway, and finally, straightening her body out and looking forward once again, wondered if that really was Officer Lopez. She also wondered what had happened to bring that many fire trucks and police cars out to the area.

"I hope it wasn't anything serious," she said to Mic. "I would hate for anyone to be in trouble on such a beautiful day."

Chapter Ten

The partial crew of Fire Station 19, including the two paramedics and the police officer, Terry Dirkson, started up the Cinnamon Ridge Trailhead within minutes of arrival at the base. Two firemen from Station 27 followed closely behind, and three of each team remained at the base, preparing themselves for whatever might be needed of them throughout the hours that lay ahead. All of the crew carried heavy packs of equipment and medical supplies needed to, first of all, save a life, then to get the injured down this steep trail safely. There was little conversation during the hour that it took the crew to get to the ranger station. Their goal was to get to those who needed their undivided attention as quickly as possible.

At the ranger station, they stopped for a few minutes for water and continued on to the bottom of the staircase. Officer Dirkson went up the staircase first, and one by one the others followed. Upon reaching the top, Dirkson went directly to the man he presumed to be the husband, introduced himself, and knelt down beside the injured woman.

"Ma'am," he said softly to Jill, "I am Officer Dirkson with the Buffalo Springs Police Department. There are two paramedics coming up the staircase at this very minute and they will make you as comfortable as possible. They will check you out thoroughly and as soon as they give us the okay, there will be several firemen to get you down the mountain. Do you understand what I am saying?"

Jill blinked her eyes, softly said yes, and attempted to thank him, just as two uniformed men bent down beside her.

"Ma'am," Jake said. "I'm Jake Hudson, a paramedic, and I'm here to help you. Can you tell me where it hurts? Are you having any problems breathing?"

Jill said, beginning to cry again, that she didn't hurt anywhere, but that she couldn't feel her legs.

Jake asked her to tell him her name, and when she responded, he continued. "I'm going to take your vitals now, your blood pressure and your temperature and I'm going to put a cervical collar around your neck to stabilize it. All the while I am working on you, my partner, here, John Dawson, will be speaking directly with a doctor at the hospital in Buffalo Springs."

Jake continued by asking her if she was on any medications, did she have any allergies, or any other medical conditions that he should know about. When she weakly said no to all of the questions, and with Dawson's approval from the ER doctor, Jake gently cleaned her arm, inserted a needle and started the intravenous feeding. He told her that this would make her feel better in no time. He also suggested that she take the oxygen mask, due to the high altitude, even though she said she was breathing just fine.

Dr. Christian Slager, at Pike's Peak Medical Center, in Buffalo Springs, was on the line with John Dawson. John told Dr. Slager Jill's vital statistics and the doctor told John what medications to start her on. The paramedic and the doctor knew that if Jill was not already in shock that she could go into shock at any moment, and, although she currently had only slight pain, that too, might increase at any time.

Jake, looking over at Tom, asked if he was Jill's husband, asked his name and told him not to worry, she was in good hands. He also asked him if he hurt anywhere. Tom said no, but the paramedic noticed blood on his arm and on his leg and said the fireman standing to his right should check him out, and that he should go to the hospital as well.

"The fireman can check you out, sir," Jake said, noticing Tom's facial disagreement. "Since Dawson and I are busy attending to your wife, please let the fireman see to those injuries."

"We're going to get your wife down the mountain as soon as she's stable," he continued. "We're going to put her in a neck brace, stabilize her onto a padded backboard, and these six men will get her down the trail. Please don't worry; we have all done this before. We'll take good care of your wife. Please, let us do our jobs, and you need to step over to that fireman right there and see to your injuries, okay?"

While the two paramedics worked to make Jill as comfortable as possible, the other firemen checked on Tom and the two other couples at the scene to make sure no one else was injured. He put a bandage on a large cut on Tom's left arm—a cut he hadn't even realized he had, and cleaned out, and bandaged a deep cut on his leg as well. He informed Tom, too, that he also needed to be checked out at the hospital as soon as they got his wife down the mountain.

All the other people seemed to be fine, and the officer asked for their names, telephone numbers and, as he wrote down their information on a small note pad, he asked which of them had contacted 911. When a taller, slender man raised his hand, the officer thanked him for his assistance and assured him that, due to his help, the injured women would most likely be okay.

He suggested that they should now all go down the trail and check in at the ranger station, pick up any belongings they might have stored there and get down to base. There would be an officer at the base who would speak with them further. He thanked them for all their assistance and reminded them to be cautious getting down the staircase.

"Please stop at the ranger station and borrow flashlights." The officer ordered. "There will also be a police officer to help escort you all down the trail. Now you be safe, and thanks for all your help."

The sun had set, and was well behind the mountain when Captain Simpson made the decision that even with flashlights, it was going to be entirely too dangerous to try to get the injured woman down the trail before it was completely dark. There was only one other way to get her down the mountain safely and that was by helicopter. Simpson knew that a chopper could not land on the mountain, but they could get her out by cable. They would need to wrap her up tightly in blankets, strap her to a backboard, and place her in a basket type device shaped like a rowboat. This basket, tied to several cable lines could gently lift her up into the air, then fly her over the mountain and drop her down the mountainside next to the waterfall and onto the highway. There would be six firemen waiting for her at the bottom of the mountain to guide the basket. That way they would have her down the mountain in less time and into the waiting ambulance.

The Captain radioed dispatch and asked for a helicopter with sensory nightlights and the proper equipment for a basket rescue. The chopper could hover over the area and light the way as the cables were lowered and the basket was hooked up. He then radioed his crew standing by at base, told them of the plan, and immediately a police cruiser, fire truck and ambulance drivers were sent the five miles up the canyon to block off the west side of the highway, direct traffic and prepare for Jill's descent.

The Captain then told Tom Casey of the decision. Tom didn't agree with their decision to bring her out by chopper. He felt that she could be injured worse than she already was. He had, however, no choice but to go along with what he was being told. After all, it was Jill's life at stake here and he had to put his trust in these qualified firemen and paramedics.

Jill was told that she would be taken out by helicopter. She was naturally frightened, but seemed to understand what the captain was telling her. The oxygen tank was placed securely in the basket next to her and the intravenous bag was temporarily disconnected. She was wrapped in heavy blankets and placed on a backboard. Six firemen lifted her carefully into the basket and securely strapped her in. She was now ready for her descent down the mountain. All they needed now was the helicopter.

As the paramedics and firemen made final preparations for her journey, Tom stood by her side. With tears in his eyes, he told her that he loved her and would be there for her when she got to the hospital.

"Don't be afraid, baby," he said lovingly. "I'm right here. I love you. Jill, do you hear me, baby? I love you. I'll always love you baby, I'll always love you."

Chapter Eleven

In only eight minutes; a medical helicopter arrived above the accident sight. The pilot had turned on the enormous lights, which showed brightly onto Jill and the emergency crew. Captain Simpson, having been in contact with the pilot all along and with his radio still in his hand, gave the high sign for the paramedics to drop the winch with the attached cables to the waiting fireman. Immediately Jill's basket was attached to the heavy cables and she was securely strapped in. After checking all of the cables one more time, Captain Simpson radioed the chopper pilot that all was a go, and Jill was gently lifted off the ground and several feet into the air. Simpson continued speaking to the pilot, who assured him that they would have her down safely onto the highway in just a matter of minutes. At the drop off point, the other set of paramedics already on the scene would take over. Her intravenous tubes would be re-connected, her vitals checked and once loaded into the ambulance, she would be on her way to the hospital.

Tom watched as his beautiful but injured wife was lifted into the air, and as he watched the chopper go higher and higher into the night air, tears began streaming down his face. He began to sob. A fireman walked up to Tom, placed his arm around his shoulders and told him that she was safe in the basket and for him not to worry. She would be down onto the highway in just a matter of minutes, and for him to stay strong. Tom thanked him, wiped his tears with his shirts sleeve walked toward the staircase and began the long walk down the Cinnamon Ridge Trailhead. The firemen and paramedics still on the scene packed up their gear and also headed down the trail.

Remembering their rented bicycles, Tom stopped first at the ranger station.

"You can certainly leave them here until tomorrow," the ranger suggested.

"No, I'll take them now." Tom said adamantly.

He picked up one bicycle while a fireman offered to take Jill's bike down the trail. Tom realized at that moment that he was angry, that he and Jill might never ride bicycles or hike together again. He asked himself why this accident had happened to him, to his wife? What had he ever done to deserve this?

Then, just for a fleeting moment he thought of the woman he and Jill had met at the hotel—the woman in the wheelchair. He thought to himself, what if Jill never walks again? What if she has to use a wheelchair? He didn't think he could bear it.

Jennifer was just coming out of the bathroom after showering, a towel wrapped around her wet hair, when Mic motioned for her to watch the television broadcast.

"All those police cars and fire trucks we saw this afternoon," he said. "There was a rockslide on a mountain above Manitou Springs, and someone was injured. A chopper had to come in and take the injured person down off the mountain. It must have been a really bad slide. Come look."

Jennifer asked Mic if they had given any names or mentioned how badly the person was injured?

"They haven't given out any names," Mic commented. "But it was a man and a woman who were injured, and the women's injuries are thought to be serious. This telecast is live, and it shows the helicopter dropping the basket with someone in it next to the ambulance on the highway."

The young couple continued to watch the news for a few more minutes, then turned the television channel to a game show. After Jen dried her hair, they ordered a movie and spent the rest of their evening lying in bed. They ate snacks, talked about the past few days, and admitted that they were sad to be heading back to Chamberville so soon.

"It's been a wonderful honeymoon so far, Mic," Jen said, reaching over to kiss her husband. "I wish it could last longer, but it will be fun to go home and look at all of our wedding gifts and get our apartment in order.

"It will be fun, Jen," Mic said. "By the way can you cook?"

She slapped him lovingly across the face and said he'd find out soon enough. Before they even watched a quarter of the movie, they were in each other's arms, holding each other and making love on the third night of their honeymoon.

As the medical helicopter lifted off the ground, Captain Simpson radioed his crew below that the chopper was in the air and for the patrol officers to close off the highway in both directions so the chopper could land. With one lane of the highway already closed down, it took only a few more minutes for more barricades to be set up and traffic diverted through downtown Manitou Springs. The highway was closed and the area readied for the chopper's landing.

The helicopter flew over the top of Cinnamon Ridge, over the beautiful waterfall that poured into the river below, and within thirteen minutes was hovering over Highway 24. Four firemen, arms in the air, grabbed hold of the basket carrying Jill Casey and gently guided it down to the highway. As soon as the basket was down the cables were disconnected and, although still asleep, Jill moaned just a little as the paramedics took off the restraints and uncovered her arms. Her arms were uncovered just long enough to check her blood pressure and re-insert her intravenous tubes. She needed to stay warm. The paramedics checked her oxygen mask and immediately lifted her out of the basket. While still strapped to the backboard, she was placed on a stretcher and into the awaiting ambulance.

With sirens wailing, Officer Lopez in his patrol cruiser led the ambulance down Highway 24 to the Pike's Peak Hospital, where a medical team was already assembled and waiting. An operating room had been reserved, and an orthopedic specialist was standing by. The team was used to this kind of trauma and accidents such as this one were not uncommon in the Rocky Mountains. Still, every patient was different, and they needed to be prepared.

The helicopter had landed. Jill was transported into Pike's Peak Hospital and was already being tended to by the time Tom had made it only part way down the trailhead. As they reached the base, a police officer informed the concerned husband that his wife had been taken off the mountain safely, was in an ambulance and so far was doing fine. He had offered to take him to the hospital in his cruiser, but Tom thanked him and said his car was at the base of the trail, and he would rather drive and have his car available. He also had to place the bicycles in the bike rack before leaving for the hospital. He did ask the officer for directions to the hospital, and the officer said that he could do better than that— he would escort him. The officer also wondered why this guy was more concerned about returning the rented bikes than hurrying to the hospital to see his seriously injured wife.

"Every guy handles things differently, I guess," the officer said to himself.

The ambulance driver turned right into the emergency room's parking area and entrance. Jill mumbled something to the paramedic watching over her, and unable to understand her, he asked her to repeat her words.

"Where am I?"

"You are in an ambulance, Mrs. Casey, and we are just now pulling into the emergency room at Pike's Peak Hospital. You are doing just fine. How is your pain?"

Jill answered that she was a little dizzy, and that she had some discomfort but not a lot.

"Where is my husband? Is my husband with me?"

The paramedic, Jason Duran from the Manitou Springs Fire Department, told her that her husband would be coming soon. He would be meeting the ambulance at the hospital, but that it would take him a little longer to walk down the mountain.

"You got the quick ride, Mrs. Casey," he said, smiling. "Your husband and the rest of the fire crew and paramedics had to come down the slow way. I promise, he should be at the hospital soon."

Jill had no recollection of the helicopter ride nor did she remember all the details of what had happened to her. She asked a few more questions of her attendant, and he assured her that she would be given all the details later. Right now, it was important that she concentrate on getting into the emergency room so the medical team could see her and her treatment could begin.

The two paramedics carefully lifted Jill out of the ambulance and took her directly into an empty room. She was unwrapped from all of the blankets, her intravenous tubes and oxygen mask were attended to, and she was transferred onto an emergency room table. Immediately, without asking any questions, the medical team began to cut off her clothes. She so badly wanted to ask them to save her new Rocky Mountain blue and white sweatshirt, but there was no telling this team anything. They had a job to do, and they were doing it.

"I am so thirsty," Jill mumbled. "Can I have some water?"

The nurse apologized, said no, that she couldn't have any water, but if she gave them just a few more minutes, she could have some ice chips. The nurse did get a wet cloth and pressed it up against Jill's parched lips, for which she was very grateful.

For over an hour, Jill laid in the emergency room being poked and prodded. Feeling incredible embarrassment lying on the table with only a cervical collar at her neck, a doctor, without saying a word, walked to the head of the table, got behind her, and placed his hands under Jill's arms. Another doctor went down to the end of the table and placed his hands around Jill's ankles. Together, they both pulled on her body at the same time. She let out a blood-curdling scream. "We are so sorry, Mrs. Casey", one of the doctor's said. "We were hoping that if something in your back is only out of place, if we were to pull hard enough, it might pop back in place. We're very sorry, but it didn't work. We'll now order more tests and hopefully we can give you some answers."

Had Jill been even been the slightest bit coherent, she would have thought – what a stupid move!

The doctor also discovered that one of her lungs had collapsed, and a catheter was inserted to re-inflate her lung. This helped her breathing, but did nothing for the pain elsewhere in her body or the fact that she couldn't move or feel any sensation from her chest downward. She didn't complain nor did she ask for much. Tom however, wanted answers, and wanted them now.

She was taken to x-ray for more scans and more tests. By this time the pain was intense. She tried not to cry but the tears would just not stop. She wanted Tom. She wanted her mother. She wanted to know why she couldn't move her legs. She wanted some answers. It would be four to five days before she and Tom got any answers, and then their world would fall apart.

Jill was still in emergency when Tom, an hour and a half later, finally made it to the hospital. He was told that Jill was stable that she had been asking for him, and that he could see her in just a few minutes. First, he needed to fill out some paperwork. He showed them his insurance card, his driver's license, and answered all the questions that were asked of him. Only after all of the paperwork was completed did they take him to his wife.

Jill sobbed when she saw him.

Chapter Twelve

$\mathcal{M}$ ic and Jennifer slept until 8:30 a.m., packed up their suitcases and, by 10:00 a.m., had checked out of the Dream Lodge and were sitting at a restaurant table having ordered a late breakfast. Their plan was to drive to the Air Force Academy on the way back to Chamberville, where they would spend a few hours touring the museum, seeing the chapel and an informational video about the Academy and then go to their new apartment. They had rented the apartment two weeks before their wedding. They had shopped for and purchased a new Early American style couch and overstuffed chair, a beautiful wooden kitchen table with four chairs, and a television. They had also moved Jen's bed and dresser— one that she had purchased shortly after graduating high school, from her parent's home. Jen had been showered with many gifts, both personal and domestic, and she and Mic agreed not to buy anything else for their new apartment until after the wedding.

"I know we're getting new lamps and end tables for the living room from my parents, as well as a vacuum," Jen had said. "I also know that we'll be getting glassware and an eight-piece place setting of dishware, as well as money from your parents, so we should just shop after we get home and see what we need."

The young couple discussed a number of things on their way to the Academy, including the fact that their apartment was not completely wheelchair accessible. There was only one small step getting into the apartment. Jen could roll up to the doorway, do a wheelie, placing her front wheelchair casters onto the step, and, by gripping both sides of the door jam; she could easily pull herself through the door and into the living room. She did have to get out of her wheelchair, crawl into the bathroom, and hoist herself onto the toilet, however. As she sat on the toilet, she could access the sink and also swing herself onto the ledge of the bathtub and drop herself into the tub. Jen was very strong, and none of this seemed to be an issue or an inconvenience.

"I can easily build a small ramp for the front door," Mic had told her. But she said for now it was just fine for her and pulling herself in and out kept her in shape. The landlord had also told the couple that in no way did he want the bathroom door remodeled, and either they took the apartment the way it was, or they would have to find something else. For now, Jen was satisfied. If and when she got pregnant and could not pull herself in and out or crawl around the bathroom floor, that would be just be another challenge for her to take on.

On the way to the Academy, they watched three airplane gliders peacefully gliding through the blue Colorado skies. They saw a few white-tailed deer eating grass along the highway, and after spending two hours at the Academy headed home. Traffic was light, and before their arrival at their apartment on Louisiana Street, they stopped at a neighborhood grocery to pick up a few items. Jen mentioned a few items that they needed, and Mic went into the store and came back with not only the essentials but with a single red rose in a white cylinder vase and a quart of chocolate mint ice cream.

"I plan to get you a rose for every year that we're married, Jen," Mic said as he handed her the vase. "This is the first one, and I plan to shower you with flowers every year on our anniversary and maybe on other special occasions throughout the years until I can't remember to do it anymore!"

Jen chuckled, accepted the rose, gave Mic a quick kiss, and they headed for home.

"I'm one lucky lady," she thought to herself.

There were two handicap-parking spaces in the parking lot of the Louisiana Apartments, and Mic pulled the Chevy into the one closest to their front door. Their apartment was on the end of the complex, making it a little bigger than the other apartments and giving it two more windows on the street side. It had only one bedroom, but the rent was perfect for them and for now one bedroom would work. Jen could also push herself to work, the school being just two blocks away, making it very easy for her. She left for work at 7:45 a.m., pushed home for lunch and to use the bathroom, and then back. The school's staff restroom was not accessible to a wheelchair, so, when needed she used the student's restrooms, not exactly what she liked, but workable. Students would ask her questions at times, and it gave her an opportunity to educate them about her disability. She did worry a little about pushing her wheelchair back and forth during the winter months, but for now, pushing her wheelchair (walking to work as she would tell people), worked perfectly. She got exercise, and they saved on gas money.

Mic got Jen's wheelchair out of the car, and as they walked hand in hand to the front door, Mic stopped her, unlocked the door, and then putting his arms under her bottom, lifted her up and out of her chair and carried her over the threshold of their first home. He kissed her softly and, as she kissed him back, he sat down on their couch with her on his lap, flower vase still in her hand.

"I love you so very much Jen," Mic said smiling. "I hope we'll be in love forever. You are the most important person in my entire life, and I hope you feel the same. You are my angel."

Mic would call her angel more often than she could ever remember in their marriage, and as in the movie **Ghost**, where Demi Moore used "ditto" rather than saying I love you. Jen also used "ditto" rather than saying "I Love You" back to Mic.

"Ditto," Jen said, lovingly kissing Mic. "Ditto".

Once back in her wheelchair, Jen set the white vase with the single red rose on the kitchen table, and the newlyweds spent the rest of the afternoon and evening going through their wedding gifts. Her parents had stacked them neatly in the living room—neatly, so that Jen could easily move her wheelchair throughout the apartment. Jen wrote an immediate thank you note after they checked each present, monetary gift or gift card, so as to not forget anyone. There were sheets and pillowslips, blankets, towels, pots and pans, beautiful glassware, dishes and even three beautiful sterling silver items. There was the cutest cookie jar she had ever seen, three flower vases and the most beautiful hand-made quilt— handed down from her grandmother on her dad's side of the family. All total, there was over $500.00 in cash and gift cards, and they both were so thankful for all the items they had received. They found a place for everything, and then made a list of items they still needed. They planned to go shopping on Saturday.

"It will be our very first shopping adventure as man and wife," Jen said, giggling. "Get ready, Mic, I know how you **love** to shop."

The couple ate tomato soup and grilled cheese sandwiches and, of course, chocolate mint ice cream for a late supper, and Mic kiddingly complemented her on not burning the soup. They said a blessing before their meal and, afterward, Jen stood up on her braces, leaned up against the sink and washed as Mic dried the dishes. They turned in early, as they both had to be on the job by 8:00 a.m. the next morning.

"The last three days have been wonderful," Jen told Mic as she got into bed. "What a great beginning to what I hope will be a forever and ever love affair."

Jen reached over to turn out the table lamp, then turned back to the love of her life, kissed him goodnight and wished him sweet dreams.

Chapter Thirteen

After six hours in the bright and cold emergency room, Jill Casey had been moved to room 302 of the intensive care unit. The doctor hadn't as yet made a decision on surgery or treatment. He told her and Tom that he was waiting for more test results.

Once in the ICU, Jill laid flat on her back, unable to move. No one turned her on her side or her stomach, and later on in life she asked herself why she had not developed serious pressure sores from lying on her back for so many hours, and then days. She found out later that the doctors were hoping that her paralysis would be temporary, and they hadn't wanted to make any rash decisions concerning her injury or form of treatment.

A nurse stayed in Jill's room most of the time, and when Tom left the hospital room and Jill needed tending to, Jill would bang her wedding rings on the bed rail to get the nurse's attention. She was angry, she was hooked up to intravenous tubes and heart monitors, had a tube inserted into her lung and was in intense pain. There was no movement or feeling in her lower extremities, a catheter had been inserted, she was not allowed anything by mouth, and all the while she waited for a diagnosis and prognosis from her doctors.

Tom stayed at the hospital night and day for the first three days. He slept on the couch in the waiting room and made sure he was available for the ten minutes each hour he was allowed into his wife's room. He had telephoned Jill's mother, Loren, in Booth Bay Harbor, Maine, and although she wanted to catch the first flight to Buffalo Springs, Tom convinced her to stay in Maine until they had some plan for Jill's treatment. She agreed.

On the fourth day, Tom asked to speak to Jill's doctor. He had asked him the question that had been haunting him the entire time—could Jill ever again have sexual intercourse? Could she have an orgasm? Could she be sexually active? The doctor's answer was short and to the point—she would most likely be able to bear children.

On the fifth day in the intensive care unit, a decision was made to move Jill to the spinal injury unit. After admission, and a day full of more tests, an orthopedic surgeon came into Jill's room to tell her that she had a "complete lesion of the spinal cord."

"Just exactly what does that mean?" Jill asked.

The doctor informed her that it meant only one thing—that she would be paralyzed for the rest of her life and that she would never walk again.

Tom asked again, this time so Jill could hear the answer. "Will my wife ever be able to have an orgasm?"

The doctor politely told both him and Jill that she would most likely be able to get pregnant and have children. Again, that was not what Tom wanted to hear.

The doctor went on to explain that Jill would have to have surgery to repair the vertebrae in her back, that she would have to use a wheelchair for mobility, therefore drastically modifying her life. He did not offer to set up counseling for the young couple—he just walked out of the room, leaving them on their own.

Tom took a seat in the chair next to Jill's hospital bed without saying a word. He had a blank look on his face when finally he asked her if she wanted him to call her mother, or did she wish to call her. Jill said she wanted to make the call. Tom stood up and left the room.

Jill didn't cry; she didn't break down. She just asked the nurse to hand her the telephone and dialed her mother's number.

Loren promised to leave for Colorado on the first available flight. She asked Jill if there was anything she needed from her apartment in Portland, and Jill said no.

"Just please come as soon as you can mom," Jill said quietly. "I think Tom is struggling with this whole ordeal, and he needs you, too, mom. I'm sure my surgery will be tomorrow, and if you don't make it in time, please don't worry. I'll be fine. I'll see you when you get here."

The next day Jill had surgery to place two plates, one on either side of her injured spinal column. They also molded her body into a two-piece

Plexiglas body cast. Later on, they would place the body cast around her, attach it together with velcro strips so her bones would have support when she learned to sit up on her own.

So began the rest of Jill's summer. Her mother stayed with her for the first two weeks after surgery but then returned to manage her restaurant. She telephoned her daughter daily after her return to Booth Bay Harbor, which helped lift Jill's spirits immensely.

"I am here for you, baby," she told her lovingly. "I'm not sure what the future holds for you, but you are strong, Jill. You can handle it. Just make sure and talk to Tom, or to me, or ask someone for help when you need it. Don't keep your feelings inside—let it all out."

Jill left her hospital room very little over the next several weeks. The view from her hospital room window was not of the beautiful Rocky Mountains, but of a solid, red brick wall. Her husband, the handsome, loving man who for the last year and a half had become her friend, her lover, her soul mate and her husband, spent most of his time playing tennis with some of the nursing staff or coming up with every imaginable excuse not to be with her. Jill wondered what had happened to that sensitive, loving man she had recently married.

After Jill's third week in the hospital, Tom left for Portland. He assured her that he loved her, that he would call daily, and that he would try to fly back and forth at least once every ten days—but flew back only three times during Jill's four-month hospital stay and rehabilitation.

On one of those visits, Tom was pushing Jill through the hospital corridor and he asked her what she thought of their starting a family as soon as she was discharged from the hospital and living back in Portland.

"I think it would be great for us to have a baby right away, Jill, or at least try to have one," his emphasis on the word, **try**.

"Are you kidding me, Tom?" Jill asked, somewhat irritated. "I can't walk, I can't pee on my own, and I have to learn how to do a bowel program because I can't do any of those things on my own yet. I can't feel anything! Do you remember Tom? I have no feeling below my waist! Tom, get real! I have to learn how to cope with my disability first before we can even consider having a family!"

Tom apologized and lovingly said. "I just want things to be like they were before, baby."

"Well, Tom, things are not going to be like they were before," Jill said calmly. "I can't walk, but they tell me I can learn to do almost everything from this wheelchair. I will just have to do things a lot differently. I also have to find another job. I certainly can't be a cruise ship hostess anymore, and I'm not sure they have another position for someone using a wheelchair. Our apartment isn't accessible to a wheelchair. We have stairs, Tom, we have thirteen stairs getting into our apartment!"

Tom returned to Portland the next day.

Chapter Fourteen

Officer Lucas Lopez had been to the Pike's Peak hospital once again after Jill's accident. One of the paramedics, John Dawson, who had assisted Jill during her transition off the mountain, had been in a serious off-duty motorcycle accident and had suffered a broken neck. Lucas had checked in with John's family shortly, after the accident and had also stopped in at the intensive care nurses station to check on Jill. He had checked on her one more time after she had been transferred to the spinal cord unit. Being the investigative officer on her case, he liked to check up on not only the victims, but also their families, especially if their injuries had been severe or life threatening, like Jill's. Many times, as soon as accident victims were stabilized, they were sent by air-ambulance to a trauma center or rehabilitation center in another city or even back to their hometowns. In Jill Casey's case, she had remained in Buffalo Springs and would be moved when she was ready, he heard, to a specialized spinal cord injury center in Chamberville. He had gotten permission to say hello to her on one of his visits, but she had been asleep when he had checked in on her.

Lucas had not seen Jill's husband on either visit and had been informed by Jill's nurse that he had gone back home to resume his position as a lieutenant in the Coast Guard. He had been back once or twice to see Jill, but wasn't sure if and when he would return.

Lucas thought it rather strange that a husband, especially a newly married husband, would not have made arrangements with a commanding officer in the Guard to take time off to spend with his severely injured wife. It was none of his business, but yet he was curious.

One Thursday morning, about eleven weeks after Jill's accident, he stopped in at the Pike's Peak Hospital to check up on the paramedic who had been injured. He asked the receptionist after his initial call was completed if Jill Casey was still a patient. When the receptionist had said yes, Lucas asked for her room number. After a few more pertinent questions from the lady in charge, including asking if he was a family member, she had given out the room number.

Lucas waited for the elevator and after a trip first to the third floor, and then to the basement where the physical therapy department was housed, he located her. Jill was standing between a set of parallel bars, trying very hard to learn how to stand and move her motionless legs in a set of full leg braces. Lucas knew that she would have no idea who he was, so rather than going up to her and introducing himself, he asked the therapist in charge to do so.

"I was the investigating officer at Mrs. Casey's accident site," he had told the therapist. "I would like to see how she's doing if it's okay with you?"

The therapist assured him that it was fine, and most likely Jill would be happy to have some company.

"No one has been to see her," the woman replied. "She is not from around here, and her husband has gone back to their home in Maine. Just let me check with her and see how long she needs to be on the bars."

In a few minutes, Lucas was taken to where Jill now sat in her wheelchair, and introductions were made. Jill seemed excited that someone she didn't even know would take the time to come to see her.

"How nice of you, Officer Lopez," she said, taking a deep breath. "I'm sorry, you have to see me like this. I'm just learning to stand up again, and as you can see, I'm not at my best today. This is hard work. I'm not sure I will ever be able to stand or walk with these braces, but I'm sure going to give it a go."

Wiping her brow with a towel and pushing her long blond hair back behind her left ear, she asked how long he had been a police officer? Where did he live in Buffalo Springs?

"Do you make a point to see all of your accident case victims?" she asked, smiling.

Lucas chuckled, answered all of her questions, and for over thirty minutes, he and Jill had an interesting conversation. She told him what she remembered about the accident, which was very little. She asked him questions about the helicopter, the ambulance, how long had he been an officer, and he, in turn, told her a little about his life, his wife, and then towards the end of the conversation asked her how her husband was.

Hesitating just a little, Jill shared with Lucas that Tom was struggling with her disability and that he had gone back to Maine and was working again and trying to find them an accessible apartment.

"Our apartment was beautiful," she commented. "It overlooked the harbor in Portland, and it was close to the Guard and to where the cruise ships set out to sea. I am, or was, a hostess on a cruise ship. Not sure I'll be able to do that job anymore."

Lucas realized that Jill was starting to get emotional so he changed the subject immediately. He stood up from the chair he had been sitting in, told her to keep up the good work, and that if she ever needed a visitor to give him a call.

"My wife is a news anchor on CBS television here in Buffalo Springs," he told her. "She is on the road a lot lately, but perhaps she and I could both come and visit you. Would that be okay?"

Jill assured him that she would love it and would love to meet his wife. She would let him know when she was being discharged from the hospital and being transferred to Chamberville.

"I'm not sure how long it will be before I head for Chamberville," she told him. "I'm told it will be soon. I want my husband to be here when they move me too. But I understand Chamberville is a short distance from Buffalo Springs, so maybe we could still see each other."

Lucas told her that he and his wife had friends in Chamberville that it was about 65 miles from Buffalo Springs, and they went up at least once a month. He promised to keep in touch, gave her his business card with his telephone number both at the Patrol office and at home.

"By the way, Jill," he said smiling. "Just for the record, I am not a police officer, I am a highway patrolman. There is a difference you know."

They both laughed, and, as Jill watched this handsome uniformed officer leave the physical therapy department, she wondered what her handsome, uniformed Lieutenant was doing back in Maine.

Lieutenant Tom Casey was struggling, no doubt about it. He had returned to Portland a few weeks after Jill's accident, hoping that if he returned to work, he would not have to think so much about what was happening to his perfect life. He had hoped all along that Jill's injury would only be temporary, that she would walk again and that their lives would return to normal. He felt guilty about leaving her; but he'd left her. He felt guilty about not being there to support her; but he didn't know how to support her. He felt guilty about being unable to handle anything that had to do with Jill's accident. How could he be so weak he asked himself? He was a lieutenant in the Guard for heaven's sake. He was strong, capable, the best at what he did, and yet he could not imagine his life with a disabled woman—even Jill, the love of his life. He wanted to feel ashamed—but he didn't know how.

He had worked as many hours as he could at the Guard—working during the day on board and out to sea and after hours in the offices, doing whatever was needed of him. He tried looking for another apartment. He went out with a realtor, looking at houses with no stairs, with wide bathroom doors, everything Jill would need when she came home. He hated it. He didn't want to leave their apartment. It was their home, the home they hoped to share until they outgrew it. He stopped looking after seeing two accessible apartments and one house, none of them overlooking the harbor.

He went on-line, checking out all the information he could on paralysis, paraplegia, spinal cord injuries and anything else related to a "lesion of the spinal cord". He read what seemed like volumes on catherization, bowel programs, and sexuality for the physically impaired—and realized that he hated that word—impaired.

"I'm not going to be able to handle this," he said to himself. "I can not be married to a disabled woman—a woman who can't pee on her own, or has to wear a diaper, or can't have normal sex! I just can't!"

Lucas Lopez left the Patrol Offices after his shift ended, and on the way home thought about his visit with Jill Casey. She had left a serious impression on him, and he wasn't sure why. Yes, she was pretty and had a kind of "draw-you-in" type of personality. But, there was more to it. He was sure that when she completely healed, at least emotionally, she could be a very fun-loving, out-going person—one who could charm her way into any situation. Her husband is a lucky man, he thought, and then he figured it out—why Jill had left such an impression on him.

"Jill Casey reminds me of Erica," he said out loud as he drove through the winding streets of Buffalo Springs. "My beautiful wife who is gone on assignment, **again,** is just like Jill Casey! That's it. Except for the color of their hair, they're so much alike, I can't believe it."

Lucas smiled as he turned the corner into the parking garage of his and Erica's condominium, sighed a deep sigh and said aloud. "Gosh, Erica, I miss you. Please come home soon."

Chapter Fifteen

For the first several weeks after the honeymooners returned to Chamberville, Mic and Jen worked on their little apartment, adding wall hangings and wedding photos to the décor. Jen sewed new white curtains for the single kitchen window, and they purchased a washing machine with part of their wedding money. They both returned to work on a daily basis and, on the weekends, they played cards or board games with several of their newly married friends. Several couples got together, usually on Friday evenings, taking turns fixing dinners or desserts, and sharing their stories about weddings and honeymoons. When they met each other at a friend's inaccessible home, Mic and two more of the guys would simply lift Jen and her wheelchair up the stairs and into their home. Jen made no waves about accessibility issues or the lack of accessibility in her life. It's just the way she was.

Mic continued his quest to become a professional bowler, bowling on four bowling leagues a week, pot games (bowling for money), every other weekend, and signing up for as many bowling tournaments as he could afford. He had always dreamed of being a professional bowler, having started bowling when he was a teenager, but the sport of bowling was an expensive one. When he did well, the winnings were nice, but when he wasn't winning, it could be an expensive venture. Now with a wife to support, the pressure of bowling in that many leagues plus tournaments became a financial burden. He had dropped out of two leagues shortly after the wedding, and Jen felt bad for him. She wished that they could bring in more money to support his incredible talent for bowling, but even with financial help from Mic's parents, he'd had to cut back.

Jen in the mean time spent a lot of time learning to cook, and bake, using many of her mother's and grandmother's Dutch recipes, including the infamous Dutch Letters—sugary, almond filled pastry made and baked in the shape of an "S". She continued to sew and knit, make crafty items both to decorate their little apartment and to sell. She and several women friends made crafts one evening a week and planned to have a large craft show towards the end of October, hoping they could all make extra money for holiday shopping. Jen stayed in shape, pushing her wheelchair at least three miles every other night through their neighborhood. She pushed her wheelchair on the sidewalks or on the side streets, making sure she did not impede traffic. She weighed 105 pounds when she got married, and she was determined to stay slender and get into her wedding dress on their first anniversary.

During the middle of November, five months after their marriage, the young couple made the decision to look for and purchase a small house. Their apartment was nice, but very small, and definitely not accessible to a wheelchair. They had signed a six-month lease, hoping that they would be able to have their own place by the beginning of the New Year. Jen's parents had promised to help them with a down payment and, after looking at several affordable houses, they found one they really liked. Mic and his father checked out the cost of building a small ramp that would lead directly from the driveway into the laundry room, and with a small amount of reconstruction, they both felt that the bathroom door could be widened for Jen's wheelchair. The house stood on a corner lot, had plenty of room for their two cars in the driveway, and Jen could have a clothesline—something she had always wanted.

"I love hanging my clothes outside," she told her father-in-law. "I love the way sheets and shirts smell after they have been dried by the wind and the sun—so fresh. We always hung our clothes outside when I lived in Iowa on the farm. Can you and Mic, please, please, build me a clothesline? You just have to hang the wire a little closer to the ground so I can reach it. Please, please?"

With help of a down payment from her parents, Mic and Jen had applied for a home loan, and, hopefully, would be approved and Jen would get her clothesline.

It took a little over a month to get all of the paperwork on the loan completed and turned in, and with Christmas just around the corner, the young couple purchased their first Christmas tree. They realized that it was a rather early, silly purchase, knowing that their loan would most likely be approved the first part of December and they would be moving before the holidays but they were so anxious to decorate and spend their first Christmas together that they bought and put up the tree anyway.

Jen wanted a white-flocked tree. Mic wanted blue decorations. On the day after Thanksgiving, they purchased a four-foot, white-flocked tree from the corner Christmas tree lot, drove to Wal-Mart where they purchased three boxes of blue lights, blue and white bulbs, and blue and silver garland. Jen borrowed her mother's Singer sewing machine, and having learned how to sew in 4-H, she sewed a blue and white Christmas tree skirt. Mic added several of his childhood decorations to the tree, and Jen did the same. Being avid football fans, they also purchased their very first Bronco Football Club decoration—the first of fifty Bronco Football Ornaments to follow.

Two weeks later, their home loan having been approved and in a lightly falling snow, they moved all of their belongings, including the little white-flocked tree, in the back of their friend's pickup truck to their first home.

Two days before Christmas, Tom Casey flew from Portland Maine to Chamberville to spend the holiday with his wife. Jill had been moved to the spinal cord center in Chamberville in late October. Tom was not there to help with the move. She spent almost every day in therapy, and the evenings in an apartment provided by the center, learning to care for herself. She learned to dress, cook and to clean her apartment on her own. She went to the grocery store and to the mall with other people at the center, and she started learning how to drive again.

With the adaption of hand-controls—a device that allowed her to control the gas and brake pedal of the car with her hands—she slowly learned how to drive. She learned how to dismantle her wheelchair, first placing the wheels and then the frame in the backseat behind her. She needed to first of all be able to put her wheelchair into the car by herself and then pass the driving test with hand controls.

Jill was determined. Still being very weak and having lost over twenty five pounds since the onset of her injury, she lifted weights in the center's weight room, pushed her wheelchair time and again up and down the halls of the center every day, all the while receiving physical therapy and learning how to live her life as a women in a wheelchair. She was very careful to check her bottom side daily for pressure sores. She would lie on her side, hold a mirror underneath her, and watch for red spots, or pressure spots. For someone with no sensation, who sat day in and day out in a wheelchair, a pressure sore could become a medical nightmare.

She had learned how to do daily pressure point checks and take the pressure off of her bottom while at the center. She checked herself often.

Jill knew that Tom would be in Chamberville before the holidays, and since she had not seen him in over six weeks, she made extra special plans for his arrival. With the help of her aide and her therapist, she went shopping and purchased a small holiday tree. She found a few unused decorations in the recreation hall, and bought popcorn to pop and cranberries to string on the tree—something romantic and something she and Tom had done before their marriage. During her weekly outing at the mall, she had purchased a romantic holiday card, a small bottle of his favorite cologne, and a pretty white, low-cut nightgown. The young couple had not been intimate since her accident. Yes, Tom had kissed her, told her that he loved her, but that had been the extent of it.

Jill was not sure of how their sex life would be. She had been in several sexuality counseling classes during her stay at the center, but Tom had not been around to attend any of those classes. She wasn't sure he wanted to be. Now, she had her own apartment and they would be alone for the first time since her accident. Jill was sure that their love was strong, and that, with a little encouragement from her therapist, she and Tom could learn how to be intimate again, even though Jill had no sensation below the waist. She knew that she could still make Tom happy, that they could have great sex again; it would just be a little different. It would also take some extra effort on both their parts to be satisfied. Tom had agreed to attend two sexuality-counseling sessions with her over the Christmas holidays. Jill hoped and prayed that everything between them would be as good as it originally was.

At 4:30 p.m. on the afternoon of Christmas Eve, Lucas Lopez left his and Erica's condominium on the south side of Buffalo Springs for the 80-mile trip to Chamberville International Airport. Erica was coming in on the 7:00 p.m. flight from New York City. She had been on assignment in London for the second time this year and had promised to be home in time for the holidays. Her flight had left Heathrow Airport at 9:00 a.m. that morning, with a short, scheduled layover at JFK in New York City. Her presumed arrival time was for 7:00 p.m. in Chamberville.

Erica could have taken a jumper plane from Chamberville to Buffalo Springs, but Lucas had suggested that upon her arrival they stop for holiday drinks and dinner at a nice restaurant in Highlands Ranch, on the outskirts of Chamberville. He also hoped to surprise her with a dozen red roses and a beautiful diamond necklace. He had missed her so much. CBS had promised Erica that once she gave up her CNN assignment and came on staff with them, she would be sent on assignment just a few times a year, but this was the fourth trip already this year. Tom wished she would change from CBS to another media outlet. He wanted her to be home more so they could be together, and also, so they could really work on starting a family. He smiled as he visualized his beautiful wife great with child. He was ready to be a daddy. What fun it will be, he thought to himself to try to make a baby during the week he and Erica were together during the holidays.

Chapter Sixteen

Jen and Mic joined his parents for a light supper on Christmas Eve, and then they left in Mic's Chevy for the candle light service at his parent's church. Mic had been raised Episcopalian, but over the past few years his parents had become very involved in a Church of Science. Jen had never been very comfortable worshiping at their church, it seemed that Jesus Christ was the last thing this church taught, and she wondered what a Christmas Eve service would be like if they could not celebrate the true meaning of Christmas.

Upon entering the church, Jen noticed that someone had taken a great amount of time to beautifully decorate the sanctuary. There were evergreen boughs with twinkling white lights and red sashes, red and pink poinsettias in beautifully decorated pots, and on the altar a small, empty manger. Throughout the evening, there had been short prayers and special music, and although the Bible story of Christmas had not been read, the younger children had taken part in the Christmas story, acting out all of the parts, and a baby had been laid in the empty manger. At the end of the service with a grand entrance of "Ho, Ho, Ho", and "Merry Christmas." Mic's father had portrayed Santa, handing out goodies to all the eager children. As she watched Mic's dad handing out candy and toys, she thought back to her own childhood, first on the farm, and then at their home in a small Iowa town. Her family had never believed in a Santa Claus, rather, on the 5th Day of December, they had celebrated Saint Nicholas Day—a day when you set out your shoes on the front porch. By the next morning if you had been a good little girl or boy, the shoes would be filled with fruit and nuts and all sorts of homemade sweets. In a way, I guess the two are similar, she thought to herself as Santa made his way over to where she and Mic sat. Mic's father handed her a candy cane and a small stuffed polar bear, and she chuckled and thanked him as he let out another "Ho, Ho, and Ho."

Jen and Mic spent the rest of Christmas Eve alone—their choice—opening gifts, and starting what would become a yearly tradition—watching **Scrooge, A Christmas Carol**, on television. They made eggnog shakes in their new blender—the first time it had been used—adding a little rum to make it festive.

"You know I'll be sloshed after just one of these drinks," she told Mic, laughing. "I can't hold my liquor and you know that. Are you trying to take advantage of me?"

By the time she went to bed after celebrating their first Christmas Eve together, Jen was feeling no pain whatsoever and Mic did take advantage of her.

Jen hated the thought of going back to work after her two-week holiday vacation. It was great working for the school district as she always had the same time off as the students, but these two weeks had gone by so quickly, and she was not ready to go back. She also hadn't been feeling the best. She seemed to be sick to her stomach a lot, had way too many headaches, and she wondered if she needed to see her doctor. The birth control pill program she was on was not working the best. She had been spotting lately, before and after her periods, and she was sure the pills were the reason she felt nauseous all the time. She had stopped her exercise program—pushing her wheelchair through the streets where she now lived—as the weather had been very cold and snow covered the streets and sidewalks. She had taken to driving her car every day to work and doing very few exercises at home. She wondered if she needed to exercise more, and for sure eat better. She had set up an appointment to see Dr. Patterson on the next Thursday.

On Thursday nights, while Mic was bowling, she had begun playing wheelchair basketball. She loved the game, and it really did add to her exercise regime. She played at the Spinal Cord Injury Center ten miles from their house, and Mic kidded her all the time that she was "just one of the guys", because she was the only woman playing on a men's wheelchair basketball team.

"If you cut all your hair off, sweet thing," he had said, "then you'll look just like one of the guys, cuz you know, you don't have very big boobs!"

She had lovingly slapped him, said he was just jealous that she was with seven other guys every Thursday night, and as far as she knew, he liked her breasts just the way they were.

Jen knew that the only reason she had been accepted on the basketball team was because of her strength. She had been pushing a wheelchair since she was eight years old, had very strong arms, and could maneuver her manual wheelchair as good as or even better than the men on the team. She could also shoot well, and was one of the higher scoring members of the team.

The team was called the Rocky Mountain Spokebenders. Jen pursued a sponsor so they could purchase matching basketball uniforms, and she learned how to completely take apart and fix any part of her wheelchair that did not operate well. After only six months on the team, she had already become a designated starter, competing against other wheelchair basketball teams in the area.

One Thursday evening after basketball practice, Jen had noticed a young woman sitting on the sidelines of the gymnasium, watching the team practice. She had smiled at her when the young woman seemed to be watching her specifically, and Jen wondered if she knew her, or if she had seen her somewhere before. It was not unusual for several wheelchair users to be at the gym on Thursday nights, watching practice, but most of the time she knew the other disabled women. This young woman gave her a strange feeling, a feeling that she had known her from some other time in her life. She had hoped to speak with the woman at the end of the practice session, but after Jen had showered and gone back into the gym, the young woman was gone.

Jen had kept her appointment with Dr. Patterson shortly after the Christmas holidays, and she had been correct—the birth control pills were causing her to feel sick and causing the spotting. She and Mic had gone to see the doctor together, and together they had decided that Jen would no longer use the pill as a contraceptive, that Mic would either use protection, or they would keep track of Jen's cycle and be cautious during that time so as to not get pregnant. Jen knew that would be difficult, as she had never had regular menstrual cycles. Sometimes she could go two or three months without a period, so she wasn't exactly sure when she was on her cycle. They decided to use protection, and if indeed she did get pregnant, it would be God's will.

Jen and Mic celebrated their first wedding anniversary the end of June. They had drinks and dinner with another couple at a quaint little mountain restaurant, twenty miles west of Chamberville, and after returning from dinner, Jen had put on her wedding gown, Mic had turned on the stereo, and as Jen stood up on her braces, Mic had lifted her up and stood her up on top of his shoes. He had carefully moved her around their living room to the soft sounds of Elvis and "Love Me Tender".

"Am I too heavy for you, Mic?" she had asked sweetly, her arms around his neck. "I don't want to hurt your feet, Mic, please stop when I get too heavy. Okay?"

"Hey, you!" she said, having gotten no response from him. "You're supposed to tell me that I am as light as a feather! I'm not heavy. I still got into this wedding dress a year after our wedding!"

For five minutes, Mic danced with his beautiful wife, and when she did get a little heavy on his feet, he stopped, picked her up in his arms and carried her into their bedroom.

That evening, a baby was conceived.

Chapter Seventeen

Tom Casey's plane landed at Chamberville International Airport at 4:30 p.m. on Christmas Eve Day. He had made arrangements at Hertz Rental Car for a Toyota with hand controls. He wasn't sure how Jill would handle driving her own car by this time, but her telephone calls about driving an adaptive car at the center had been very positive over the past several weeks. He had hoped to surprise her with a car they both could drive, and perhaps he would get a better perspective about his handicapped wife. The Hertz representative had given him a ten-minute crash course on how to drive with controls, and Tom left for the center with time to spare. On the way across town, he had spotted a flower shop, where the owner informed him upon entering, that he had always stayed open late on holidays and weekends. "For that last minute special gift," the owner had said. He had purchased a beautiful pink poinsettia plant, a card and a bottle of wine.

He had promised Jill that he would arrive by 7:00 p.m. on Christmas Eve. They would go out for a nice dinner somewhere, and then spend the evening at her apartment. He had brought a few small gifts with him, but his biggest gift would be a surprise—he had investigated a house in Portland that was accessible, and although not quite what he had originally wanted, he was sure that it would work for her. He had been working really hard lately to change his attitude concerning Jill and her disability. He had spoken several times with co-workers at the Guard and had driven to Booth Bay Harbor twice to speak with Jill's mother, Loren, about her daughter's disability. He had flown into Chamberville and was driving to the center with an open mind and a positive attitude. It had been almost two months since he had seen his wife, and he was anxious to see her and tell her about the house.

Tom parked the Toyota in the center's handicapped parking lot, even though the car did not have a designated parking tag, took the keys from the ignition and got out. Arms filled with gifts and flowers, he walked up to the apartment building, pushed the button to announce his arrival and when asked whom he was there to see, proudly gave the attendant on duty Jill's name.

He tapped lightly on Jill's apartment door, and when she opened the door Tom was once again taken aback. His wife of only six months was as beautiful as ever. She was dressed in a long, silver strapless, dress. Her long hair was curled and swept up behind one ear, and on her ears were the earrings he had given her for a wedding gift. She backed up her wheelchair so Tom could get through the doorway, and before he even set down the flowers and gifts, he was bending over and kissing her.

"You look wonderful, Jill" He said, kissing her again. "You look so much better than you did just two months ago! Are things going well? How do you feel?"

"I'm getting so much better, Tom. I really am," she said, smiling and taking his hand. "I couldn't wait for you to be here. I miss you so much. I want this first Christmas to be the best one we will ever have. I know I'm different, Tom, but really I'm not different. I'm still me. I'm the same old me."

Tom sat down on a chair next to the kitchen table, and Jill rolled her wheelchair up next to him. He told her that he couldn't wait for the plane to land; he was so anxious to see her and had lots of things to talk with her about.

He noticed the little Christmas tree and commented on how cute it was, but that it was a little bare. She assured him that, after this evening, it would no longer be bare, that she had popcorn and cranberries to string, and it would be the prettiest tree he had ever seen when they were through with it.

"I know this isn't how we expected to celebrate our first Christmas together. It's Colorado instead of Maine, Tom," she said, squeezing his hand. "But Christmas is wherever we are together, right?"

Tom agreed and took two plastic cups out of her kitchen cupboard and poured them each a glass of wine. After a little more small talk, Tom told Jill that he had his first surprise for her in the parking lot and was she ready to go out to dinner? Tom helped her with her jacket, and she signed out of her apartment building. A light snow was falling as they headed for the parking lot, and Tom, somewhat unsure of how to approach the subject, asked Jill if she needed him to push her in her wheelchair. She said no, that she was fine as long as the snow didn't get too deep.

When they reached the rented Toyota, Tom opened the door for her and watched as she pulled her long dress up over her knees, showing her full leg braces. He watched as she lifted her legs and transferred herself into the passenger seat. Jill then showed him how to take the wheelchair apart and place it in the back seat. Once behind the steering wheel, he told her that he had rented this car with hand-controls just for her and that in the next two weeks, he wanted the two of them to go driving often.

"Can you show me how these controls work, Jill?" he said turning on the ignition. "I want to see how you drive now, baby, and I want to learn too. Will you be able to drive this car a few times while I'm here?"

Jill looked at the controls, said that they looked similar to the ones she was practicing with, and said if her instructor and counselor said it was okay, she would love to take him driving.

"I still don't have a new driver's license. My counselor has to be with me when I drive, but I'm legal," she said, laughing, "I still have my old license."

There was only one problem, she informed her husband—we will need a two-door car for me to drive by myself. She told him how she had to take her wheelchair apart, lean over into the passenger side of the car, and put the wheels in first and then the frame into the backseat.

"When we buy a car, Tom," she said calmly. "It'll have to be a two-door. Otherwise, I will always have to have someone with me when I drive, and I want to become independent."

The Caseys laughed and talked all the way to the restaurant. Tom agreed that his pickup truck, back in Portland would never be adapted for her to drive, and neither would her four-door Buick.

"How about a convertible?" Tom asked his wife. "That way you could just throw your wheelchair over the top of the backseat? We'd have to move to where it never snowed, however—could be a little cold and wet with the top down all winter in Maine."

The evening was going beautifully. Jill was positive that their marriage could still work, even though she now had a disability. She shared with Tom how busy her weeks at the center were. The therapy sessions, walking in the pool on the parallel bars, learning to cook and clean the apartment. And then she mentioned the sexuality sessions.

"I'm learning a lot, Tom," she said quietly. "I am learning that sex, well that sex is really mind-over-matter. I will no longer be able to feel you inside me when we are making love, but mentally, I know exactly how making love with you feels, and the sessions are really helping me to understand myself. I hope that the two sessions we are going to take together this week will help you to understand more, too."

Tom was quiet for a moment, but then said of course he would take the sessions with her, and how he couldn't wait to get her back to the apartment and make love to her.

After a lovely dinner, Tom and Jill returned home, popped popcorn for an hour, strung it on red thread, and did the same with a bag of cranberries. She helped string the decorations on the bottom of the tree, and Tom hung them on the top. When the tree was entirely decorated, Jill pushed her wheelchair into the bedroom and came out with a beautiful white paper angel, one she had made in occupational therapy. She handed it to Tom, and he placed it on the very top of the tree.

Jill gave Tom the gifts she had purchased for him, and then Tom gave her a beautiful black box with a green ribbon. Excitedly, she opened the box. Inside was a set of beautiful diamond post earrings. Along with the diamonds, there was a set of beautiful pearl earrings as well.

Puzzled, Jill looked at him and said. "Tom, they are beautiful, absolutely beautiful, but my ears aren't pierced. I only wear clip on earrings. Have you forgotten? You gave me clip-on's for a wedding gift."

"I know, sweetheart. I know," he said. "But, you're such a beautiful woman, and I thought these earrings would make you look even more stunning, even more sexy. I want to take you one morning next week to get your ears pierced. Please, will you do that for me? It's the trend, Jill, to have two or three posts in each ear. You'll look so fantastic. I've always wanted you to get your ears pierced!"

Jill set the box down on her lap, and tears filling her eyes, said softly to her husband, "Tom, they're beautiful earrings, and I love them, but if you gave me these earrings thinking that it'll help you forget that I'm not a whole person anymore, that these earrings will help you forget that I'm paralyzed, it won't work. You can't make my injury go away; you can't make my legs work again. You can only love me for who I am, for who I have always been, and not because part of me doesn't work anymore. Making my face or ears look more beautiful to you, or making me look like an able bodied woman because my face looks prettier to you won't make my paralyzed legs come back to life. Tom, you're giving me these earrings for all the wrong reasons."

Tom stood up, and turned his head toward the window of Jill's apartment and said, "Jill, I've always wanted you to have your ears pierced. I think pierced ears are sexy. I just want you to look beautiful for yourself, and yes, for me too. I'm sorry if I hurt you. You don't have to get your ears pierced if you don't want to."

He then walked back to his wife, bent over and gave her a hug and gently kissed her on the lips. "Let's go to bed," he said. "It's been a long day. We can talk more tomorrow."

Jill was disappointed, no doubt. She had wanted Christmas Eve to be perfect and it wasn't turning out that way. She got ready for bed, and even though the mood had changed, she decided to put on the new nightgown anyway. It took her longer to get ready for bed than it had previously, but within twenty minutes she was ready. Tom was already in bed when she came out of the bathroom, but he immediately got up, asked her if he could help her in any way, and once again complimented her on how beautiful she looked. Once in bed, she laid back and curled up in Tom's arms. Once she had to have him help her sit up so she could reposition her legs, but it was just a matter of minutes before they started kissing and getting into heavy petting. Tom caressed her breasts underneath her gown, and then gently helped her out of it. Jill's body showed no signs of trauma or scarring. Her body was just as perfect as it had been six months before. Tom began kissing her all over, on her neck and breasts, and realized how long it had been since they had made love.

Only a few minutes into the sexual act, Jill's bladder went into a spasm and Tom suddenly stopped, immediately getting off of her and getting out of bed.

"What the…!" he exclaimed. "Jill, what just happened? What is this? Did you just pee all over me?"

"I'm not sure, Tom," she said fearfully. "I'm on medication to relax my bladder so I can catheterize myself on a schedule, but sometimes I have accidents, Tom. I can't feel it when I pee, so maybe I did. Tom, I'm so sorry, but it's no big deal. It's part of being paralyzed. It will get better, I promise! Next time, I'll make sure I empty my bladder before hand."

"I'm going to take a shower."

Jill got herself to a sitting position on the bed and realized that she had voided, but it wasn't the first time she had had an accident. Her bladder had most likely gone into a spasm during sex and there was nothing she could have done to prevent it. She wished that she had forewarned Tom about the possibility of an accident, but it was too late now. She transferred into her wheelchair, pulled the soiled sheet from the bed and took another from the hall cupboard. She would ask Tom to help her remake the bed when he finished with his shower.

Chapter Eighteen

*L*ucas had taken a shower, dressed in a pair of khaki slacks and a light brown shirt and sweater and made sure the apartment was picked up before he left for the airport. He took his Jeff Gordon #24 jacket out of the closet, put it on, and picked up the small, brightly decorated package—his gift for Erica, and headed out the door. He hummed a few bars of "I'm Dreaming of a White Christmas" as he walked down the stairs to the parking garage. He unlocked his vehicle, got in, put the key in the ignition and started up the black SUV, turning the heater on high. He immediately turned on the radio to his favorite country music station, hoping to hear Christmas music all the way to Chamberville International Airport. A few minutes later, he was on his way.

A light snow was falling and there was an inch of snow covering the grassy areas as he drove through his Buffalo Springs neighborhood, but the streets were clear, and, once out on the highway, there was very little traffic and the highway was also clear. He stopped on the outskirts of Crested City to pick up roses, and, with flowers and a card featuring Harry Potter characters in hand, he continued towards Chamberville. He took the toll road—C-470 across town to CIA to save time.

Lucas sang along to his favorite country artists as they sang a number of his favorite Christmas melodies, and before he knew it he was at CIA. The long-term parking lots were filled with cars parked there by Christmas travelers, but the short-term lot was only half full, and he quickly pulled into a parking space. He left the Christmas box on the front seat of the SUV but took the beautiful bouquet of red roses with him.

It took Lucas only a few minutes to access the elevators from the short-term parking area into the airport. Once inside the airport, he took a minute to purchase coffee at Starbucks, and then checked the American Airlines flight schedules from London and New York. He knew he was over an hour and a half early, but he wanted to make sure her flight was on time and be there to greet her.

As he looked over the arrival board for Flight 1437, he noticed, "delayed" typed across the scheduling board.

"Delayed flights are nothing new," he thought to himself, and after getting a boarding pass, he continued on to the gate and Concourse-D. He would enjoy his coffee, perhaps pick up a NASCAR magazine and read for a while as he waited for Erica's plane.

As Lucas continued his walk, first through security and then to Concourse-D to Flight #1437's arrival gate, he noticed several airport security officers scurrying ahead of him. He then saw several men and women in blue blazers with the American Airlines logo on their lapels also walk running ahead of him. He wondered immediately what was happening or if there might be a problem somewhere. He picked up his step just a little, and as he approached the arrival gate there was not only a long line of people at the AA desk, but several of the security officers and AA personnel he had seen previously gathered about the area. He stood quietly for only a few moments before an AA representative spoke into the microphone.

"Ladies and gentleman," the calm voice announced. "All of those who are waiting for Flight #1437 from London and New York, would you please follow these two gentleman here to my right, to the American Airlines hospitality room directly across the hallway?"

The representative pointed out the two men dressed in the traditional blue blazers representing AA, and immediately people voicing excitement and concern began gathering around the two men.

Lucas also walked towards the two men.

Erica boarded her flight in London, and the plane had taken off right on time. She was so excited to finally be heading home to Buffalo Springs and to the waiting arms of her husband—especially now that it was the Christmas holidays. She had missed Lucas terribly, and she had made the decision to talk to her supervisors at CBS as soon as the holidays were over. She would ask for a more permanent position at the station, which would include no more overseas travels and only local reporting and newscasts. She admitted that she loved her job, loved the traveling, but she loved Lucas more and wanted to be at home with him.

As the aircraft soared through the air high above the Atlantic Ocean, Erica sipped on hot tea and read from the latest Harry Potter novel. "Yes," she admitted quietly and then chuckled and thought, "Lucas continually tells me that I am a Harry Potter freak, and I know I am. He is always kidding me about it. We've seen every Harry Potter movie at least twice, and I've read every book in the series at least three times."

She smiled, thinking about her handsome husband, and how everything about him was so perfect, from his incredible physique and good looks, to his crooked little toe. She loved everything about him and had for years. "Yes," she thought to herself, "I am either going to have to convince my superiors to stay on task at the station or look for another position."

Just as Erica was engrossed in her thoughts, a severe pain went through her abdominal area. She dropped the book and bent over, thinking she just might vomit. She grabbed the paper bag out of the seat pocket in front of her and although she gagged and gagged, nothing came up. Noticing her distress, the woman seated next to her asked if she was okay or could she help her in anyway?

"I guess I may be airsick," she replied, taking a deep breath. "I've been flying my entire life though, and I've never had this feeling before. If you'll excuse me, I think I'll go to the restroom."

The woman stood up to let Erica out of her seat and into the aisle of the plane, and Erica proceeded to the back of the aircraft and into the lavatory. Once inside, she sat down on the toilet seat and wondered just exactly what was happening to her. "This is the third or fourth time this past week that I have felt nauseous," she said to herself. "I hope I'm not coming down with the flu or a cold. I can't be sick for Christmas!"

Then, all of a sudden, like she'd just received a vision or a proclamation from above, she smiled, looked down and touched her hand to her stomach.

"Oh my gosh!" she said aloud. "I wonder! What if…what if I'm pregnant? Just maybe!" she thought excitedly, "Just maybe Lucas and I are finally pregnant!"

A few minutes later, having splashed her face with cold water and feeling much better, she returned to her seat and continued reading her book. Her stomach seemed to settle down, and when her light supper came, she ate her sandwich, drank another cup of tea and afterward fell sound asleep—a deep, deep sleep where she dreamt of a handsome prince and a beautiful princess, alone in a castle, high up in the Rocky Mountains of Colorado.

After she had been asleep for almost an hour, Erica was awakened by a hard thumping sound and an announcement being repeated by the Captain to "fasten their seatbelts."

"Ladies and gentleman," came the calm voice of the Captain. "This is your captain speaking. This aircraft is experiencing some difficulties at this time. You may feel some turbulence and hear some unusual noises. We ask that you stay in your seats with your seatbelts securely fastened. This also goes for all airline personnel. Please stay seated with your seatbelts securely fastened. Please do not be alarmed, and we will keep you informed."

Everyone on board seemed to fasten their seatbelts at once and passengers, their voices filled with excitement, could be heard talking loudly throughout the plane. Five minutes after the first initial announcement from the captain, his voice came through the intercom once again.

"Ladies and gentleman, this is your captain speaking," he said, his voice not quite as calm this time. "We're having mechanical problems with the aircraft. We have lost an engine, and are having problems with another. We're in contact with JFK and are preparing for an emergency landing, but we're still three hundred miles from New York City. Our plan is to attempt a landing at JFK with only two engines. Please be aware that we **can** fly and land with only two engines, but it will be a bumpy descent and difficult landing. When the time comes for us to land, please listen carefully to everything the aircraft personnel have to tell you and follow their instructions explicitly. I'll continue to keep you abreast of the situation."

Immediately, the airline personnel began to collect leftover supper paraphernalia and asked everyone to make sure they were securely strapped in and to put their seats in the upright position. They prepared all of the passengers for a difficult landing and attended to those who were already starting to panic.

Erica looked at the woman next to her who seemed very calm, considering the situation.

"Are you doing alright?" she asked the older woman.

"Yes, thank you miss, I am doing just fine." she replied.

"How about you? Are you okay?" she asked.

"Yes, I think so," Erica replied calmly. "I've flown thousands of miles and never had any problems. I guess there's always a chance that something will go wrong, but no, right now I'm not panicking at all. I'm thinking of getting home to Colorado and seeing my wonderful husband for Christmas."

The two women introduced themselves and shared light conversation for another five minutes when once again the voice of the captain came over the intercom.

"Ladies and gentleman," he began. "I am sorry, but we have just lost the second engine and the third engine is giving us a slight problem. We are trying very hard to make it to JFK, but be prepared, as it will most likely be a rough landing. Personnel at JFK are preparing for a crash landing and they'll do everything they can, as will my co-pilots and myself, to keep you all safe and secure during a possible crash landing. We are now making our descent into JFK. We'll be landing in approximately fifteen minutes. We're now asking the aircraft's personnel to prepare all passengers for a crash landing."

As Erica watched the aircraft's personnel scurrying around and heard screams coming from a woman sitting three or four seats ahead of her, she looked at the older woman next to her who had introduced herself as Irene Wilson. She seemed very calm, as was Erica.

"Do you think we'll make it down okay?" Erica's new friend asked.

"I'm not sure Erica. I have a somewhat bad feeling about this, but no matter what happens, I'm okay with it. I've lived a very long life, over seventy-five years in fact, and I've always been ready to meet my Lord and Savior whenever he called me. If this is the time, then let it be."

"You have a very strong faith," Erica said, taking her hand in hers. "I too have faith, but I guess I've never thought much about dying. I'm only in my late thirties, have only been married less than ten years, and my husband and I so much want to have a baby. In fact, I think I just might be pregnant. I think that may be what caused my illness a little while ago."

Erica patted Irene's hand, which was still clasped in hers, and Irene asked if they shouldn't perhaps exchange addresses and telephone numbers?

"Who knows what is going to happen in the next few minutes, Erica," she said calmly. "God willing, we'll both make it through this situation, but if perchance only one of us makes it, it would be nice for the one who survives to try to contact the other's husband. Do you think that would be smart?"

Erica let go of Irene's hands, quickly took a note pad out of her purse, wrote down her information and handed the pad to Irene. The two women, strangers only a short time ago, not only put down pertinent information but also began to write a short personal message to their loved ones

"Do you mind if we have a prayer together?" the older woman asked Erica.

Nodding her head yes, then taking the older woman's hands in her own, Erica smiled, and said she would like that very much. In silence at first, each woman bowed her head, and prayed her own personal prayer, and then out loud they recited the Lord's Prayer together. Two other passengers, perfect strangers sitting a row in front of the two women joined in the prayer.

In the cockpit, the captain of Flight #1437 had just contacted the JFK airport tower, reporting that the third engine of the aircraft was now on fire.

"We have flames," he yelled into his radio. "We have flames in engine number three! We'll never make it in to JFK. I can no longer control her! We are going down!"

Erica, still writing her note, did not finish it.

Chapter Nineteen

More than one hundred people gathered into the small AA hospitality room where they were asked to get comfortable while another AA employee handed out coffee and snacks. In the back of the room, a handsomely dressed, kind looking man with a satchel stood quietly by.

"Folks?" the representative asked calmly. "Folks, I need your attention. I need to inform all of you who have someone coming in on Flight #1437 from New York City that there have been mechanical difficulties with that aircraft. The aircraft is about three hundred miles from JFK airport, and the crew has reported two of their four engines as being out or on fire, and another engine in danger of stalling. The crew at JFK are preparing for a crash landing."

Before the AA representative could say any more, those gathered—loved ones, friends, corporate executives, strangers and many military family members—began talking among themselves. Some started crying or looking around the room for help, and one elderly man passed out and fell to the floor.

"People, people, please!" the representative called out, trying to bring some calmness to those gathered. "Please, I know this is very difficult, but you need to know that the plane is still in the air; it has not crashed. You need to be prepared for the worse but hope for the best. We are in constant communication with those at JFK and we will keep you posted. If you will take your seats, we will try to answer any questions you might have."

A man in blue dress slacks and a white, long sleeved shirt, at the back of the room, quickly walked over to the elderly man who lay lifeless on the floor. People gathering around him were asked calmly by the man who introduced himself as an AA doctor, to please give his patient breathing room. Evidently skilled at working this type of an event, he opened his satchel, took out a stethoscope and began to check the man's heart rate. He checked his pulse and the doctor motioned for one of the AA representatives. He immediately told him to call 911 and to get the on-call ambulance to Concourse-D. He then broke open a small capsule, placed it under the man's nose and the man began to stir.

"I think he'll be okay," the doctor said to the AA representative standing next to him. "He has passed out I'm certain because of the news he just heard, but I want to make sure he's okay." The doctor continued. "He should come around in just a few seconds. Then let's ask him who he is and check his identity. I'm sure he has a loved one on board flight #1437."

Lucas stood in silence, listening to the words but not actually comprehending all that was being said. He accepted a cup of hot coffee, took a sip, and then walked over to where the doctor still knelt at the side of the elderly man on the floor.

"Can I help in any way, doctor?" Lucas asked. "I'm a highway patrol officer and have my Red Cross certification if that helps you in anyway."

The doctor thanked him and said he would certainly call on him if any more of those present had problems, but for now he was fine. Lucas turned around, went back and sat down.

The elderly man, now in a sitting position on the floor took out his wallet, handed it to the doctor who then handed it to the AA clerk. The clerk pulled out his license, which identified him as Marlow Wilson from Littleton, Colorado.

"How are you feeling now, sir?" the doctor asked. "Do you know where you are? Can you tell me your full name?"

"I believe I am alright, sir," he said, his voice shaking. "I am Marlow Wilson. My wife, Irene, is on the flight coming in from New York City. She was visiting her sister in London."

The doctor and clerk assisted Mr. Wilson from the floor to an empty chair and asked the clerk to bring him a glass of water. When the paramedics arrived, they checked him over, said he should be fine and offered to stand by in case any others might be in need of medical assistance. The doctor thanked them and told them that just might be a good idea, considering the situation.

"I'm on call here at the airport all the time," he mentioned. "Not only just for a crisis like this one, but if there are people who become ill or injured. I'm thankful that we don't get very many of these situations, but I'm always glad to be of service to those who need it. Keep an eye on Mr. Wilson, will you please? I believe there is a young man I should check on right now."

The doctor walked over to where Lucas sat and asked if he could join him for a few minutes. Lucas' eyes were staring straight ahead, a blank look on his face, but he nodded his head yes, and the doctor sat down.

Offering his hand to Lucas, he introduced himself as Dr. Jim Ashton.

"Are you doing alright?" Ashton asked. "You look a little pale."

Lucas shook the doctor's hand and told him who he was, and that he was fine, but worried.

"I'm waiting for my wife," he answered.

"We live in Buffalo Springs," Lucas said. "My wife, Erica, has been on assignment with CBS in London for the past two weeks."

And then, after a few moments of silence, he asked the doctor, "What do you think, sir? Is there any chance at all that a plane with only one or two working engines can possibly land safely?

Chapter Twenty

*R*ather than staying the entire two weeks, Tom Casey stayed in Chamberville for only three more days after Christmas. Jill was devastated when he informed her that he was leaving early, but she knew there was no changing his mind. Tom would have to find a way to accept her disability before they could go forward. They said their goodbyes at her apartment, and he took the rental car back to the airport—without her ever attempting to drive it.

Tom promised his wife that, when he returned to Portland, he would sign a contract on the accessible house and would also look for and purchase a vehicle that could be readily adapted for her. Unknown to Jill, what Tom actually did upon his return to Maine was immediately to get better acquainted with the woman he had been seeing on a regular basis.

Jill continued with her rehabilitation, getting stronger every day, and soon she was driving the center's adapted car on a daily basis, going to the grocery store or to the mall, to dinner out with friends she had made while in rehab, and learning to get her wheelchair in and out without assistance. She knew it wouldn't be long before she'd return to her home in Portland and start life anew. She had not only improved physically and emotionally while at the rehabilitation center in Chamberville, but she learned to accept life as it now was, to go through it with a good outlook and a positive attitude, and that there was nothing she would not be able to handle—yes, life, would have to be handled differently, but she had learned that, even from a wheelchair, life was definitely doable.

She had mixed emotions, however, about returning to Maine. She no longer had a job, nor had Tom signed the lease on the accessible house, and she wasn't certain if she even had a loving husband to go home to. He had flown to Chamberville only once since the holidays to see her, staying only four days, and calling on average of once a week, and seemed very distant. He admitted each time he spoke with her on the telephone that he was struggling with the whole "disability" thing, but he would keep trying and maybe things would be better when she got home. She constantly assured him that all would work out fine, but as time went on, she wasn't too sure.

Tom flew into CIA early on a Friday in the middle of January, and by Saturday morning they were packed and ready for their trip to the airport. They had both been instructed by her therapist on what to expect at the airport; Jill would be loaded onto the aircraft before all others, placed in an "aisle chair", strapped in, and then two attendants would roll her onto the aircraft, undo the straps, lift her up and into the aircraft seat. Her wheelchair would be placed in the baggage compartment and upon arrival in Portland, she would be the last passenger to leave the aircraft, going through similar procedures to get off the aircraft. There would be no chance for her to use the restroom on the aircraft, but having catheterized herself prior to leaving the center and wearing a protective pad, she was confident there would be no "accidents". Tom, however, wasn't as sure. He now had to handle the baggage and her wheelchair, see to all the arrangements, talk with the airline personnel about Jill's needs, and watch the humiliation when she was lifted in and out of her wheelchair—like a sack of flour. He was embarrassed and uncomfortable—for her, but most of all for himself. Jill noticed his discomfort immediately and tried her best to calm him down.

"Tom, baby," she said lovingly. "It's no problem. I don't mind being lifted in and out. I'm getting used to this. These people are being very helpful to me. I'm just sorry that I can't help you carry all of this luggage and medical supplies. Please, please, baby, you need to just go with it. Our lives are a little different now, but if it doesn't bother me, it shouldn't bother you."

Tom bent down, kissed her on the check, said he was sorry, stood back and watched as the airport personnel assisted his beautiful but disabled wife into her aisle seat. He placed the overnight case into the compartment above their seats, closed the door, and attempted to step over her motionless legs without hitting them. As he sat down beside her, he looked out the window of the aircraft, daring not to say a word to his wife of less than a year. He knew, deep down inside, that this marriage would not work—he could not be married to a woman in a wheelchair.

Lucas opened a can of tuna fish, took off the lid, and with a fork scraped the contents into a bowl. He walked over to the refrigerator, opened the door, took out a jar of sweet pickles and the jar of mayonnaise and set them on the counter. Without doing anything further, he sat down at the kitchen table, looked out the window to the north, and watched two squirrels scurrying around his deck for food. Unlike them, he had no appetite and no desire to prepare or eat a tuna fish sandwich. He had no desire, really, to do anything. He just wanted his life back, the life he had enjoyed with his wife of nearly ten years—the life that had been taken from him so suddenly on Christmas Eve—the night of the airplane crash just outside of New York City. The night when 217 passengers, including his beloved wife, Erica, had been killed.

Chapter Twenty-One

Three months after Christmas and having suffered through many weeks of serious morning sickness, Jen was certain she was pregnant and scheduled an appointment with her gynecologist. Mic took off work early the afternoon of the appointment, and with Jen being on spring break from school, they went together to see Dr. Patterson.

"I think the rabbit died, Doc," Jen, smiling, told her doctor as he came into the examining room. "I wasn't quite ready for this quite this soon, but if I'm pregnant, Mic and I will be elated."

After a thorough exam, blood and urine tests, Dr. Patterson told her and Mic that indeed she was pregnant, and that the baby would be due sometime around the middle of September. He started her on a vitamin regimen, told her to eat right, continue exercising, working out by pushing her wheelchair through her neighborhood, and that she could continue to play basketball for a few more months.

"I don't see any problem in the foreseeable future," he told the young couple. "I really think you'll handle this pregnancy just like any other woman, Jen. If you do have any unusual pain or spotting, just call me right away, but I think you'll do just fine. I want to see you monthly, and then at seven months, I want to see you twice a month until the baby is born."

Mic and Jen asked the doctor a few more questions, and then went out and celebrated with a nice dinner. They decided to let their parents know right away. This would be the first grandchild on both sides of the family. As expected, they were all excited, and yet concerned—especially Mic's mother. She hadn't ever been excited about having a disabled daughter-in-law in the first place and now, although she was excited for her son, she wasn't sure that Jen and a new baby wouldn't be more work for Mic. She wasn't convinced, even after fourteen months of marriage, that Jen was the right woman for him, and Mic knew that he might have a real problem with his doubting and interfering mother.

Jen was excited about being pregnant and immediately shared the news with her co-workers, her neighbors and her close friends at church.

Her parents, too, were elated at the news, not only because Jen had been able to conceive, but that they would be grandparents in just a few months. Jen's mother immediately started making a baby afghan and bought baby clothes, and even Jen's mother-in-law, insisting that it was going to be a girl, purchased darling little pink outfits, booties and blankets for her. Jen accepted them gracefully, wondering what she would do if it was a boy. The soon-to-be parents bought a used baby bed and dresser at a local thrift store and repainted them both in baby-safe white paint. Jen sewed new curtains for their spare bedroom in a blue and yellow pattern. Jen continued to play basketball and exercise and had a horrendous appetite. She gained weight almost immediately, but Dr. Patterson didn't seem to think the weight gain was a problem.

At nearly six months into her pregnancy, she and Mic signed up for a pre-birthing class. The class was held on Tuesday evenings for a total of six weeks and, although they couldn't participate in all of the pre-birth procedures due to Jen's disability, they did participate in all of the breathing and counting exercises. Jen even managed to readily get out of her wheelchair for some of the exercise programs.

During the second week of classes, Jen started having minor back pain. She didn't say a thing to Mic until they arrived at home. A few hours later the pains worsened, and although she wasn't exactly sure what labor pains were supposed to feel like, she was certain something was happening and that she might be in premature labor.

Around midnight, Jen's water broke. She tried not to panic, but she admitted on the telephone to Mic, who was at work, that she was very concerned.

"It's too soon, Mic," she said, tearing up now. "This baby is not due for three more months. It just can't be coming so soon!"

Mic tried to calm her down and mentioned to her, sweetly, that she should call the doctor and call her parents. Realizing that it was late, Jen figured Dr. Patterson wouldn't be available and that worried her. She wanted to have the doctor who knew her case best, and understood her disability as well. She wanted this baby more than anything and felt that, even though her water broke, this little one would be born healthy. She said a silent prayer as she prepared an overnight bag, left a message on the doctor's on-call message machine and called her mother.

A nurse returned Jen's call within minutes, advising her to leave for the hospital right away. She would call ahead to notify the maternity ward of her arrival.

Mic left the brewery and arrived at their house just as Jen's parents were pulling into their driveway. He kissed Jen gently, smiled, and asked if she was ready. Nodding her head yes, he immediately assisted her out the front door, lifted her gently into the front seat, after placing several towels on the front seat to absorb the water and blood. By this time her contractions were coming every five minutes, and Jen and Mic both realized that they would be lucky to make it to the hospital in time for the early birth of their first baby.

Chapter Twenty-Two

$\mathcal{U}$pon Tom and Jill's return to Maine, and even though Tom had promised to sign a lease on an accessible home earlier, he had not done so. He insisted that she live with her mother in Booth Bay Harbor for a few weeks while he looked for an apartment in Portland. Jill wasn't upset about going to live with her mother, but she was upset that he had procrastinated so long and had lied to her. Tom purchased a small ramp for the one front step, allowing Jill access into her mother, Loren's, home, as well as a bath chair that she could use in the shower.

Loren was excited to have her daughter back with her. She was cautious about asking her questions at first, but as the days went by, their conversations about all that had happened in the past several months went smoothly—until Loren asked her about Tom and their marriage.

"Mom," Jill said somewhat sternly. "I love Tom, and I know he loves me. I admit that he is struggling with my disability, but he promises to try really hard to accept the "new me", and I believe him. I know he should have found us an accessible home by now, but I have to be patient. This is a big change for both of us, so please, mom, let us work all this out ourselves, okay?"

The discussion was put to rest, and three weeks after Jill's return to Maine, Tom rented a two-bedroom, fairly accessible apartment that he had seen earlier in Portland. He and another friend from the Coast Guard moved all of their belongings into the small apartment, and Tom drove to Booth Bay Harbor to pick up Jill.

Jill was impressed—Tom had come through for them. He even lifted her out of her wheelchair, kissed her and carried her across the threshold into their new place. However, after getting into bed and talking for a few minutes, Jill started kissing him and making more romantic gestures toward her husband, but he turned over on his side, commenting that he was too tired to make love.

For the next several months, Jill settled into her new life. Her husband, however, spent more and more hours at the Guard and away from home. At first, Jill gave Tom the benefit of the doubt, presuming that he still needed time to adapt to her disability and their new life together. On a Friday morning in May, Jill drove herself down to the Coast Guard, planning to surprise her husband with a picnic lunch. She drove into the Guard's parking lot, knowing he was not going out on the water, so there would be a good chance of surprising him. She got herself out of the car and rolled into the Guard offices. The secretary greeted her with open arms, giving her a huge hug, but when Jill asked to see Tom, the secretary, somewhat surprised, told her that Tom had called in that morning requesting a vacation day.

"I'm sorry, Jill," the secretary said rather sheepishly, "I figured you two were together today. I have no idea where he is."

Jill thanked her, stayed a few more minutes for idle chat and then excused herself. When she got back into her car, she hesitated before starting the engine and wondered where her husband could be and why he had not confided in her. She sat in the car only a few more minutes when she decided to check on her husband's whereabouts. "Stupid me, stupid me," she said to herself, smacking her hands against the steering wheel. "I guess I've known all along what you were up to, I just wouldn't or couldn't admit to myself that you might be cheating on me. Well, enough is enough Lieutenant Casey. Enough is enough."

Chapter Twenty-Three

Spring had come and gone, and Lucas's heart was no closer to healing than it had been the night he received the news of Erica's death. He and all other family members or friends had been asked to stay at the airport until the early morning hours of Christmas Day. Airport personnel, airline representatives, ministers, priests, rabbis and many others trained to deal with this type of tragedy, had all been brought in to counsel with the families and friends of those killed in the airplane crash. The AA representative asked if he could call someone for Lucas, a minister or a family member? He had said no, there was no one. Then, on second thought, he gave the young woman in a blue blazer Ken Porter's telephone number, and even though it was Christmas Day, Ken and his wife drove to the airport immediately to be with Lucas in his grief.

Lucas took a month's leave of absence from the Highway Patrol, hoping that he would have time to grieve fully and get his life back to normal. Now, it was summer in Buffalo Springs. The trees were leafed out, flowers were blooming everywhere and, for tourists and residents alike, it was a beautiful time of the year—but not for Lucas. His heart was broken and nothing or no one seemed to be able to help him recover from Erica's death. He worked long shifts, he went to movies, he even volunteered on his days off at the local children's home, thinking that being around children would help mend his broken heart, but nothing seemed to help. Then in mid-July, Lucas received a letter in the mail, a letter that would finally show him a way out of his grief and into a new beginning. The letter began:

> "Dear Mr. Lopez, my name is Irene Mercer. I was on Flight #1437 the night it crashed. Yes, thankfully, I was one of the survivors, having only suffered a broken leg and severe bruising. I met your wife Erica on that flight from London, and although we only talked for a short while, we became quick friends, even sharing a prayer together before the plane went down. We had exchanged

telephone numbers and addresses and placed those in our individual purses. We planned, that if one of us survived and the other did not, we prayed that our purses would be found and our loved ones would be contacted. That way they would know how we spent our last minutes in the air. Erica also wrote a personal note to you and she asked me to place her note in my purse. Of course, we weren't sure that this plan would ever work, but now it seems that it did. Unbelievably, after all this time, some of my belongings were returned to me, including my purse. I found the telephone number and your address, as well as the note that she wrote to you. I took it upon myself to read her note, and rather than calling you, I am sending you the note Mr. Lopez. I hope you don't mind that I read it first. Please know that I felt a kindred spirit in Erica, and I know that our Lord and Savior took her to be with Him on that day, and that she now rests in His loving arms. I hope and pray that you, too, have found peace and consolation in knowing that Erica knew her Lord Jesus in those last few minutes. Please call me at anytime, I have included my number and would be happy to speak with you."

Lucas then went on, tears filling his eyes as he finished reading the first letter and began reading the dirty, crumpled note from his beloved wife:

"My darling Lucas. I am sending this note to you, not sure if it will ever be discovered, but wanting to write it anyway. The Captain assures us that he will get us on the ground safely, but I'm not so sure. Two engines are already gone and one is on fire. But please know my love, that I have no fear of crashing or that I might die. Irene, my new friend, has assured me that she is not afraid and that I should not be afraid either, as we're both resting in the arms of Jesus, and I believe that to be true. There is one thing Lucas, my darling, that you need to know. After all these years, I am almost positive that I am pregnant. Irene believes it to be true also. Wouldn't that be something?

> *You and I finally having a child together after all these years of trying? I'm not sad, Lucas; I am thrilled. If I don't survive this crash, I know that this baby and I will make it safely to Heaven. I also know that if we do not see each other again, we will meet in Heaven one day. I will never stop loving you, and I know that after you recover from my death, you must, yes, hear me my love, you must find another person to love in the future. You have so much love to give, and I want you to give it to another woman, just like you gave your love to me. Promise me, Lucas, promise me...I lo...."*

"Erica, Erica," Lucas sobbed. "My beautiful Erica."

The letter was not finished or signed. Lucas, tears now streaming down his cheeks, presumed that she hadn't had enough time to finish the note before handing it to her friend Irene. He could not help but ask, "Why God, why Erica, why finally bless us with a child of our own and then take them both from me?"

Sobbing, Lucas clutched the note to his chest and fell to his knees, continuing to ask God why. It would be a long, long time before Lucas would receive an answer.

Chapter Twenty-Four

Five hours after arriving at the Porter Memorial Hospital in Chamberville, Mic and Jennifer's first son was stillborn. It had been a painful and trying time for the young couple. Sometime during those hours, and for no apparent reason, Jen's labor had stopped, and during that period of time, the baby's heart also stopped beating. Entirely too small to survive, and no longer, even with Jen's pushing, was he able to help himself get through the birth canal, Jen's tiny child had lost his battle to survive. Having not had air for several hours, the one-pound, five-ounce baby boy was completely blue when he entered the world, and although Jen's pediatrician had been on hand for the untimely birth, there was nothing anyone could have done to save the life of little Timothy Jay Collins.

Jen was devastated. She and Mic held each other and cried, and it would take months before they recovered from the loss of their firstborn son. Jen was immediately transferred off of and out of the OB-GYN area, hoping this would aid in her healing, and although it did help some, Jen found herself in tears most of the time. Two days later, the tiny baby boy was buried in a small white casket in the baby section of the local cemetery. The grave marker, paid for by Mic's parents, read, "Our son, Timothy Jay Collins, Resting in the Arms of Jesus".

Jen stayed with her parents for the first week after Timothy's stillborn birth. She suffered slightly from the "baby blues" especially knowing that her father and Mic had immediately taken down all of the baby furniture in the nursery. But the biggest hurt of all was when her parents began receiving "hate" mail—letters stating that they should have had their daughter "fixed" prior to her marriage, that she, a disabled person should not be 'allowed' to have children—a disabled woman could never take care of a child. The doctor had assured Jen that in no way had her paralysis had any bearing on the stillbirth; it had to do with her "afterbirth" getting more nourishment than the baby—just one of those freakish wills of nature or God's will, as Jen believed. But still the letters were heartbreaking.

"Why, why would anyone write such hateful letters?" she asked her mother, sobbing. Her mother had no answers, but shared with her daughter that there were definitely unkind people in the world, people who didn't understand what having a disability was all about. She should just forgive them for what they had done or said. Of course, none of the letters were signed.

"Cowards," she thought to herself, "unbelievable cowards!"

Jen, as always, picked herself up, quickly got back to her normal routine and, after just three weeks, prepared to go back to work. She started to play wheelchair basketball again after only being off the team for a month, and a few months later heard that the Colorado Paralympics Team were having tryouts.

"Oh my gosh, Mic," she exclaimed one day. "I've always wanted to be involved in sports, not just basketball. What do you think? Should I check it out?"

Of course Mic said yes.

She found information on the Paralympic Games and learned that they had been going on for many years, virtually since shortly after World War II. Veterans coming home from the war with missing limbs or paralysis were learning how to participate in sports from their wheelchairs or with their artificial limbs, and reading further, she realized that there had never been any women competitors.

"Until now," She thought to herself, smiling.

"Wow, this is just what I need, Mic," she said one weekend morning at breakfast. "I think there should be women in wheelchair sports competition, and I think I should be one of those women who sets a precedent and is selected for the Colorado team."

Of course, Mic agreed to that, too.

So after initially signing up to be a part of the Colorado Team with a higher goal to make the national team, Jen's first challenge was to lose all of her pregnancy weight. Although little Timothy had only weighed slightly over a pound, she had gained over 45 pounds during that six month time period. She began a workout regiment until school started, and then worked out before and after work. She started eating healthier, and pushed her wheelchair over 50 miles a week throughout her neighborhood. Twice a week she worked out at the local high school with eight handicapped guys and two other disabled women who also used wheelchairs, and two Paralympics coaches. Within four months, Jen had lost twenty-five pounds, but then, shortly into her newfound challenge as an athlete, she realized she was pregnant again.

She was only a little disappointed that she would have to put off her tryouts for competition for another year, or for at least another nine months. She worried a little about this pregnancy and actually slowed down her activities some. She stopped crawling up and down her stairs, and Mic widened the bathroom door so she could get in and out in her wheelchair rather than having to transfer. Everything went well until her seventh month, and once again Jen went into early labor. This time however, even though little Lennie Jay was only four pounds, he was healthy, a fighter, and remained in the hospital for a month after his birth. Jen pumped her breasts, placing the milk in bottles, freezing it, and taking her milk up to the neonatal ward at the hospital and feeding him her breast milk once a day, sometimes twice. When Lennie Jay was only a month old, he joined her and Mic in their little house on Zenobia Street. She continued to nurse her beautiful baby boy, and although he was somewhat fussy at times, she bonded with him immediately and motherhood came easily. Having to balance herself in her wheelchair with one arm, she adapted early how to pick him up out of the crib with one arm. She would strap him onto her lap while she vacuumed the carpets or did the dishes. She placed him in his carryall in the front seat of the car, and then went to the other side to get herself and her wheelchair into the car. She did the shopping, took Lennie Jay to his and her doctor appointments and checkups—she was as capable as any other "normal" mother. She was so thankful for this beautiful little boy, and in her prayers at night, she asked God to forgive those few people who had written those hateful letters about her. Her life was truly a blessing, regardless of her disability, and she was so thankful to her family, to Mic, and most of all, to God.

On a beautiful but blustery day in September, Mic and Jen Collins dedicated their miracle child to God, as he was baptized at the Holy Shepherd Lutheran church.

Chapter Twenty-Five

The young couple, married only a short time, had not been intimate since Jill's return to Portland. Jill was heartbroken, but she finally realized that the love of her life was really not the man she thought he was—a man unable to love her for what and who she was, a man who no longer found her sexually attractive, a man who no longer loved or wanted her.

One evening, at dinner, only a month after Tom was not at the Coast Guard offices on the day of her surprise visit, she planned to approach him about their future. However, Tom brought the subject up first, telling Jill that he was in love with someone else and wanted a divorce. Although not surprised, Jill was deeply hurt, and she cried openly. Tom stood up from the dinner table, touched her lightly on the shoulder and left the room. He packed a bag, told her he would return later for the rest of his things and stepped out of her life—forever.

Jill had prepared herself for Tom's departure. Over the past several months, even before leaving Chamberville, she had applied for Social Security Disability benefits, taken two computer classes, a communication skills class, and had spoken with the director at the Spinal Cord Injury Center in Chamberville about a position. She had also applied for two positions in Portland, but had been turned down.

She was preparing herself for a new life, a life without Tom. She was seriously hurt but not broken. How could someone who had declared his undying love for her be so callous, so cold, and so unsympathetic to her needs? How could he not love her for who she was, for whom she had always been, who she continued to be? He should have been able to cope with her disability, after all she was.

Life as Jill knew it was now over. Tom filed for divorce, and she didn't contest it. Within three months of his leaving her, alone and crying at the dining room table, their marriage was over, but Jill's new life was about to begin.

With assistance from her mother and two of her friends, she moved out of the house she and Tom had shared for only a few months and moved back in with her mother. She planned to stay with her mother only long enough to secure a position either in Portland or in Chamberville in the communication field. She was ready to move on, to move forward with her life. So, when the director of the Spinal Cord Injury Center in Chamberville called her and invited her to come to Chamberville for an interview, she readily accepted. She boarded the airplane and flew to Chamberville on her own, where upon her arrival she was driven to the center in an adaptive wheelchair van and checked into the very same dormitory she had lived in during her rehabilitation. Immediately, she felt right at home.

The interview over and a position in the administration offices offered and accepted, Jill asked to stay in the dormitory for a few more days. This way she could get reacquainted with some of the center's staff and check out more of the activities. There were events held every day at the center—crafts, and oil painting in the recreation room, swimming and aerobics in the pool, trips to the mall or theatre, and evening entertainment twice a week. The events, however, that interested her the most were the sporting events being held daily in the gymnasium. There were teams of both men and women practicing wheelchair rugby and basketball, wheelchair fencing, and others. She was enthralled by what these wheelchair athletes could do.

On the Friday before she was to return to Portland, she stopped by to watch a women's wheelchair basketball game. There was the local team from Chamberville and a team from Chicago. She loved basketball, had played in high school, and became instantly interested in the way the game was played in a wheelchair. She stayed and watched the game for over an hour. As a young, blond woman rolled down the court, stopped her wheelchair and put up a shot—a shot that hit the backboard and dropped in, she found herself clapping, perhaps not for the two-point basket but for the young woman who had made it. As she watched her come back down the court, the two of them made eye contact, and Jill realized that she had met this young woman somewhere before. At first, she wasn't sure from where, but then she realized who she was. It was the girl she and Tom had met on their honeymoon—the young bride from the Sky City Hotel.

"My goodness," Jill said to herself. "That's the woman Tom and I met on our honeymoon." She continued in her thoughts, and what came to her mind first of all was that, after meeting this young woman and her husband at the Sky City Hotel, Tom had told her that he could not imagine how anyone could be married or have a relationship with someone who had a disability.

"I guess he was right. He couldn't be married to someone in a wheelchair."

The game continued and Jill so badly wanted to stay and not only finish watching the game, but most of all she wanted to get reacquainted with the young woman she had met a few years earlier. However, now was not the time. She had a plane to catch. She was certain that they would meet up again in the near future, as within the month Jill would be moving to Chamberville to start her life over. A tear slid down her cheek, and she gently wiped it away.

Chapter Twenty-Six

*J*en noticed the young woman in a wheelchair sitting on the sideline of the basketball court but didn't recognize her. She did wonder, however, who she was. She put her out of her mind, continued to play basketball and, when the game was over, got into her car and went directly home. She sometimes showered at the center, but she chose to shower at home tonight because it would be time for Lennie Jay's feeding when she arrived, and she wanted to breastfeed him before he was put down for the night. She knew the time for breastfeeding was about to end, as he was nearing a year old.

She loved being a mother. Lennie, although a "preemie", was gaining weight, eating well, and the pediatrician said he would catch up to normal weight and size by the time he was two years old. He did have colds and high fevers often, and on many occasions went into fever-seizures. These seizures scared Jen, but the doctor assured her that the seizures caused no damage, and he would outgrow them in time. One day, while she was driving to an appointment, Lennie had one of his worst seizures while strapped into the carryall in the front seat of her car. Jen stopped the car, controlled his head and his tongue as she had been taught, then drove to the nearest emergency room where they put the little guy in an ice bath, medicated him, and this time admitted him for three days. There was no brain damage due to the high fever, but the doctor told Jen that because of Lennie's premature birth, he would most likely have seizures until his body and brain caught up to a normal child's weight and size, and that he would most likely have colds and sore throats until he was old enough to have his tonsils removed. He continued to have the seizures for another year. Jen blamed herself for his condition, knowing full well if she had carried him to full term he would not have had them. Her doctor assured her that it was only an act of nature that he had been born early. It had nothing to do with her disability, and she should not blame herself, but more often than not, while holding her precious son, Jen cried after every seizure.

She continually blamed herself for Lennie's early birth Since the male organs are the last body parts to develop in a boy baby, and since Lennie had been just short of three months premature, his testicles had not dropped before his birth and, although doctors would surgically try to drop them over the next few years, there was a pretty good chance that little Lennie would be sterile. It took Jen a long time to convince herself that it was just one of those things that happen in life, that it was not her fault, and she finally was able, with God's help, to let it go.

Lennie celebrated his second birthday and Jen decided to take a leave of absence from her job. She had returned to work when he was three months old because they needed the money. Her mother had watched Lennie, and although Jen knew he was in good hands, she missed him. She wanted to be a stay-at-home mom, and when Mic had secured a better position at the brewery, she was able to stay at home with her son. She could also workout more on the sports team, play more basketball and keep trying out for the Paralympic Games. She was very busy being a wife and a mother and trying out for the Paralympic team, but she was happier than she had ever been—if that was possible. Mic continued in his bowling career two nights a week, and she and Mic joined a wheelchair/able-bodied square dance club. On practice nights and for exhibitions Jen would dance with her partner who was also in a wheelchair, but for fun and after Monday night practices, Mic would also get into a wheelchair and together they would dance the nights away. Jen sewed beautiful yellow square dance skirts for the women wheelchair dancers, did most of the public relations work for the club, and on the nights Mic had to go to work early or needed extra sleep, she would take Lennie Jay and go to the dance club meetings/practices by herself. Grandma would babysit or Jen would take Lennie along.

Mic continued to work seven days a week, sometimes ten hours a day. The money was wonderful and after Lennie's third birthday, the Collins family purchased a newer home. It had four bedrooms, a double car garage, and was the most beautiful house Jen had ever seen. The payments were a little more than they were used to paying, but Mic assured her that they could handle it. They sold their old home and moved into the new one. Having had only two bedrooms in the old home, Jen decorated the other two bedrooms, making one into an office and another into a guest room. This way, they could have guests over and not have to use Lennie's room for their overnight guests.

She worked on the house all day, sitting on the floor to paint, then sitting back in her wheelchair to paint the next level of walls, and even transferred up and onto a bar stool to paint the higher levels. When Mic had time, he painted the trim and the high spots Jen couldn't reach. When Jen wanted the furniture changed, she would move the pieces around by either getting out of her wheelchair onto the floor and pushing tables, chairs, even the couch with her strong arms, or she would line up her wheelchair footplates with the bottom of the piece of furniture and move it around until she got it into the right position. Jen figured she had the will power and the strength to do it, and Mic was gone so much, she could readily take care of some things herself.

Jen was a very independent woman and Mic told her so on a daily basis. He was also feeling the guilt of not being the complete husband he should be. He was always tired, didn't help her much with the "honey-dos" that all wives require, and working the night shift was taking its toll on the young couple. Mic needed a lot of sleep, and although he seemed to get plenty of rest during the daytime hours, daytime sleep wasn't as refreshing as sleeping during the nighttime. More and more, Mic would tell her to go places on her own, and so Jen would take Lennie and go to events while Mic slept, then hurry home to wake him up, fix him supper, and get him out the door on time.

A man and a woman, married with a little one, need to spend much more time together than Mic and Jen Collins were. One night, after a square dance exhibition, a night when she had left Lennie with her mother, Jen accepted an invitation to go out for a drink with her dance partner. It was only for a drink and conversation, but her dance partner was having marital problems, and Jen was very lonely with Mic working all of the time. It would only be a matter of time if they continued to be together on dance nights that their relationship would become more than just a friendship. Jen promised herself that, that, would never happen.

Chapter Twenty-Seven

Lucas Lopez spent many hours at the local cemetery where his darling Erica had been laid to rest two years before. He brought flowers at least once a month—red roses—they had been her favorite—and he read at least one or two chapters out of a Harry Potter book—also a favorite—each time he visited her grave. He also teared up each time he visited his wife. He tried everything in his power to control his grief, but nothing seemed to work.

After a year and a half, his supervisors on the Patrol finally insisted that he see a grief counselor—no questions asked. He was still carrying out his duties as a Highway Patrol Officer in perfect order, but they could tell by his actions day after day, that he was lonely and still so devastated, that finally he agreed to get counseling.

Sheila Grayson was a 55-year old woman who had been with the Patrol for over twenty years. She had counseled hundreds of officers, their wives and families on a multitude of different subjects, but grief counseling was her specialty.

Lucas saw Sheila once a week for almost three months. During this time period she let him share his feelings and gave him ideas on how to get on with his life. She told him he needed to accept the friendship of others—something he had been refusing. He needed to write down his feelings, feelings before Erica's passing and his current feelings, feelings about the horrible airplane crash, feelings of anger and guilt. She even suggested that he write a journal or perhaps start writing a book about his and Erica's life together. He also agreed to go visit a few children's homes. Perhaps it would help him in the loss of his unborn child to see other babies and small children waiting to be adopted. Sheila also suggested that perhaps he should begin to go to church once again, spending time with God, all the while asking for His guidance and grace. Lucas agreed to at least try all of the things she had suggested.

After a Thursday shift and wanting to see his good friend Ken Porter again, Lucas changed his clothes, got into his own vehicle and drove the sixty-five miles to Chamberville to have dinner with Ken, his wife and daughter. They had come to Erica's funeral, but during the months following the service, each time Ken had called to speak with Lucas, Lucas had the message machine pick up the call. Now, after his sessions with Sheila, Lucas was determined to get in touch with Ken and his family again. He called early in the day to let them know he was driving down and had met them at a local diner in the south part of Chamberville. They talked for hours. Ken hadn't done any drugs in years, seemed to be very content with his job and his family, and they could have talked way into the night. However, at 8:30 pm, Ken was reminded that it was a school night, and they needed to get home. As Ken paid the ticket for their dinner and as Lucas was walking towards the door, he noticed three young women sitting at a table near the back of the room—one sitting in a wheelchair. He recognized her immediately. It was Jill Casey, the young woman who had been injured over two years ago on Cinnamon Ridge.

"My gosh," he said out loud, "she must have not fully recovered from her injuries and ended up using a wheelchair."

He asked Ken to hold on for a moment, that he recognized someone and wanted to go over and say a quick hello. He walked slowly over to the table where Jill and her friends were definitely enjoying themselves with heavy chatter and laughter. As he approached their table, the three of them looked up at him almost simultaneously.

"Hi cutie. Can we help you?" one of the women asked, chuckling."

"Yes", Lucas said somewhat embarrassed. "Jill? Jill Casey?" he asked. "Jill? It's Officer L…"

"Officer Lopez?" she exclaimed! "Officer Lopez, it's really you? Oh my gosh!! I can't believe it!! I haven't seen you in forever!"

Excitedly, Jill pushed her wheelchair away from the table, maneuvered to the side where Lucas was standing and held out her hand to him. He took it in his, held it tightly, and smiling, thought to himself how warm and comfortable it felt.

Chapter Twenty-Eight

Shortly after celebrating their fourth wedding anniversary with a romantic dinner at a local restaurant where Mic had given her four beautiful purple roses—one for each year of their marriage—and an evening of lovemaking, Jen conceived once again. She was elated and so was Mic. This pregnancy, just like the two previous ones, had not been planned, but it seemed to make her pregnancies all the more special, and she hoped that this time there would be no complications, and she would give birth to a beautiful, healthy baby. They both hoped for a baby girl this time, and once again her mother-in-law gave her several pink items, as if pink gifts would make having a little girl possible. Jen chuckled to herself, as she knew her mother-in-law meant well, but with Mic having a brother and several male cousins, and she only having a brother, having a little girl was probably not in God's plan. She continued to play basketball, stay in good health, and this time she only gained 28 pounds during her entire pregnancy. When she entered her last trimester, she prayed to God that this baby would make it to full term. She did have to quit driving the car, as she couldn't lean over far enough to pull her wheelchair into the backseat any longer, but most of all she didn't want to take any chances on another early labor.

A week after her due date and after only two hours of labor, another beautiful baby boy came into Jen and Mic's life—little Mickey Lee who weighed in at over seven pounds and was a perfect picture of health. Taking care of two children was not easy for Jen, but she managed. Lenny would help her out at times in his "big boy" ways, and most of the time gave his baby brother many more hugs and kisses than necessary. Jen loved it. Her life was so perfect. When Mickey was four months of age, Jen began to have serious morning sickness, she realized quickly that nursing Mickey was not a foolproof type of birth control, and she was most likely pregnant again. At first she became a little more than panicked.

"Just how am I going to handle two babies, only a year apart?" she wondered to herself.

However, with Lenny walking alongside her wheelchair and Mickey strapped, with a dishtowel around her waist, she continued to do the grocery shopping, go to doctor visits, and all other duties performed by "normal" mothers. It took a little longer to load and strap her two sons into their car seats and pull her wheelchair into the backseat, but she always seemed to manage. It wasn't until at seven months into her pregnancy that she admitted she could no longer strap Mickey onto her expanding lap, nor get in and out of the car by herself. Mic helped her more than usual, even though he seemed to require more sleep than most men who worked nights, and her panic on having a third child began to subside. When little Ronnie Alan was born and Jen came home from the hospital with her their new bundle of joy, she quickly realized that handling three children was going to take a little more maneuvering. Ronnie was so little in comparison to Mickey, and Mickey hadn't begun to walk, so along with double the number of diapers, she also had two "lap" babies. She soon learned to strap Mickey to her legs on her wheelchair footplates strap Ronnie around her stomach, and with Lenny walking and helping her to open doors and strap himself into the car by himself, she managed once again—it just took a longer time to get things accomplished.

Mic and Jen did agree, however, even though they hadn't been blessed with a little girl, that three children, three healthy little boys were enough, and Mic had a minor procedure to assure both of them that there would be no more little ones in the Collins household.

Chapter Twenty-Nine

$\mathscr{F}$our years after the accident that left Jill Casey a paraplegic, and although most of her friends and family had reminded her that it was just an "Act of God", Jill was awarded an appropriate sum of money because of her accident. With extra money in the bank and money to live on for a few years, she quit her job at the center, purchased a modest home in a Chamberville suburb, and enrolled in college. With her previous college credits and after going to school two days and three nights a weeks for nearly two years, she received her degree in education. After several interviews, and finally finding an accessible high school with a principal who realized that her disability would have a positive impact on her students, she was hired. She loved working and teaching English and Advanced Writing, and shortly after her hiring, was asked to be the lead teacher in the school's Drama Club. Her first task was to put on a junior/senior play, and after three months of teaching and learning the script, she and her students received a standing ovation at the end of the two-night dramatic performance. Her life, once in turmoil, had done a complete turn-around. She had adjusted to her new life as a wheelchair user, had a great position at the local high school, had several very close friends, and had even heard from her ex-husband once or twice, the second time to tell her that he was getting married again. Jill felt no remorse. She was happy for him and told him so. His news did, however, spark a lonely feeling in Jill. She had not dated since her accident, figuring that it would take time for her to adjust to her new lifestyle, and, to be honest, no one had really shown an interest in her, nor, had she found anyone that she was really interested in—except maybe for Officer Lopez.

Ever since her untimely encounter with him several months earlier, she had thought of him often. She heard his name mentioned on the evening news once in awhile, and she had read the newspaper articles of the New York/JFK airplane crash in which his wife had been killed. She had not realized when she read the list of fatalities, which included an Erica Lopez, that she had been Officer Lopez' wife. It was not until she scanned the obituaries and read her funeral notice, where Lucas' name had been included as her husband, that a deep sadness settled in over her. She had wanted to call him, but did not feel at the time that it was appropriate—maybe now that time had passed, it would be.

One afternoon, when her classes were excused early, she looked for a Lucas and Erica Lopez in the Buffalo Springs telephone book. To her dismay, there was no listing.

"I guess, for safety reasons police officers don't have their phone numbers and addresses listed," she reminded herself, and put it off for another time.

Chapter Thirty

$\mathcal{L}$ucas Lopez had driven to Chamberville several times to see his good friend Ken Porter and his family after Erica's passing. Taylor was growing so fast and he enjoyed being around this lively youngster. However, it was hard to imagine what life could have been like with a child of his own. Had Erica and his unborn child survived the air crash, the baby would be over two years old. Erica would've decorated a nursery, and they would've been shopping for clothes and gone to pre-parenting meetings, and he tried to imagine his beautiful wife great with child, what labor and delivery might have been like, and how he would have felt holding their child for the first time. But it was not meant to be, and he could understand that now. He had been in grief counseling for many months and would continue for sometime. He had also been back to church, something he hadn't done regularly since he was a kid. He not only enjoyed the services, had met some nice single women his own age, but realized how important God was to him now, and he prayed daily that he could stay the Christian man he had vowed to become. Erica would have been so proud of him. Each time he visited her grave, which was still at least once a month, he not only took red roses, but he would recite or read a scripture verse to her and their child. At least once or twice, he would read aloud the inscription on her stone, "My Beloved Wife, Erica Jordaine Lopez and Our Unborn Miracle Child. We'll Be Together Again in Heaven." The tears came less frequently now, and he prayed that in the days and months ahead, they would stop completely, and he could get on with his life.

Dating was not important to him. There were several lovely ladies, either single or widowed, who had approached him at work and at church, but although he was friendly to them, he did not encourage them in any way. He took out Erica's last note to him every now and again. He would run his finger across her writings, but most often, he would skip the writings asking him to go on with his life to find someone else. He just wasn't ready for another love in his life. Erica had been his only real love, and he doubted he could ever find another to take her place.

One sunny afternoon around 1:30 pm, he drove south into Crested City and had just turned left onto the main street in front of the high school when he saw Jill Casey coming down the sidewalk. He wondered what she might be doing in this booming Colorado town, as the last he'd heard she was working at the center in Chamberville where she'd received her rehabilitation. He slowed down and watched as she pushed into the high school's staff parking lot. Not wanting to scare her, but really curious as to what she was doing in Crested City, he turned into the lot, and as she went up to a newer blue Mustang, he pulled up behind her car, rolled down the window and asked if she had called for a highway patrolman. Surprised, and very pleased to see him, she smiled and turned her wheelchair around and rolled up to his window.

"Nope, I didn't call a cop," she said, laughing. "But I could cause a ruckus if you'd like me to."

Laughing now and slowly opening his car door as she backed her wheelchair away, he got out, leaned against the front fender, crossed his arms and looked at her in disbelief. She was beautiful. She had cut her long blond hair into a short bob, had on just a touch of green eye shadow, wore bright pink lipstick, and had on a stunning pink and turquoise pantsuit. Turquoise earrings dangled from her ears. He thought she was absolutely stunning.

Realizing that he was staring, he coughed a fake cough, asked her how she was doing, and then asked what she was doing so far away from home?

"I'm not that far away," she said, rolling closer to him. "I now live in Littleton; I have my own place, and I'm an English teacher here at the high school. We only had half-day classes today, so I was just heading home."

Smiling even more now, he said. "Jill, you look amazing. I just can't believe how wonderful you look. Living in Colorado must agree with you."

They chatted in the high school parking lot for another ten minutes, and sadly Lucas said he had to get back to work.

"I have to work until 10:00 pm tonight," he said. "That's my schedule for the next three days, but next week, I work the day shift. Do you think we could get a cup of coffee one afternoon next week, after you get out of school?"

They talked a few minutes longer, exchanged telephone numbers, and agreed to meet the next week on Friday at 4:00 pm.

"There's a Village Inn just a little way up the street. Could we meet there?" She asked?

"Sounds great," Lucas said, his heart beating faster. "I look forward to it."

With that, the two parted ways. Lucas asked Jill if he could help her in any way, and she said no, that she could manage quite well, and smiling, told him she would anxiously wait their coffee date for next Friday.

Pulling out of the school parking lot, Lucas got another call, and with sirens blaring, he headed out onto I-25 to another accident scene. The siren on his patrol car was not the only thing that was blaring. His heart was beating so fast, that he could hardly get his breath and could barely answer the next call that came through on his radio.

Chapter Thirty-One

The days and months seemed to fly by, and on a Tuesday night, Jen gathered up her sons, grabbed the diaper bag, a few toys, the box of Cheerios, and rolled out to her car. It was Tuesday night basketball practice, and once again Mic couldn't watch the boys, so she was taking them along. Sylvia Brenner, a wife of one of the players, had offered to watch the boys for two hours at the gymnasium. That way, if she had to nurse the baby, she could. Sylvia had watched them before, when Mic was asleep or, when his parents couldn't watch them, and Jen had all the confidence in the world in her, plus the older boys loved her.

It wasn't easy trying to get in shape physically, play basketball two nights a week and keep a busy family and home going, but somehow she managed. No, her house wasn't always tidy, and she didn't fix 5-course meals, but her husband was happy, and her boys were well fed, clean and most of the time contented. Ronnie was a fussy baby, and at times almost more than she could handle. The doctors were sure it was allergies, and besides mother's milk he could only handle small amounts of yellow fruits and vegetables, and chicken, without becoming horribly sick and cranky. But she seemed always to have extra energy to get the tasks of a wife and mother completed. Her goal right now was to be the best wife and mother she could be, all the while trying to get in shape and then within the next year or two try out for the Paralympic Games.

She recalled, as she loaded herself, her wheelchair, and the three boys into the car, how she had worried alot about how she would handle doing all the daily chores, grocery shopping, going to doctor appointments, running errands for her and the boys, all without Mic's help. But she'd learned to manage. Yes, it took a bit longer than an able-bodied mother, but she did it, and was proud of it. It took almost twenty minutes each time she loaded her and the boys into the car to run errands. She first put the baby in the infant seat and strapped him in. Two older ones climbed into the back seat. She strapped them in, made sure their little feet and legs were up on the seat and secure, before she herself transferred into the driver's seat. She then pulled her wheelchair into the back seat behind her. She didn't want her wheelchair hitting their legs and feet. "We are scrunched," they would mumble sometimes, but soon they would be laughing and playing together. She thanked God every time she got in and out of the car with her darling little boys that she was strong enough to handle these beautiful babies He had blessed her with.

Just a few days before she had been grocery shopping, and Lennie was helping her push the grocery cart. She had Mickey standing on the footplates of her wheelchair with one of Mic's narrow belts strapped around his little body and her legs, and Ronnie secured on her lap with a large dish towel holding the baby carryall in place around her stomach. Lennie had somehow managed to tip the cart over—most likely because he turned a corner too fast. Eggs went air-borne, landing and breaking all over the floor; the milk carton exploded as it hit the floor, and as she asked a near-by stocker to please get a broom and a mop, an older woman approached her and sharply told her, "A person like you should not have been allowed to have children". Jen was upset at the remark, and as the young man came to her aid, rather than making a nasty remark back to this seemingly unhappy human being, she placed a protective shoulder around her son and helped the grocery stocker clean up the mess.

"Why did you let her speak to you that way?" the young man questioned.

"This kind of accident could happen to any mother with children," she said, smiling. "Calling her down on her comments would've made me just like her, and I'm definitely not like her."

Jen drove the twelve miles to the gymnasium, went through the entire procedure once again of getting her little bundle of boys out of the car and proceeded into the playing area. Most of the guys had already arrived and were shooting hoops, but waved at her as she entered. Anticipating her arrival, Sylvia walked swiftly to the door to greet and help her.

"How are my favorite little boys?" she asked, taking the carryall from Jen's lap and helping Jen untie Mickey Lee from her legs.

"Hi Sylvie," Lennie said, as he gave her a big hug. "Did you bwing the dominos for us to play wif?"

She gave him a big hug and assured him that, yes, she had brought the domino game for them to play. She carried the baby and took the other two boys to a corner of the gymnasium where they would be safe from flying basketballs. So far, Lennie hadn't shown an interest in the basketballs, and the other two were too little to understand what their mommy was doing. She really enjoyed their time together and knew that Jen appreciated the help. She also knew that Jen wanted desperately to make the Paralympic Team, both in basketball and in track and field, and with her large family, it was going to be a real challenge. So, anything she could do to help, she gladly would.

Jen, knowing that the boys were in good hands, rolled onto the gym floor, picked up a loose ball and began shooting. The guys all liked her and appreciated her as a real asset to the game. She was tall in her wheelchair; she was strong, almost as strong as they were, and she could take a hit or a fall like the rest of them. They also knew that there were very few local wheelchair women who could play basketball like she could. They all hoped that for Jen's sake, she would make the Paralympic Team, and that in time there would be enough stronger women in wheelchairs to have their own women's team. But for now, they enjoyed having her play basketball with the Spokebenders.

As the evening progressed and the team took a short water break, Jen checked on Sylvia and the boys. The baby was still sound asleep, and after a few games of their style of dominos, Sylvia was reading them a story.

"Mommy, mommy," Lennie called as he saw her approaching, "Sylvie's reading us a stowy of Jack with the beans. Come listen."

Jen rolled over to them, gave Lennie and Mickey a hug, checked on Ronnie and then listened to a few paragraphs of Jack and the Beanstalk. She smiled as she thought how much she loved these three little guys, and what it might have been like with one more. She couldn't imagine having to take care of four boys, but every now and then, she remembered Timmy. She had even written a poem about him, and she thought of it again just then.

…And One Is Missing

A rock fireplace stands still and alone in the living room
A stone is missing
The inner fire gives off a warm glow
On one side of the red stained mantle
Sets a photo in a black and silver frame
A mother a father and three sons
On the other side of the mantle a frame stands alone

Empty, without a photo
There's only a memory there
Through pain and toil a tiny babe entered the world
He was blond, blue-eyed like the others
Shown on the mantle
He was the firstborn son, too small to survive
Wrapped in a blanket of baby blue, cheeks only slightly pink
Cradled in his mother's arms
There was no time for photos
A blanket of rich, black soil now covers the tiny form
Cradled in a coverlet of grass and clover
Mother earth now rocks him in her arms
The fire is a dying ember and
The sun slowly peaks through the open window
Reflecting on a silver and black frame on the mantle
A mother, a father, and four blond, blue-eyed sons.

"Jen, Jen," Sylvia asked, the tone of her voice rising. "Jen, are you alright?"

"Yes, yes, Sylvia, I'm fine." Jen answered, somewhat embarrassed. "I just had a flashback; a memory from a long time ago. I'm okay now, and thanks again for keeping track of these guys. I appreciate you so much."

Wiping tears away from her cheeks, Jen prepared to go back onto the floor. She noticed three women coming into the gymnasium. One, an attractive blond woman, probably close to her age who used a wheelchair and the other two who were able bodied. She stared at them for just a few minutes and then went back to the scrimmage. On the next time out, Jen asked Jason Brenner if he knew the women standing at the doorway. He turned, looked, and told Jen that he knew the woman in the wheelchair but not the others. She had been a patient at the center when he was transferred there for his injuries, and they had been in rehabilitation together for a few months.

"I haven't seen her in a while," he commented. She's been in out patient clinic once and a while and I heard that she moved a while back, I think out to Littleton or Crested City, some city close to Chamberville, but I'm not sure where. She's come to watch us a few times but has never shown any interest in playing. It took her a little while to acclimate to this whole wheelchair thing. If I remember right, she wasn't from Colorado; she came to the center for rehab from somewhere out east." He continued to tell Jen that he thought Rich Lamanski knew more about her than he did, and she should talk with him after practice. Jen thought that she just might do that, as she was sure she had seen her somewhere before.

Chapter Thirty-Two

Lucas finished his shift, stopped at the grocery store for a few items, and after arriving at his small apartment and taken a refreshing shower, he picked up the paper with Jill Casey's number. He sat down, staring not only at her number, but also, looking lovingly at the photo of Erica and him taken on their last trip together to Rome—the week after their wedding. He stood up, walked slowly over to the silver-framed photo, picked it up, touched Erica's beautiful face with his finger, and then slowly set it down.

"I'm not sure if I can do this, Erica," he said talking directly to her photo. "I know you wanted me to, but I'm not sure if I can let you go. I want you to know that there's this woman, Jill; I think I told you about her once. She was in a horrible accident; her husband abandoned her, and I have been thinking of her a lot lately. Today I saw her and talked with her, and Erica, she's such a dynamic lady, beautiful inside and out, and I think I'd like to see her again. Just to talk, maybe, just to find out how she's doing. Erica, do you think that would be okay?"

Of course, there was no answer, and Lucas, feeling a little foolish, suddenly realized what he had to do. He grabbed his car keys from off the table, placed his wallet inside his back pocket, and picked a Harry Potter book off of the coffee table and headed out the door. He walked steadily to his car, unlocked it and got in. He drove to the corner store and bought two coffees and a single red rose. He sat in the car for a few minutes before putting the key back in the ignition, then with a smile on his face, started the engine and drove the fifteen miles to the Buffalo Springs cemetery. He knew that the cemetery would be closing soon, usually at sunset, but he was determined to speak with his closest and dearest friend, his wife, the woman he had loved for so long, the woman he had lived with, loved with, cried with and made a baby with—the woman who now would give him permission to go on with his life. He wanted to love again, to laugh again, to let go of the past, and get on with the future. It sounded silly, he knew, but he had to have her permission first. Then he could call Jill Casey.

Jill Casey and her two friends from Crested City had been to a teacher's conference in Chamberville on Tuesday, and Jill had mentioned wheelchair basketball to them previously, so on their way home they decided to stop in at the center and check it out. Immediately Jill recognized a few of the men she had been in rehab with and pointed them out to her friends. As the practice seemed to be coming to an end, she moved closer into the gymnasium and was immediately recognized. Several of the basketball team went over to her, hugs were given all around, and Jill introduced her friends to them as well. After a few minutes of sharing past memories, Jill noticed the woman who had been playing basketball earlier and asked Jason Brenner who she was.

"That's Jennifer Collins," Jason quickly replied. "She's a great basketball player, but really has her hands full with her boys. Her husband works nights, so when she can't get a sitter, she brings them along and Sylvia watches them for her."

Jill continued to watch Jennifer, and it looked to her like she might be nursing her baby. She also thought that she looked familiar, but realized that she may have seen her at practice before, or maybe she just had a familiar face. "No," she thought to herself, "I know her from somewhere else." Curiosity getting the best of her, she excused herself from her friends and went over to where Jennifer and Sylvia were sitting.

"Hi," she said shyly as she rolled closer to Jen. "I don't mean to intrude, but I couldn't help but notice you and your beautiful children."

She introduced herself to Jen, having met Syvia previously, and Jen in turn introduced herself. They talked for a few minutes about basketball and when Jason came over to give Jen the next month's game schedule, he asked Jill if she had given any more thought to playing the game with them.

"I don't know, Jason," she said, giving him a big smile. "I'm really busy teaching now and still trying to settle into my new house, and it's quite far to drive from Crested City to Englewood twice a week, but I promise I'll think about it."

The more Jen heard Jill speak, the sound of her voice, her movements, her smile, she was almost certain that she had met her somewhere before. As she finished nursing Ronnie, changed him, and put him into his nightie, she rolled up to Jill and introduced her to little Ronnie. Of course, the minute one boy was getting attention, the other two also came up to their mommy and her new friend.

"This is Lennie, Jill", she said patting Lennie on the back, "and this is Mickey."

"Wow," she said, holding out her hand. "What fine boys you are. Do you want to shake or give me a high five?"

Both boys laughed and tried to high five with her, and she told Jen once again what beautiful children she had.

"You really ought to play ball with us." Jen said to the stranger. "We practice twice a week, and you should come out once and just try it. It's great exercise, too, especially for me. I have lots of baby weight to lose."

Jill promised Jen that she would think about it, and as she turned away to leave, Jen asked her if they had ever met before?

"Something about you is very familiar. I'm sure I know you from somewhere." Jen said more firmly this time.

Jill quickly told her that she had been a patient at the center, and asked Jen where she had done her rehab. Jen told her that she was a post polio survivor and had never been in rehab. Jill asked what she did for a living, then chuckled and apologized, and said she meant a job, **other** than being a full time mother. Jen smiled and said that no apology was necessary, that she worked for the local school system but that she was on sabbatical for a few more months.

It was then that Jill remembered why this woman with the beautiful little boys looked so familiar. She had made a stupid comment to this woman years earlier—when she and Tom had been at the Sky City Hotel on their honeymoon. Jennifer and her husband had also been on their honeymoon and they had met at dinner that first evening. Now she had made another stupid comment to her about working when she evidently had her hands full with her little family. How dumb could she be…open mouth insert foot!

Jill took a deep breath before speaking again.

"Jennifer?" she said. "I think I know where we met. You probably don't recognize me because, first of all, I now have short hair, but the biggest change is that I was walking when you and I first met."

She continued to tell Jen about their honeymoon meeting at the Sky City Hotel during the dinner hour, and after a few more minutes of chatter, it all came back to Jen, too.

"Oh my goodness," Jen commented, as Ronnie started to cry. "No wonder I didn't recognize you, you, you…you were walking when I first met you, and you're right, your hair is shorter, but oh my goodness Jill, when did you become disabled?"

Ronnie was fussing, the two other boys were tired and getting restless, and Jen told Jill that they needed to talk more, but she just had to get her little troop home and into bed.

"My husband Mic works nights, and I have to be home to get him up and fix him some supper and put the boys down, but can you call me soon, and we can talk some more?"

With that said, Jen gave Jill a hug and told her once more how badly they needed to see each other again and catch up. Jill agreed and she watched as Jennifer and the boys, with Sylvia carrying the diaper bag, toys and the box of Cheerios, headed out the door.

Jill watched her and thought of that beautiful evening over five years ago when they had first met. Jill had been so happy then, so in love, so secure, and as she wiped away a tear, she thought of Lucas Lopez.

Chapter Thirty-Three

$\mathcal{L}$ucas drove the speed limit all the way to the cemetery, and when he pulled into the parking lot, he stopped and whispered a short prayer of thanksgiving for his life and for the life he and Erica had spent together. This prayer stuff was all new to him, but he continued by asking God to help him through the next few minutes as he ended not his love for Erica, but the past—he would always have her memories, but he was asking God to help him put that life behind him, and that with God's help he could start a new life—perhaps with Jill Casey.

"If it is your will, dear God, please show me the way to a new life." he asked. With that said, he got out of the car, picked up the coffees and the red rose. He placed the Harry Potter book under his arm and walked the few feet to where Erica and his child were buried.

There were no tears this time. He sat down in front of her memorial stone, set one coffee down on her grave along with the red rose and the book and began to sip his coffee. "Erica," he began, "For all of those coffee dates we used to have, for all those roses I used to bring to you, and for all those years that I loved you, I will never, ever forget our love for each other, and the years we had together, and for the years we were cheated out of…"

He stopped. Tears came first, then sobs wracked his muscular body, and he could not continue. After a few moments, however, he stopped crying, and continued.

"I want to ask you, well, maybe tell you," his voice shaking, "that this might be the last time we have our coffee and chat, and I may no longer read your favorite book to you, and although I may bring you roses every now and then, I want to tell you that I am letting you go—not your memory—no, I will never forget you, but, I have found a lady, and I think that I not only need her in my life, but she may need me as well, and I am asking for your permission to do just that."

At first he felt comfortable in what he was doing. Then he thought to himself, "what am I doing here? My love for Erica will never completely die, and I believe that she and our baby are in heaven, but can she really hear what I am saying to her? Has she ever heard what I say when I come to visit her? I don't know, maybe I've been silly all this time, letting my grief get in the way of reality. I guess I'll really never know for sure, at least not until we meet again."

With that said, he sat next to Erica's grave a few more minutes, said goodbye to his wife, stood up, and with a smile and one last touch of her grave marker, he left. He left the coffee, the book, and the red rose. He also left behind the terrible sadness of the past years, and with a brisk pace, he walked to his car and headed home.

Chapter Thirty-Four

*J*ill Casey drove into the Crested City High School staff parking lot the next morning humming "You Are My Sunshine." She felt so good, like there was an uplifting of her spirits. She was thrilled to have seen some of her old friends from rehab days the previous evening, and she was thrilled to have seen Jennifer Collins again. "What a coincidence," she thought, "after all these years, that we should meet again." However, the one thing that excited her most was seeing Officer Lopez again. She had thought so much of him the first time he had come to see her in the hospital. "What a nice gesture that was for him to come by after my accident." The nurses had mentioned him to her on a few other occasions when she had been asleep during his visits, but when she saw him again in Chamberville at the restaurant, there had been a little skip of her heart beat. He was incredibly handsome—his dark black hair, his physique, his smile, but most of all it was his sweet demeanor that attracted her, unusual she thought for a "cop".

She chuckled when she remembered that she had called him a policeman years ago, and he had politely corrected her and said that he was a highway patrol officer. "There is a difference, you know," he had said.

She had given Lucas her home and cell telephone numbers, and they had promised to meet up on Friday after work, but she wondered if he would call her before their coffee date. With a light heart, she worked throughout the day, giving her English class a free time to write poetry for their assignment, and then having them share their writings with the rest of their classmates. She was a great teacher, and her students loved her and told her so on many occasions. In return, she allowed them to do some "off the record" assignments every now and then. As the school day came to an end, and she turned her cell phone back on, it rang almost instantly.

"Hi Jill?" the woman asked.

A little disappointed that the caller wasn't male, she answered yes, that she was Jill Casey.

"This is Jennifer Collins."

Surprised that she would call so soon after their meeting up again, Jill gave a greeting back, and told her how great it was to hear from her again. Jen shared that the boys were all napping, and she had a few quiet minutes to herself, and she wanted to set up a time for the two of them to meet soon. She also wanted to encourage Jill to come out to basketball practice.

Jill said that this week was really full, but she would try to come to the next Tuesday night's practice, and asked Jen if she could get a sitter. That way they could meet an hour before practice, perhaps right there in the center's cafeteria.

Jen said she had her in-laws lined up to watch the boys next week, and she would ask them to come by early that night. "Three little guys are a handful for my in-laws," she said, "but I'll try to feed them supper before I drop them off. I do have to take Ronnie, as I am still nursing him, so they'll only have two of the boys that night. Will that be okay with you?"

Jill assured her that it would be great to see Ronnie again, and deep down inside she thought, "I have a lot of questions to ask Jen about being pregnant, giving birth and just being a mom." She looked forward to seeing Jen again and told her so before they each said their good-byes.

Jill had just made it to her car when her cell phone rang again. "Wow, I'm a popular girl this afternoon," she chuckled as she answered on the third ring.

"Hi Jill, it's Lucas".

"Officer Lopez, what a nice surprise, is it Friday already?"

Lucas laughed and told her he was just going on duty and had thought about her a lot the last twelve hours and wanted to say hello. "You really should start calling me Lucas, that is, if we're going to be friends," he said humorously.

She agreed to call him Lucas from then on, and asked how his day was going. He assured her that it had been fine, that he'd just gone on shift at 3:00 pm, and was just leaving the patrol station and was headed her way. He had some paperwork to drop off in Crested City at the police station, would be in town for about an hour, and did she want to meet him for just a half hour or so?

She said that she was just leaving, had an errand to run at the downtown druggist, and she knew exactly where the station was. She promised to park at the drugstore and just push the few blocks to the station. She would meet him out front.

"You won't get in trouble will you, Officer? If you meet someone that's not in jeopardy or causing trouble in town?"

He laughed at her, said no, he would be safe seeing her for a few minutes, and that he would be there in about thirty-five minutes.

Jill hung up, put her cell phone back in her backpack, and got into her Mustang. She drove the eight blocks to the drugstore, parked, and went in to pick up the prescription her doctor had ordered, as well as a few other items she needed and was back to her car within twenty minutes. She put her prescription on the front seat, looking at her watch. She realized she still had a few minutes to spare, so she stopped in at the dress shop a block down the street, strolled through the store for a few minutes and headed to the police station.

As she approached the station, she noticed Lucas pulling into the parking area. She waved at him, and he immediately waved back.

Lucas came up to her and reached out his hand to her, but rather than shaking his hand, she reached up to him, put her arms around his neck and hugged him.

Somewhat surprised, but very pleased, he hugged her back and gave her a kiss on the cheek.

"I'll just be inside a few minutes, Jill," he commented. "Do you want to come in and wait, or wait outside?"

She said it was beautiful outside, and she didn't mind waiting for him here. She watched him until he was inside the station and out of sight. "What a hunk," she thought to herself smiling, and wondered just what she was getting herself into? How would he handle her disability, her sexuality, if it got that far, and she also wondered how he was doing since his wife's tragic death? He seemed happy enough, but still she wondered. She wouldn't ask him about her unless he brought it up first, but she was a little curious. Time will tell, I guess, she thought to herself, time will tell.

Chapter Thirty-Five

Jen continued to work out, pushing her wheelchair at least 50 miles a week through her neighborhood. She needed to lose at least 50 pounds, and she needed to continue to lift weights, which she did at home when she had the time, but most of all she just needed to continue her ambitious quest to make the United States Paralympic Team. She knew that she would have to try out first at the Rocky Mountain Wheelchair Games, which were coming up soon, but her ultimate goal was to make the Paralympics. She had been throwing the javelin, shot put and discus in her back yard and once a week at the local high school, and she was also having one of her friends at the rehab center build her a racing wheelchair. She wanted to compete in basketball for sure, but track and field also seemed to be very interesting and competitive. She knew that being a full time wife and mother was her first priority and her first love, but she had dreamed of being an athlete her entire life, and if she didn't grab the chance now, it might be too late.

Jen checked on the boys as they all continued to nap. Currently, the two older boys were in bunk beds in a star-studded room decorated all in red, white and blue. The baby remained in her and Mic's room, as she could readily get to him during the night when Mic was working. She had the crib next to their four-poster bed, a gift from Mic's grandfather, and all she had to do when Ronnie woke in the night was to lift him out of the crib, change him, nurse him, and put him back into bed. Lately, though, he had not been nursing well or sleeping well. His allergies were getting worse, and the doctors were clueless as to what to do for him. He would break out with huge staph infectious sores on his face and legs, which not only looked hideous but also had to be very painful. She would medicate and bandage them every day, and after 7-10 days of antibiotics they would finally clear up, only to return again a few months later. Jen was getting more and more tired from lack of sleep, to the point that at least one night a week, her mother would come over and take care of the boys so Jen could get some seriously needed rest. It would take over a year and one half for Ronnie's allergies to settle down, but almost two years for them to become controlled with diet and medication.

Jen took advantage of her free time, cleaned up their modest but nice home, washed two loads of laundry, and had her chores almost completed when Mickey came waddling into the kitchen. He was a big boy for his age and did well in the bottom bunk bed, never falling out, and readily climbing out on his own.

"Come here mama's big boy," she said to him as she picked him up and set him on her lap. "Did you stay dry? Can we go sit on the potty chair?"

Mickey nodded his head, and Jen rolled into the bathroom, took off her two-year old's big boy pants and helped him onto the little blue potty chair. Immediately he laughed while listening to the tinkle, tinkle, into the potty chair

She had been potty training him for a little over a month, and he was doing so well with the training. Lennie had been easy to train, too, and she wished the same for Ronnie. Having had diapers now for over four years was long enough.

She had just gotten Mickey a Popsicle when she heard Lennie walking down the hallway, and then Ronnie started to fuss. She placed a popsicle on the table for Lennie, quietly went into the bedroom, careful not to wake up Mic, changed Ronnie's diaper, and rolled into the kitchen to nurse him. She loved this life, wouldn't change it for the world, but some days she wished that Mic would help her a little more. He could sleep like a baby, thank goodness, and he never woke up when Ronnie fussed or the telephone rang, and it was difficult to wake him just to get him to work on time. She knew that he loved her and the boys, and he was a good provider. She guessed she didn't really need anything else from him, except maybe some personal time, some loving, and a little attention once in a while. She was a woman. She needed more grown-up attention!

Chapter Thirty-Six

Lucas finished his delivery and left the Crested City Police Station within ten minutes of going in. Whether he was quick or the officer on the desk was quick, Jill wasn't sure, but Lucas knew, he just wanted to see her for as long as he could today, so he made sure the visit in and out of the police station was quick.

He joined Jill outside, and asked her if she would like to go to the picnic table on the other side of the building? He also asked if she would like a soda or water, and she replied no, that she was just fine.

Lucas sat down on the picnic bench, close enough to Jill so that she could roll her wheelchair up close to him, which she did. She felt so comfortable around him, and she told him so.

"I've got to believe that meeting up with you again is fate, Lucas," she said calmly. "I've been hoping to see you again, ever since I ran into you in the restaurant in Chamberville—well not ran into you, exactly, as I've been known to do that too," she said, laughing. "I think we have a lot of catching up to do. I'm divorced, have a new job, a new house; well, I guess I have a new life since you first met me at the accident, which of course, I don't remember much about."

Lucas let her talk, and then told her that he too had had a big change in his life and was now a widower, and she commented yes, she knew that his wife had passed away. Lucas looked at his watch, and she mentioned that she also had to leave, and they would see each other in a couple of days for coffee.

"I hate to go, Jill, I really do. I have to head back to the Springs and cover Highway 24 tonight, but I'm so glad you were able to meet me here for a few minutes."

He stood up, bent over Jill's wheelchair and gently kissed her, this time on the lips. He said nothing more, just walked briskly to his patrol car, unlocked the door, got in, and drove away.

Jill stayed at the picnic table for at least five more minutes before wheeling over to her car. She was happy; no, she was feeling gloriously happy. Lucas liked her; he had kissed her, and the best thing of all was that she liked him, too, and she had especially liked his kiss. She hoped that this was just the beginning of what could be a wonderful relationship.

Jen started preparing supper, as the boys seemed to be playing together very well in the living room, and she wouldn't have to check on them too often. She would try to wake Mic up in a few minutes, and hopefully, they could have a nice quiet dinner together before he had to lie down again for an hour and then leave for work at 10:30 pm for his 11:00 pm shift at the brewery. He could at least play with the boys for an hour or so before they had to go to bed. He loved giving them their nighttime baths, and it was not only good for all the boys, but really good for Mic to spend quality time with them as well. Once again, as she cut up celery for a salad, she thanked God for her life and for the beautiful family she and Mic had created.

She would never admit it to herself, but even with her busy life style, she was lonely. She had girlfriends, but hardly ever saw them; she had the basketball practices and the guys and their wives or girlfriends, but they were just that, basketball friends. She missed having a close woman friend to talk to or to have lunch with once in awhile. She also missed the closeness that she and Mic had shared in the beginning of their marriage. There was very little lovemaking anymore. Mic was either always working or always sleeping, or always tired. She was tired, too, especially these last few months with two babies and one that was extremely fussy, but just a few hugs or kisses, or just to lie in bed together talking would be better than what they had now. However, except for the few weekends Mic had off, he was gone off to work at night before she ever got ready for bed.

While she was deep in romantic thoughts and fantasies, she heard Lennie screaming at his little brother, and she snapped back to reality. She pushed into the other room where brothers were being brothers, and fighting over a favorite Spider Man toy. She settled the dispute, asked Lennie to help his little brother wash his hands for supper, and then went into the bedroom to wake up Mic. She shook him gently with no response, and then shook him a little harder before he stirred. She leaned over him, kissed him on the cheek, and told him dinner would be ready in ten minutes. She hoped he would get up, but most often he would fall back to sleep, and she would have to try to get him up again. Sometimes trying to get him up really aggravated her, but she knew that the night shifts were very hard on him, and she asked God to forgive her unkind thoughts.

After trying to awaken him three times, he finally got up, and dragged himself into the bathroom. Immediately, the boys saw that he was up, and Lennie and Mickey were pulling at his legs, asking him questions, and, without hesitation, Mic hoisted them both up on his shoulders, tickling them, and causing complete hysteria in the bathroom. Jen smiled, thinking, yes, all was really right with their family, and all was right with the world at that particular moment, and again dinner would be late.

Chapter Thirty-Seven

Lucas' remaining time on his shift today had been fairly quiet, for which he was grateful. There had been one minor traffic incident, and he had only given out one ticket to a speeder, so it had given him time to think, think about Erica, and now, to think about Jill. He thought back to his visit to Erica's grave the previous evening and thought how silly of him to leave the Harry Potter book on her gravesite...he would retrieve it tomorrow and pick up the coffee cup too...the red rose, however, would stay there until it dried up and the maintenance crew cleaned up the gravesites.

As he pulled into the garage at the end of his shift, his thoughts turned to Jill Casey. He thought about her horrific accident, the visits to see her at the hospital and at the center, but most of all he thought about her loving, caring and positive attitude. He wondered how anyone suffering such a traumatic injury could stay so positive. "She must have had a great upbringing," he thought to himself. He wondered if she still had contact with her ex-husband or if she was still in love with him. It seemed from their meeting this afternoon that she was happy, content with her life, but that she might be looking for happiness once again. He certainly hoped so. He really enjoyed being around her, and although he had many questions about her disability, he knew that if they were to have a relationship, all the questions he had would somehow be answered...in due time.

After clocking out, he drove the few miles to his home, took a quick shower and fixed himself a ham and cheese sandwich. He took a Bud from the refrigerator, turned on the television and hoped to wind down a little before going to bed. The swing shift always threw him off schedule. He had a hard time sleeping if he went to bed before 2:00 am, and tonight, especially, his mind was full of questions, possibilities, Erica, and what the future might hold with Jill Casey. He knew that he liked her, liked her a lot, and he was sure that she felt the same. "Just take it slow, Lucas," he said to himself, "just take it slow and see what God has planned for you."

With his mind settling down and his focus on what God might have planned for him, with a silent prayer of thanksgiving for his past life with Erica and a possible future with Jill, he slept one of the best eight hours he had slept in a long time. He awoke refreshed and ready to take on a new day, a new life, perhaps with this beautiful lady he knew he had already fallen in love with.

"Jill Casey," he thought to himself. "You have no idea what you're in for. Officer Lopez is at your service."

Chapter Thirty-Eight

*J*en sailed through the rest of the week. She and Mic went to square dancing together for the first time in several weeks. They took the boys along as there were plenty of other children to play with, and this way she could nurse Ronnie. She would practice with her handicapped partner for the exhibition dancing they put on monthly and then those with able bodied spouses would dance together for another hour. She loved the speed when dancing with her wheelchair partner, but it was special when she and Mic danced together. Sometimes he would use a wheelchair, and other times he would dance on his feet. Either way, she loved that they could dance together, as a couple, as a husband and wife who loved each other deeply. It also showed other couples that they could do a multitude of things together, no matter that one was disabled and one was able-bodied.

Jen had belonged to the **Whirling Wheels** wheelchair square dance club when she was in high school, but the club had disbanded and when it started again it was renamed the **Colorado Wheelers.** The club practiced twice a month at the local VFW post and went to at least two exhibitions a month; including overnight trips. Jen and one other woman sewed the beautiful skirts and blouses, as well as many of the men's western shirts for exhibitions and she had made Mic one of the western shirts as well.

On Thursday night, she once again took the boys to basketball practice with her, but she only stayed a short time as Ronnie cried constantly, and she spent more time off the court taking care of her baby's needs than playing basketball. She excused herself early and headed for home. The two little ones fell fast asleep immediately. When she arrived at home and as she started to turn into the driveway, she noticed a man hiding in the shadows and attempting to peak into their bedroom window. She waited a few minutes before getting out of her vehicle, called their home number, hoping Mic would answer, but after seven rings, she hung up. She told Lennie to be real quiet while she got out of the car, and

144

for him to watch his brothers for just a few minutes while she went into the house to get daddy.

"Why, mommy?" Lennie asked softly.

"I'm not sure, sweetie," she said calmly. "There might be danger outside, but don't be afraid; mommy will get daddy, and everything will be okay. Your brothers need you to be brave, okay?"

Lennie nodded his head yes, and Jen quietly opened the door, but prior to lifting her wheelchair out of the car, she dialed 911. She waited for the operator to answer, told her the situation, and the operator asked her to stay on the line and **not** to leave her vehicle.

"I can't see from this point if the man is still at the window," she replied. "I am a wheelchair user and have three babies in the car. I'm worried about them, not myself."

She did as the emergency operator requested, stayed in the car, and, within only a few minutes she heard sirens and saw red and blue flashing lights coming around the corner of her block. She thought it rather ridiculous to come with sirens blaring, and sure enough, as she turned her head to watch the house, a man ran directly by the front of her garage and into the night. She was only a little frightened, but somewhat relieved the man was gone; a police officer approached her, hand on his gun belt and asked if she was okay. She said that she and the boys were fine, and that a man had just run off down the street to the west. One officer stayed with her while another took off in the direction of the peeping tom, or whatever he was.

Once in the house, the officer asked her several questions, and Jen informed him that once or twice she'd received a telephone call where there was only heavy breathing on the other end of the line and then a hang up. She wondered if it had any bearing on this peeper. The officer took down notes and gave Jen his card, telling her they would follow up with her to make sure the peeper did not come back. She was to let him know if she had any more of those type of telephone calls. Jen assured him that she would do just that. He asked if she was alone in the house with her children, and she said no, that her husband worked nights and that he was asleep.

Once again, Mic had slept through the entire ordeal. Sometimes she wished he would be a little more available to her and the boys.

Chapter Thirty-Nine

*J*ill Casey taught her classes the rest of the week with a renewed spirit and patiently but excitedly waited for Friday to come. It was the end of the school week, but more importantly, it was the day she would see Lucas again. She hadn't heard from him since the meeting at the police station, but she knew his job kept him busy and he'd be at the Village Inn for coffee just as he had promised.

She dressed especially nicely on Friday, wearing a little more makeup than usual, and even added a little more perfume than normal. After all, she thought, it has been several years since I've seen Tom, or been on a date, or had any desire to be with a man, so I'm going to look extra nice today. Deep down inside, she thought, and, I'm not going to let this one get away.

Lucas left Buffalo Springs with an uplifted heart and not a care in the world. His mind was on Jill Casey and Jill Casey alone. He wondered if he should stop and buy her flowers, but decided not to. There would be plenty of time for flowers in the days and weeks ahead. He wondered how she was feeling about now. Was she as anxious to see him, as he was to see her? Time would tell, but he had a very good feeling about this coffee date.

As he drove with eyes open and down the highway, he asked God to be with him and with Jill, and to please bless their meeting today. Whatever His will for his life and Jill's life, they would be able to accept it. He also wondered if Jill was a religious person—she would almost have to be for what she had been through.

He drove a few more miles into Crested City, turned down Main Street and then west to the Village Inn. He smiled, no, almost cried, cried with joy, when he saw Jill's Mustang already in the parking lot.

Jill left school right after the last bell, only staying long enough to check a paper for one of her students, and then headed to the parking lot. After transferring into her vehicle and pulling her wheelchair into the seat behind her, she checked herself in the car's mirror, and started the car. It was only a few blocks to the restaurant from the high school, and she knew it was still over twenty minutes until Lucas would arrive, but this would give her time to get in and out of the car and into the restaurant, and maybe she would have time to calm down a little more

"I can't believe I'm this nervous," she said to herself as she rolled into the Village Inn. "You'd think I'd never been on a date before."

Well, she thought, I haven't been on a date since my accident, and I wonder how this man will see me. Will he be curious about my wheelchair, my disability, or will he be interested in me, just for me? She thought of Jennifer Collins just then, "If Jennifer can be married, have three babies and have a happy marriage, then so can I!"

Once inside, she told the hostess that she was joining someone and asked for a table rather than a booth. She was more comfortable staying in her wheelchair and not transferring. The hostess took her to a table close to a window, and asked if she would like to order a drink, but Jill respectfully declined and said that she would wait for her guest

Lucas spotted Jill as soon as he walked into the restaurant and told the hostess that he was there to meet someone and that he saw her. He walked over to her table, said hello, and kissed her gently on the cheek.

Jill smiled, then said a quick hello back, but wondered why he had only kissed her on the cheek and not on the mouth like earlier in the week. She guessed it was a "guy thing".

Chapter Forty

Mic Collins couldn't believe that he'd slept through the entire hour that the peeper and police officers had been in and out of their yard. He felt guilty for sleeping through the entire ordeal, and then felt even guiltier about leaving Jen and the boys alone so much of the time. It wasn't what he wanted, but his body just required a lot of sleep. Working nights and sleeping days just wasn't normal, and his body knew it. Jen never showed any irritation with his sleeping habits, but he knew that it bothered her, and he suspected that she wished he could be a better husband and father. He decided to try harder from now on, but darn it, he just couldn't wake himself from those deep sleeps that overtook his mind and body from working the night shift.

Jen seemed not to be overly upset from the peeper ordeal, and as she and Mic put the boys down for the night, they talked a little more about it. Jen informed Mic that she had been getting some weird telephone calls late at night, and Mic was upset for not being informed earlier.

"Since I work nights, Jen," he said openly. "Lets get an unlisted telephone number right away. It would make me feel much more at ease with you and the boys being alone at night. I promise I will do that first thing tomorrow when I get home from work."

Jen agreed, but although his intentions were good, he never made the call to the telephone company, and she called in the change herself. She let as many of their family and friends know as soon as possible that their number had been changed, and she received no more weird telephone calls.

However, about a month after the peeper first appeared, he appeared again, Mic had left for work about 10:15 pm on a Thursday night, and shortly after he pulled out of the driveway, and as she rolled into their bedroom, a man's face appeared at the window. She screamed, her heart began to race, and as she reached for the telephone and dialed 911, the man disappeared. The police arrived shortly after her frantic call, and this time the man was caught hiding in the bushes at their neighbor's home. It turned out that he was an older, somewhat senile neighbor and had been watching Jen for a long time. He admitted to the police that he was attracted to her, thought her to be a beautiful angel, and he wanted to cure her of her illness. The poor man was taken into custody, and Jen never heard any more about him. For a few weeks, however, Jen's mother and dad stayed with her and the boys at night until Jen felt relieved and safe enough to stay once again by herself.

However, over the next few weeks, Jen thought a lot about the "peeper ordeal". Most of the time she felt no fear when she was out at night, alone, with the boys, and she had always felt safe driving by herself and getting her and the boys in and out of the house. "Maybe," she thought, "I should be a little more cautious from now on, and either have another adult with me, or, make sure Mic is awake when I get home." She would talk with him about it later.

Chapter Forty-One

Jen and Mic's life continued on an even pace for the next few weeks and months, with Mic bowling twice a week in Classic Leagues, and with Jen playing basketball and working out for the Rocky Mountain Wheelchair Games. She and Mic also square danced together when they could, but most of the time she went by herself. They very seldom left the boys with a sitter, and when they did it was with their grandparents. The boys were the most important part of their lives, and they wanted to involve them in a many family activities as possible.

Jen knew that the boys were a distraction at the bowling alley, and with all of the cigarette smoke in some of the alleys, she really didn't want them there anyway. Mic was a tremendous bowler, bowling an average of 250 in both leagues. He also bowled tournaments for money when he had the chance. His goal was to join the Professional Bowlers Association, and Jen was sure that someday he would bowl the perfect score. He had bowled several 280 and 290 games, but the perfect 300 game continued to elude him. Part of the reason, Jen was sure of, was that Mic didn't think he was as good as he was, and then the pressure would get to him, and in the final frame of the game, he would blow it. The PBA would become a reality for Mic, but not for a few more years.

In the first part of May, Jen competed in the Rocky Mountain Wheelchair Games and won her first state gold medals in the 200 and 1000 meter track events and in slalom, a challenging course, but an event that she really enjoyed and did well in. Because of her wins and because of her times, she was invited to participate in the California and New York State Games as well, and although it took a lot of planning, and finding sponsors, and raising money for the trips, she and Mic, along with the boys, attended both games that summer, and once again she won several state gold medals. She also came back to Colorado with the California "Disabled Athlete of the Games" award.

Jen was well on her way to becoming a Paralympian. She would win many state medals over the next two years, compete in many summer games, and continue to play basketball with the Colorado team. At practice with her coach and other Colorado athletes, she would lay a photo of the shot put and javelin record holders at just the right marker, so as to hit the photo every time she put out the shot put, or threw the javelin. She truly believed that records were made to be broken, and laying the photo out at the record setting marker gave her all the incentive she needed to win. She lost all of her pregnancy weight, continued to eat healthily and work out, but for some reason, she would not be selected for the Paralympian Games for three more years, and even then, she would have to fight for the spot on the team.

Mic, too, continued his quest for the perfect bowling score. At one point in his career, he bowled a 299 score, just missing perfection by one pin. He would never bowl the perfect score. After going to PBA School becoming a PBA member and bowling many tournaments, a horrific accident would end Mic's dream of bowling the perfect score.

Chapter Forty-Two

$\mathcal{J}$ ill and Lucas started off their relationship by having coffee at the Village Inn twice a week, or however many times he happened to be on shift in the Crested City area for the next three months. In between coffee dates, she had invited him to the Junior/Senior play, which she had directed at the high school, and she had introduced him to many of the teachers and the principal. They had also been to dinner twice, and to a movie in Buffalo Springs. She had driven up on one Saturday afternoon and met him at his home. He would have invited her in, but his home was not accessible for her, and although it could have been a hitch in their relationship, instead it opened up more communication between them regarding her disability.

A few weeks later, Lucas once again invited her to drive down on a Friday night to Buffalo Springs. He told her they would have dinner at a new restaurant close by, and that he also had a surprise for her. As she drove her Mustang through the city, she wondered just what the surprise might be. Their relationship was advancing, and he had kissed her many times, sometimes passionately, but he had never once made any further advances, and she wondered if he was worried or scared about taking this relationship any further. She planned to share more of her disability issues with him that night.

After a lovely dinner of fresh crab and lobster and an elegant dessert of chocolate mousse with brandy sauce, they returned to Lucas' modest home, both driving their own vehicles. He had asked her to pull behind him in his driveway. That way, he could park in the garage and then assist her in getting out of the car and into his house. She had not asked any more questions about accessibility into his home she just presumed he would lift her in and out of her wheelchair, set her down in a chair, and then bring her wheelchair into the house.

Much to her surprise, Lucas had built a wooden ramp for the two steps from his garage into the kitchen. She was almost speechless, and after composing herself, rolled up the ramp and tearfully hugged and kissed him in delight.

"I can't believe you did this for me"" Jill cried.

"I did this for us, Jill," he said, kissing her gently. "I hope it's not too soon, but I want you in my life, and if that means making things more accessible for you, then that's what I want to do."

With that said, he got down on his knees and told her that he was falling in love with her, and he hoped she felt the same. Jill didn't hesitate in the least. I've loved you since that day I saw you in the restaurant in Chamberville," she said sweetly. "I just didn't know if we would ever see each other again, and now here we are."

Lucas got up, invited her to see the rest of his house, and later he poured them glasses of Chardonnay and asked her if she would like to get out of her wheelchair and join him on the couch. She said yes and transferred easily. He put his arm around her, kissed her gently, and asked if they could possibly talk openly tonight about their past lives and what their future together might be like.

"I know that I'm in love with you, Jill," he said, looking at her lovingly. "However, I don't know anything about your injury or your disability, if you have medical problems or other issues I need to learn about, but most of all, I want to be your best friend, your lover and your soul mate."

The two talked easily and long into the night. After about four hours, Jill told Lucas she needed to use his bathroom, and he asked what he could do to help. She transferred back into her wheelchair, rolled up to the bathroom door, and knowing that it was not wide enough for her wheelchair to roll through, asked if he minded lifting her onto the toilet. He of course said yes, and after gathering her purse, which contained her catheters, he lifted her gently into the bathroom. She said she would call out to him when she was finished.

Jill knew that this was the evening she would need to tell Lucas how sexuality might be between the two of them, and after the terrible experience with her ex-husband, she was a tiny bit afraid of what Lucas would say or do. She wouldn't worry long, for as the night progressed, and they became more and more passionate, Lucas asked if she'd like to spend the night. I know you're not prepared for a night away from home, but could you stay the night with me?

Jen always carried her medicines with her and always had catheters with her, but she had no protection sheets for the bed, nor was she on any type of birth control. Before she agreed to spend the night, she told him that sex together would be different with her than it had been with his wife, and that there was always the chance of having an accident with her bladder. She also told him that if he were willing to talk about this more, that she would spend the night.

Lucas gave her one of his tee's to sleep in, and after she'd taken her medications, used the bathroom and had laid one of his large bathroom towels over the sheets, she transferred into bed with him. Cuddling together, Jill shared the story of her injury, her paralysis, and pointed out her areas of non-sensation—the area below her waist to her feet.

"I'm a spinal cord injury at a level called T-12," she continued.

"I have no sensation, Lucas", she said quietly rubbing her stomach. "I might be able to feel you inside of me, and I will mentally know what is happening with lovemaking, but I have not had an orgasm since before I was injured. I could have one, however, with a little work! My ex-husband was not willing to work with me. So this is going to be as new for me as it'll be for you, but hey, getting there is half the fun, right?"

They both shared a good laugh, and Jill continued to tell him, that with intercourse and pressure on her bowel and bladder, she could have an accident. He understood. She also told him that she felt wonderful kissing him, and that it was important for him to find her secondary erogenous zones, like her breasts or kissing her neck. She also told him that she wanted the best lovemaking for him, that he was not to worry about her, and that together they could have wonderful sex. Laughing now, she told him, it just might take a lot of practice to get it right.

As Jill drove back to Littleton late Saturday afternoon, she marveled at the beautiful green rolling hills, the gorgeous sunshine, and even the lone hawk that sailed through the cloudless skies above her. She had just spent the most fabulous time with Lucas, and she thought she'd never, ever forget the time they'd spent together. There had been no actual sex act as she worried about getting pregnant. They had cuddled and passionately kissed, and Lucas had touched her body everywhere, and the sensation she did feel overwhelmed her. Lucas, being the gentleman that he was, said he would like to just hold her and sleep with her the first night, and learn more about her body. Then, the next time, after they'd discussed birth control, they'd make love.

Jill agreed with him. She loved him for who he was, for the smart decisions he made, for his gentleness, his loving heart and most of all for how honest and sincere he was. She knew she loved him, loved him with all her heart, her mind, and her soul. Her past life was behind her. She would always have great memories of her and Tom's life together, no matter how short of a time it was, but now it was over and she was beginning a new life with Lucas. God, if there really was one, was good.

Chapter Forty-Three

Lucas called Jill on Saturday night to make sure she'd made it home safely, and to tell her how much he'd enjoyed their time together. He also asked if she was free on Sunday, because he had one more day off and would be attending church in the morning, but would like to drive up to Littleton in the early afternoon. They could have a late lunch or early supper, as he had to be back on patrol by 6:00 am on Monday morning.

"I have to be back home by 9:00 pm," he said. "Next week, I work the early shift, and I need my beauty sleep."

Jill chuckled at him and agreed to have him come by early Sunday afternoon. She told him that she would try out a new recipe on him, and they could have an early supper at home. She told him that she loved him, for him to drive safely, and she would see him on Sunday afternoon. As she hung up the telephone, she wondered how long he'd been going to church and which church he went to. She would have to ask him on Sunday. Church or God had not ever been a big part of her life. Her father had been a terrible man, in fact all of her mother, Loren's, husbands had been wife beaters, and her father had been no different. They'd never gone to church, but her wedding to Tom had been a big church affair because that's what her mother wanted. Yes, it had been beautiful, and the minister had said loving, caring things about marriage and love and forever stuff, but look where it had gotten her—to a man who swore he would love her forever and who had dumped her when she was down and severely injured.

On Sunday morning, Jill slept in until after 9:00 am, took a shower in her accessible shower, dressed, had a container of yogurt and a glass of apple juice, and headed to the grocery store. She wanted to make Lucas a nice meal, and a recipe had come to mind—one that she hadn't made since she was still working the cruise ship and living in her own apartment. It had been in a Maine cookbook, one her mother had purchased at a local fundraiser, and it called for lobster and noodles, and she remembered, a pinch of dry mustard. It had been a local favorite and one that her mother always made on special occasions. Having Lucas to dinner was a special occasion, but she first needed to purchase all of the ingredients to make it.

She returned from the grocer about an hour later, and had started putting all of the ingredients together, when Lucas arrived about 3:30 pm. She had set a lovely table. Her white, gold trimmed dishes, matching goblets, champagne glasses with the sparkling bubbly on ice, and two white candles in silver candleholders adorned her table. She couldn't remember the last time she'd set a table like this, or even wanted to.

Lucas complimented her on her beautifully set table and kissed her sweetly. She kissed him back, much more passionately than he had kissed her, and commented that they just might have to hold dinner if she continued to kiss him like that.

The dinner was the best he had eaten in a long while. The Lobster Elegante was delightful, and Lucas told her so. She told him the story of this popular dish as they enjoyed their dinner, and after her third glass of champagne, suggested they move to the living room. She had rented a romantic movie and as they sat together on her couch watching the love story, she began to feel sexy and told Lucas so. As they kissed passionately, and he began to fondle her breasts, he stood up; gracefully carried her to her bedroom and laid her on the bed.

"I think this might be the night, Jill," he said lovingly. "I want to make love to you in the best way. I have protection, and I want to make love."

Jill told him she was ready, too, but hoping it would not change the mood, she needed to catheterize before they could make love and asked if he would bring her wheelchair into the bedroom. He did so, and after a few minutes in the bathroom, she came out. He had removed all his clothing and, as he stood in the dimly lit room, she thought him to be the most beautiful specimen of manhood she had ever seen. His muscular arms and shoulders, his beautifully toned legs—she thought he was gorgeous.

Jill transferred into bed, and Lucas gently removed the rest of her clothing as he gently kissed and caressed her. As the evening progressed and Lucas made beautiful and caring love to her, Jill felt like a goddess, a goddess making love to the man in her dreams for so many years now, and although she was not completely, physically fulfilled, mentally it was the most romantic night of lovemaking she had ever encountered. And that is what counted, that she could mentally control her body and mentally control her feelings, and love the man she had dreamed of for the past several years. If there was to be more, it would come with practice and patience, and even if she never, ever had another orgasm, she had all she needed for the rest of her life—but, she was sure that an orgasm was in her future.

Chapter Forty-Four

Jen and Mic made plans to take the entire family to an out of state bowling tournament. Jen was excited, as they would spend three days at the tournament site, then spend two more days with cousins she hadn't seen in awhile, and then spend two more days taking the boys to Disneyland. Mic's father had given him the money for the entry fee and also some extra money for travel expenses. Mic had two weeks vacation coming and although Mickey and Ronnie had no idea of what was happening, Lennie was excited to be going on a road trip.

Mickey was now completely potty trained and, with only one child in diapers, Jen was elated. She bought disposable diapers rather than having smelly diapers and laundry to do every other day, and as she packed a week's clothing for the five of them, she thought of how wonderful her life was. Mic had been much better the last few months, sleeping better, not being as grumpy or as tired as he had been, and although she was still nursing Ronnie, who was about to turn one, he too was not quite as fussy or sickly. Jen's weight was down to 135 pounds, and she was still actively pursuing the Paralympic spot. She and Mic had traveled with the square dance club on two separate occasions to two sites in Colorado, and they had recently been invited to perform in California. She wasn't sure the whole family would be able to go on that trip, due to their money situation. She might just have to go alone.

She and Jill Casey had spent some quality time together, too. Jill was really in love with a man named Lucas. The name had rung a bell with Jen, but then, she met so many people on a daily basis that she put his name out of her mind. The two women planned to get together one evening with their significant others, but so far it hadn't happened. Jill had asked Jen many questions about sex, pregnancy, labor and delivery, as well as how to handle a newborn, and many more questions about marriage and motherhood. She shared what she could with Jill, but also reminded her that she was a post polio survivor, so she had complete sensation.

"I can feel it when we make love," she had told Jill, "and yes, we've had to make some changes once in awhile in positioning so that both of us can enjoy it more and no, I don't always have an orgasm."

She explained to Jill that, since she could feel sex, she had definitely felt labor pain too, and that her labor had been short but hard, due to the fact that the babies always stayed low in her belly, because of no stomach muscle. She also shared the tragedy and heartbreak of losing little Timmy, and why it had happened—in no way was it due to her disability.

The Collins family, all packed and ready for a ten-day vacation, left their Chamberville home early on Wednesday morning. Mic had laid down the entire back seat of their station wagon so the boys could play with their toys and nap when they needed to rest. Jen kept the baby in his car seat, and knew that the older boys should also be strapped in, but this was going to be a long trip, and she wanted to make sure they stayed as contented as possible. She had bought plenty of snacks, juice and sandwiches to save on expenses. They planned to drive as far as Salt Lake City the first day if all went well. Everyone was so excited, especially Mic. It had been a hard year at the Brewery, and he was looking forward to this competition and time off with his family.

The road trip went exceptionally well. The boys were happy in their make-shift toy room, slept well in the hotel room, and with Mic and Jen taking turns at driving, neither one was too tired upon their arrival in California. They checked into their motel, had a light supper in the restaurant next door, and Mic left to check in at the bowling alley. His heart was beating faster than usual, as it always did at pre-tournament time, as he wanted so badly to bowl well and prove to his father and to himself that he could be one of the best bowlers around. He checked in, got his schedule for the next three days, and then practiced about ten games before heading back to the motel. He told Jen that his practice had gone well, and he admitted that, although nervous, he felt really good about this tournament.

Early on Friday morning, Mic left the motel and had a cup of coffee when he got to the bowling alley and checked in. Around 9:00 am the tournament began. He bowled head to head with an older bowler from Utah, and kept an even pace the first two games, bowling a 239 and a 257 score. He felt comfortable, was bowling well, and knew if he could bowl one more high 200 game, he would make it to the next round. He thought of Jen as he sat and waited for the third game to begin. She had been a solid rock of support for him all through his bowling career. He had begun bowling long before the two of them met, at the age of fourteen. When they started dating after graduation from high school, she had gone with him almost every night of the week to watch him bowl leagues. They had even bowled in a mixed league for two years, but bowling just wasn't Jen's favorite sport, and he realized that. When they were married and the boys were born, he dropped to only two leagues a week and an occasional tournament when he could rearrange his work schedule. She still supported him, but seldom came to the alleys anymore. It was just too difficult with three little ones.

As the third game began, he said another prayer for patience and for God's will in his life. Jen had been the strong Christian in their marriage and had taught him so much about God; the Bible had been the inspiration in their lives to attend church on a regular basis and to bring their boys up in the faith. It certainly had helped him in many areas of his life, including his bowling career. He believed that God was in charge of all areas of his life, and he went to Him now.

About seven frames into the final game, Mic was in the lead with seven perfect frames—seven strikes in a row. All he needed was a few more strikes for a perfect 300 game, but now he wanted only to strike or make his spares one frame at a time. People had begun to gather around the lanes, and although silence reigned, he could feel the pressure begin. He prayed again, eyes closed, took a few seconds to regain his composure, and stepped up to the line. One more strike. Eight in a row. One more strike. Nine in a row. The pressure on him was unbelievable. He had bowled several 300 games in practice, but never in a tournament. Was this the time for a perfect game?

Chapter Forty-Five

$\mathcal{L}$ucas was incredibly busy for a few weeks. After he and Jill's wonderful night of lovemaking, he'd only seen her twice, and then only for a few minutes when he came into Crested City. He had seen her once during her lunch hour and once after classes were dismissed. Officer Douglas Pole had been diagnosed with cancer, and Lucas had been asked to pull double shifts until his supervisor could find a replacement. Lucas was devastated, as Doug was a good friend, a great officer, and had been an officer for over fourteen years. His cancer was most likely terminal, and Lucas pondered over this tragedy often. He knew what losing someone was all about, and he worried about Doug's wife and four children. Two of the kids were already in high school, but two were elementary school age, and Lucas wondered at times where God was in this whole scenario. He knew the answer, of course, but he was still new to being a Christian, and he found it hard to understand at times. He prayed for Doug's family daily, had even stopped in twice to see him at the hospital, but it was such a struggle, sometimes he just couldn't comprehend.

He'd spoken to Jill almost every day over the past two weeks, telling her daily how much he loved her, and how much he missed her, and that they'd be together more often when a replacement for Doug Pole was selected. Jill understood, told him that she too was lonely without him, and hoped they could be together soon. They chatted about work and her final play of the season, and what they might do during her summer break.

"I really want to go back to Maine for a few weeks," she commented. "I want to spend some time with my mom. She is so busy with the restaurant, and I would love to help her out and also see some of my friends and past co-workers. It's been years. I think it's time to show them the new me."

She commented on how much she'd missed working the cruise ships and seeing the harbor, and, yes, she really did miss Maine. So many of her friends had written and sent cards after her accident and during rehab, but she hadn't had much time to see them on her last trip home—the last trip to Maine as the wife of Lt. Tom Casey.

"I love it here in Colorado," she said. "But, I still miss the ocean and the seagulls and my friends on the east coast. I really want to go home for a few weeks."

Lucas understood and said perhaps she should plan a trip for the beginning of summer break, and when he had three weeks off in late July, they could take a trip together somewhere.

Jill agreed, and with that she said the final school bell was ringing, and she needed to get to class. They said her goodbyes, and she thought, I guess, it's time to tell my mother about Lucas. I'll call her tonight.

Chapter Forty-Six

Jen looked at her watch. It was 12:00 Noon. She hadn't heard from Mic and he'd promised to call after his first three-game series and they would meet for lunch somewhere close to the tournament site. She waited until twenty minutes after noon and decided to call him. If he was still bowling the voicemail would kick in and she wouldn't disturb his concentration.

She hoped and prayed that he was having a good tournament. She knew how hard it was on him when he didn't bowl well and he'd bowled for so very long without winning a major tournament—well, she was just so confident that this would be his time to do well. She also knew that being able to pay his dad back for sponsoring him, with some of the winnings, would also help out his ego.

When he didn't answer his cell phone she fixed peanut butter and jelly sandwiches and poured juice for the boys and hoped that a small amount of food would keep them happy for another hour or so. Ronnie was eating solid food much better these days, and after feeding him junior carrots and chicken, she nursed him for a few minutes and put him down for his nap. She put a Peter Pan movie in for Lennie and Mickey to watch and laid down on the bed to rest until Mic called.

By the time Mic was up to bowl his 10th frame, at least 100 people had gathered behind the lane to watch him. He was still fairly calm, but sat quietly between turns trying to block out everything going on around him, except, for what he had to do next. He had nine strikes in a row—the most he had ever bowled in a tournament. He had already beaten his competition and would be high on the leader board going into the next three games. He concentrated on making three more strikes and bowling a perfect score.

He didn't watch his competitor bowl. He just listened for the crowd to either clap and shout or make empathetic sounds. When they clapped

Mic knew that he'd thrown a strike, so he stood up, picked up his Elite red bowling ball, wiped it off with the dirty gray towel, and threw the bowling towel down onto the floor. He took one deep breath and walked to the line. It was a perfectly thrown ball and as it hit the ten pins deep into the pocket pins flew everywhere. Strike number ten. The pressure was somewhat off of Mic now and he would bowl again later that afternoon with a lot of room to spare, but now he was hungry for strike number eleven. His competitor left a split with his final ball, and ended up with a 247. The crowd gave him a nice round of applause and as he sat back down, a hush came over the entire bowling alley. Men who were competing on the other lanes stopped. People eating and drinking at the bar turned around on their bar stools to watch. It was as though there was no one in the bowling alley but the guy on lane number 16.

Mic closed his eyes for a moment as he walked to the rack to pick up his ball. Again, he wiped off the oil, got in position and approached the line. When he released the bowling ball it took the far outside right line and hit the pocket directly on target. Strike number eleven. The crowd roared with delight. People sitting at the bar walked over to the crowded area with their drinks in hand. Then, once again, the entire bowling alley quieted down. Mic was definitely sweating at this point. He took his oily bowling towel wiped off his bowling ball and wiped the sweat from his forehead. He went through the same approach—releasing the ball and gently walking backward as he watched the ball glide into the pocket. This just could be the most perfect ball he had ever thrown. Nine pins went down. One pin wiggled and squirmed seemingly trying to decide whether it should stand or fall down. The crowd screamed, wishing with their shouts and yells to knock the ten-pin down, but it stood tall and would not fall.

Mic picked up the spare and shot a 299 score, the highest score he had ever posted in a tournament game. He also had one of the highest three-game scores in his tournament history. As he walked back to his seat, his competitor from Utah, John Simmons, shook his hand and left the area. Many others came down the few steps to the lane and also shook Mic's hand. It was definitely a game and series to remember and as he awaited the placement tally sheet for the next round, he thanked God for the patience he had been given, the stamina, and for another chance to possibly win his first PBA tournament. He stepped out into the California sunshine and punched in Jen's number.

Jen was dozing when her cell phone rang and didn't realize where she was for a moment. Lennie, hearing the telephone ring, jumped onto her bed and tried to answer the telephone for her. He picked up the ringing cell, and after saying, "haawo" said, "Daddy, daddy, did you bowe good?"

"Yes, I did little man and I'll tell you all about it when I get back. Can I talk to mommy for a minute?"

Lennie handed Jen the telephone and Jen, first taking a deep breath said, "Hi sweetheart."

"I almost did it Jen," Mic said with a perk in his voice. "I almost did it. I bowled a 299."

Almost screaming into the phone, and sitting up on the bed now. She whooped and hollered into the phone and before long Mickey was on the bed jumping up and down and hollering too.

"Mic that's wonderful!" She said sincerely. "How were your scores on the other games?"

"I'm at the top of the board after the first three games," he said smiling. "I'm right at the top Jen and if I can bowl this good again this afternoon I'll be in really good shape."

Jen could barely contain her happiness and as the young couple chatted for a few more moments she shared her happiness with him, telling him how proud she was of him and how much she loved him. They agreed that Mic should stay at the bowling alley, wait to see what time he bowled the second round and she would take the boys for a walk, maybe get them some ice cream and Mic said he would call to let her know about dinner.

Jen hung up the phone, hugged her two boys and tickled them as they all rolled and laughed together on the bed.

"Daddy did really, really good at bowling today," she said, hugging them and kissing them and saying again with a thankful voice, "your daddy did really good today in the tournament."

Chapter Forty-Seven

*J*ill finished off the school year by having lunch with four of her closest teacher friends, cleaning out her desk and stripping all of her bulletin boards. She thought how lucky she was to have secured this position and how far she had come in the past few years.

She didn't dwell on the past, but memories of the beautiful blue waters of the Harbor, sailing with her friends, and even memories of Tom haunted her every now and then. She hadn't seen him in a long while, but he had called to tell her that he was happily married and that he and his new wife, Samantha, were expecting a child. She truly believed that he didn't call to brag or to hurt her feelings but to share his new life with her, and he would do that now and again for many years to come. Tom and Sam would have three daughters and would spend many happy years together—Jill was happy for him and the nightmares of their first year together began to completely fade away.

She left two weeks after the end of the school term to spend time with Loren, her mom. The two had a close relationship, always had, and Jill was anxious to see her. Her plane left Chamberville on a sunny Thursday morning. Lucas had driven her to the airport after an evening of wine, dinner and lovemaking. They had once again talked way into the early morning hours, and she was definitely feeling the lack of sleep. She didn't mind one bit—spending as much time with Lucas as was possible with his schedule was wonderful. No, she thought, it was fabulous, and she knew she would miss him terribly.

He had lovingly seen her off, waited until he could no longer see even a wisp of the airline in the early morning sky, and then walked to his car. He'd thought seriously of asking her to marry him before she left for Portland, but thought better of it after their night together. They both still needed time. He had closed the door on his life with Erica, but even so, once in awhile he found himself comparing the two women, and he wanted that to end before he talked of marriage. He knew the time would come, just not quite yet.

Loren pulled into the airport-parking garage just as American Flight 209 landed. She wasn't real happy about being patted down but realizing that Jill would be the last person off of the plane, Loren took her time getting to Concourse C-15, sat down and waited. She thought about the past few years, Jill's broken marriage and the horrific accident which caused her paralysis. Now she was anxious to hear about Jill's new career, her new home, and most importantly, the new man in her life. She hoped that her daughter was not moving too fast, but she figured she was old enough and smart enough to make the right decisions—still, she was a mother, and a mother never stops worrying about her children.

About ten minutes after the last passenger walked through the doorway, Loren spotted her beautiful daughter being assisted by airline personnel up the walkway. She noticed her new hairdo right away and kind of wished Jill hadn't cut that beautiful long hair, but realized it was a part of Jill's new beginning. As she walked towards her daughter, Jill was thanking the attendant for his services, and then rolled up to her mom. There were hugs and kisses, more hugs and more kisses, and tears streaming down Loren's face before any words were spoken.

"Hi, mom." Jill finally said. "You look great; wow, it's so good to see you and to be home again."

Between sobs and blowing her nose, Loren managed to tell her how good it was to have her back home and how absolutely marvelous she looked.

"I feel great, mom," she commented, all the while holding on to Loren's hand. "I really do feel great."

After picking up Jill's luggage, loading it all into the car, Loren helped Jill transfer, although no help was needed, and placed her wheelchair into the trunk. Jill's wheelchair was very lightweight with pop-off wheels, and Loren commented to Jill how easy her wheelchair was to handle. Jill agreed and said she had no problem getting it into her little blue Ford Mustang. Her mom chuckled, imagining this cute young daughter of hers driving around the big city and turning the male population heads as she drove about in her cute little sports car.

Loren and Jill stopped at a café just outside of Portland, had a light lunch and continued their trip towards Booth Bay Harbor. Jill couldn't breathe in enough of the salty sea air. She watched out the open window, focusing on the beautiful seagulls flying over and into the sea for food. She had to admit that she really missed the sea, and as a tear slid down her cheek, she wondered if she would ever have a chance to sail again or do all of the things she once did in this part of the country—things that had meant so much to her as a child.

Loren drove into her driveway, turned off the ignition and assisted Jill out of the car. Loren had rented a portable ramp once again, and Jill rolled easily into her childhood home. Loren had turned her office into an extra bedroom during Jill's visit, and much to Jill's surprise, a few of Loren's customers from the diner had widened the bathroom door.

"Oh, mom," she said, hugging Loren. "You're the greatest."

Chapter Forty-Eight

$\mathscr{M}$ic bowled his next set at 1:30 pm, and bowled well enough to stay in the top five on the leader board. After signing his score sheet and talking with several other PBA members, he called Jen, asked her to be ready at 4:30 pm, and then they would go to dinner and spend some quality time with the boys. He was feeling the best he had ever felt after a tournament of this caliber. God was definitely with him. He closed his eyes for a moment, said another short prayer of thanksgiving, and drove home to those who were the most important to him.

After a fairly quiet dinner, as quiet as dinner could be with three little ones, they went back to the motel and played dominoes with the boys—dominos made up of a four year old and a two year old's rules. The family laughed and cheered, and finally when the games were over, they bathed the boys, tucked them into bed, and Jen and Mic finally had some time together. They readied themselves for bed and laid together for over an hour talking about the tournament and what the possibilities were if Mic continued to bowl as well as he had today. Finally, the young couple, as quietly as they could, and with three children asleep in the same room, made love before falling asleep in each other's arms.

The next day, Mic was up and out of the motel before Jen or the boys woke up. He wanted to practice before his set, have a little time to himself, and eat something before he bowled. Once again, he averaged 255 and stayed at the top of the leader board. On the afternoon set, however, he lost his concentration and his patience. An older man watching the tournament, and with too much alcohol in his system, had caused a scene. He had been asked to leave the alley, but prior to his dismissal, he had caused Mic and several other professional bowlers to lose their trains of thought and bowl lower numbers than they had the day before. Mic was angry, distraught, and highly irritated by the time he went back to the motel.

Jen tried her best to calm Mic down but with little boys wanting their daddy's attention and his mind so set on the afternoon's devastating scores, he told Jen he needed time away and was going for a drive—no matter that three kids and a wife were tired of being shut up in a motel all day and were very hungry!

Jen watched him go with no more said. She had been with him before when he bowled badly and she knew it was best to leave him to his thoughts. She made up a story about why daddy had to leave for a while and said she would play a game with the boys if they were really good. She first nursed Ronnie, told the older ones that they were going on a hunt and they were to look for certain objects on this hunt.

"Just like on a jungle Safari," she had explained to them. "We have to be on the prowl. Are you two ready to head into the jungle?"

The two boys agreed wholeheartedly. Lennie found his plastic sword and Mickey his Batman cape, and she quietly laughed to herself as she watched her blond little boys prepare for a Safari.

As she put needed essentials into the diaper bag and hung it on the back of her wheelchair, she also asked the older boys to hold hands, stay close by her, so they could safely head out on this excursion.

The boys loved this game. Jen left the motel room, children in tow, and first told them to look for a green light—a sign of safety on this Safari. At the corner of the first cross street, Lennie spotted the first stoplight, just as it turned green.

"I see, I see gween," he exclaimed.

"Yes, you did, sweetheart", Jen assured him. "Now, we're safe to cross this scary trail, watch out for lions or tigers because I bet they are as hungry as we are. Now, we need to hunt for a sign that shows people food. Mickey, do you think you can find a sign that shows a picture of a hamburger or a hot dog or maybe a chicken or a cow?"

He assured her that he could. Jen had seen a Chick Filet drive through the day before and knew it was only two blocks from the motel. She also knew she could push that far and keep three active boys in line for a few blocks, and so, the game continued.

After seeing the ice cream parlor from the day before and presuming that was a win on his behalf, Mickey agreed to now keep on looking for a cow or a chicken. Jen chuckled at her second oldest son, who asked for an explanation as to why he should find a cow.

"Are their cows in the jungle, mommy?" He asked. "Are there hambuggers in the jungle, mommy? Where do hambuggers come from mommy?"

"In this jungle, there may be cows," she said trying not to laugh. "We need to find at least a sign of a cow or a chicken so we can find fooooooood fast!'

"And for your inquisitive little mind," she said touching his cute little face, "hamburgers come from a cow and chicken tenders come from a chicken." But of course he still had more questions. He wanted to know what part of the cow did they use for hamburgers, and all the way to the Chick Filet they had a lesson in where hamburgers and chicken tenders came from.

The young mother and her little family enjoyed a nice chicken dinner, and she exclaimed that the hunt had been a tie, that both Lennie and Mickey had spotted the Chick Filet sign at the same time, and they could have a special treat at the end of their dinner. Once again, they both chose ice cream. She also wondered if Mic had eaten dinner and prayed that he would be back at the motel when she and the boys returned.

Mic returned to the motel when Jen and the boys were already fast asleep. He had spent an hour alone with his thoughts, but had also returned to the alley to watch more of the tournament and practice again. He was calm when he returned to the motel. He showered, crawled into bed and kissed Jen on the cheek. She stirred but never woke up.

Chapter Forty-Nine

Lucas returned to Buffalo Springs after dropping Jill off at the airport. He truly wished she would have a wonderful time with her mother and her friends, but he wondered how he would manage without her. She had consumed him—body and soul. He loved her smile, her laugh, her personality, her hair, her cute little ears, her back scars; he just plain loved everything about her. Yes, Officer Lucas Lopez was smitten, and he knew it.

He called her the first night of her arrival in Booth Bay Harbor, and they talked for over an hour. He asked about her flight, her mother, and whether she missed him. She told him of her plans for the next few days and that Loren's significant other was going to take her sailing on Sunday. She wasn't sure how she would access his sailboat, but they were going to give it a try, and, of course, she missed him terribly.

With her mother in the room close to her, she didn't talk too openly with Lucas about her feelings, but she told him she loved him and that she would call him tomorrow after his shift. He blew her kisses through the telephone and hung up.

Her mother made no mention of Lucas until later on in the evening. It was at that point that Jill shared her feelings for Lucas with her mom—her closest friend. She shared everything that had happened with the two of them over the past several months, and that she knew one day she and Lucas would marry. She told Loren that they both wanted children and that she planned to get pregnant as soon as they did marry.

"I plan to waste no time having a family, mom," she said openly. "I've wasted too many years already, and Lucas and I agree that children will be a part of our lives." However, she also added that he had not asked her to marry him.

Loren asked no questions about what pregnancy for her disabled daughter would be like or what labor and delivery would be like for her. She knew that in time, Jill would share all those issues with her, but only when the time was right. For now, Loren was elated that her only daughter had found happiness once again.

Barbara Roose Cramer

Jill was exhausted from the lack of sleep the previous night and from the long flight. She turned in early and dreamt of sailboats, white caps, seagulls and a tall dark stranger escorting a woman wearing a beautiful white dress.

Chapter Fifty

*J*en woke early on Saturday morning, got out of bed, showered and was completely dressed before Mic or the boys even stirred. Ronnie had slept through the night, something he very seldom did, and she moved about the room, refreshed and ready for whatever the day might bring. She took out her Bible, read a few passages, prayed for peace and harmony in the world and in her family, and thanked God for all her blessings. She said an extra prayer for Mic and for his day to be successful, but most of all she prayed for God's will to prevail.

She made coffee in the motel's small coffee pot, poured two small glasses of grape juice for the two boys, and filled a bottle with apple juice for Ronnie. She was trying desperately to wean him from nursing, but with his allergies she either had to take him off of breast milk and put him on soymilk, or continue to nurse him for a few more months. He was over a year old, and she felt the time was over for breast-feeding, but her little one didn't seem to be cooperating. As she rolled throughout the small motel room, Mic woke up, sat up on the bed and looked at her lovingly.

"I'm so sorry, Jen," he said quietly, and walking over to her, got down on his knees at her level, kissed her gently on the lips. She kissed him back, and told him it was okay, and asked how the rest of his night went.

"I prayed a lot, Jen," he said, getting back on his feet. "I was just so angry. I need to learn to control my feelings when bad things happen, and I just can't seem to do that. I'm just so sorry that I put you and the boys through this—again."

He asked if the boys had been good. Did they walk somewhere for supper? Did she forgive him? She said everything was fine, and asked what time he had to bowl this morning?

Looking at his watch, he saw that it was already 7:30 and that he had to check in at 8:45. He suggested that he run out for some breakfast for her and the boys, for her to awaken them and get them dressed. They could eat, load up and she should drop him off at the alleys and keep the car. It would be rushed, but Jen knew she could handle it. Lennie was such a great help to her, and she agreed to Mic's suggestion.

After dropping Mic off at the bowling lanes, she found a laundry center close by and decided to spend a few hours doing the washing. It was amazing how many clothes a family of five went through. There were storybooks in the car, and as she did the washing, she read books to the boys, took them outside the laundry for a short walk and then reloaded everyone and the clean clothes back into the car. She had seen a park close by the bowling lanes with a large play center, and for several hours, she and the boys enjoyed the beautiful park and the California sunshine.

Around 1:00 pm, she returned to the motel, put away the clean clothes, and after another round of juice and peanut butter/cheese crackers, the boys settled down for one more time with Peter Pan, and slept the entire afternoon away. The fresh air had done them all so much good.

Jen missed a telephone call from Mic, and by the time she picked up and heard his message, it was too late to call him back. She figured that he would be bowling another set of games, so she didn't return his call. The message had been positive; he was bowling well, and Jen silently thanked God.

At 4:30 pm, Mic called again. He was coming back to the motel and asked where would she and the boys like to go to dinner?

She said there was a nice buffet advertised in the motel lobby and suggested they try it. She cleaned the boys up, put away the trail of toys and books across the floor, changed into a smart blue and lavender outfit, and was ready when Mic walked into the room.

He was smiling, no grinning, when he walked into the room, and Jen knew that he was about to share some really good news with her. He'd kept up his average, had one more set to bowl, and had an excellent chance of making the final four. The final four. The final four meant that Mic would make it to the Sunday finals, bowling live on national television—something he had never accomplished before.

Chapter Fifty-One

Lucas left the patrol offices early on Saturday afternoon. He had requested a few hours off and promised that he'd make it up the following week. He had spoken with Jill every day since she had been in Booth Bay Harbor, and he had come to a decision—when she returned, he would ask her to become his wife. He realized that their relationship was new and that they shouldn't marry for some time, but he loved this woman more than life itself, and he wanted to keep her for his very own.

He drove to the jewelers close to his Buffalo Springs home, got out and shopped around for a few minutes. He finally asked a smartly dressed older woman for some assistance, and although he had no idea of Jill's finger size, asked to look at a few rings that had caught his eye. The jeweler introduced herself, then showed him four or five beautiful engagement rings, a several engagement and wedding ring sets, and when she showed him a beautiful diamond and pearl ring set, he knew for sure that this was the one he wanted. He would have to have it sized after she said "yes", but asked how much of a down payment it would require to hold the set, and he would return in about ten days to purchase it.

Lucas stopped at the Carlos Bistro in Buffalo Springs and made a reservation for dinner on the 1st of August. It was one of his favorites and had great seafood, and he knew Jill would enjoy it too. This way, Jill would be back in Colorado, and classes at the high school would not have started for the school year. He planned on a wonderful evening with dinner at the Bistro, perhaps yellow roses—her favorite— and then after taking her to his home where he would have champagne and chocolate covered strawberries waiting, he would give her the cruise tickets. He had already made reservations to fly to Miami, spend one night at the Marriot Hotel and then leave on a seven-day cruise to the Caribbean. He had been careful to check out the boat's accessibility including boarding ramps, the staterooms, restrooms, the pool and hot tub areas and the restaurants. He was assured that everything, minus the hot tub area, was accessible. There were three steps up onto the pool and hot tub deck.

Lucas figured on lifting Jill out of her wheelchair and up the stairs and into the tub if she wished to do so.

Lucas also planned to call Jill's mother and tell her of his plans. He was certain that Loren and Jill would be having long talks about him during Jill's visit to Maine, and he hoped those talks went well—well enough so that when he did call Loren, she would be prepared for what he was about to ask.

Lucas called Jill that evening, and she was so high-spirited that he could almost see her smiling through the telephone.

"I went sailing today, Lucas," she said cheerfully. "Joe Spencer, my mother's friend, well, her boyfriend, he made a wooden ramp so I could access the boat, and he took me sailing all day. He lifted me into the bathroom, had lunch all prepared for us, and oh, wow, Lucas, it was awesome!"

Lucas could tell how "awesome" it must have been by her voice. He was almost envious that she was having such a good time. However, he told her that he was thrilled for her and asked what else she had been doing.

She had seen friends, gone shopping with Loren, then out to dinner with Loren and Joe Spencer, which reminded her to have Lucas ask her more about Joe Spencer when she got home. "He's got quite a story to tell," she said.

She admitted she was so happy to be back home, but she also reminded him that home would always be where he was. "I will always need you and want you in my life, Lucas," she said lovingly. "I love being with my mom and seeing my friends again, but I'm anxious to get back to Colorado and to you. I love you Lucas. I've been telling my mom all about you, and she loves you already."

It's exactly what Lucas was hoping for, and he told Jill that he would love to meet her mother and Joe sometime soon.

Chapter Fifty-Two

Mic was at number three on the leader board by Saturday afternoon, and knowing that the next day's set would be the most important three-game set of his bowling career, he first called Jen and then sat in the lounge area, sipping on iced tea and praying. He had enjoyed lunch with two other PBA members, who most likely were not going to make the cut, and they had given him a shot of confidence; something Mic appreciated and needed. He told Jen to come down to the bowling lanes and pick him up, and they'd go to the Buffet for supper. He also told her that he wanted her and the boys to come to the alley in the morning for the early set. She insisted that the boys would be a distraction, but he said he wanted his family with him, and if the boys did get rowdy, she could leave. If he bowled well, he would bowl again at 3:00 pm on national television; if not, he was at least guaranteed around $8,000.00 in winnings.

Jen was in shock—$8,000.00? The most prize money Mic had ever won was $3,000.00 and even that amount amazed her. He loved the game and he could make this kind of money by winning? Wow! She realized that the money would be helpful, but she also knew what kind of pressure Mic would be under, and she prayed that he could handle it.

The Buffet turned out to be a good choice. The boys ate very well, were exceptionally well behaved, and before returning to the motel, Mic took them all back to the bowling alley to meet some of his friends. He also wanted the boys to see the lanes, to talk to them about being quiet when they were watching, and more or less have a trial run before Sunday morning. Mic's friends and acquaintances marveled at his beautiful wife and the fact that she was in a wheelchair—nothing new to him and they played openly with Lennie and Mickey. Jen wasn't too worried about the older boys being quiet during the tournament, but she couldn't guarantee how Ronnie would be, and she shared her concern with Mic on the way back.

Early Sunday morning, the young family was up and out the door by 7:30 am. They ate breakfast at a Dennys and entered the bowling alley thirty minutes before the start of the tournament. There were television crews mingling about, several sports reporters interviewing bowlers, and Jen was certain that she should've remained back at the motel. However, their daddy had made up his mind, and as she took the boys into the restroom so she could change and nurse Ronnie, she told the boys once again how important being quiet would be when daddy and his friends started to bowl. They seemed to understand the severity of the situation and agreed that they would be good boys—and they were.

Mic was as cool as she had ever seen him during a tournament. He averaged 259 for the 3-game set and made the final four. Jen waited for him in the back of the bowling alley, but when he was asked to do a press interview, she took the boys outside and not only praised them for their behavior, but bought them a soda, something she never did, as a reward. Fifteen minutes later, Mic found her outside, ran up to her, hugged her, and almost pulled her out of her wheelchair. Never had she seen him so excited.

Jen left Mic at the bowling alley and took the boys back to the motel for naps. Mic was scheduled to bowl again at 3:00 pm, and once again he wanted her and the boys at the alley. She disagreed again, but he insisted. So, after short naps, she loaded up the diaper bag with books, snacks and juice. As she entered the alley, she was astounded at the number of spectators, security officers, news and television camera crews who filled up the bowling alley. Mic had asked a friend to watch for Jen, and then escort her and the boys to their seats. Most of the seating area was not accessible, and that was fine with Jen, as Fred Meyer showed her to an area behind the main seating where she could watch Mic but also keep the little ones close and out of sight. The older boys stood on their chairs at first to get a glimpse of Mic, but after the national anthem was played and the match started, they sat quietly watching and then cheering along with the other spectators.

Mic bowled a 232 the first game, and his competitor bowled a 219. He was doing okay, but a 232 wouldn't be enough too win the second round. As the crowd was asked to settle down and the announcers asked for quiet, Jen closed her eyes, prayed a prayer of contentment and patience for Mic and for herself. She opened her eyes and looked at her boys who were being perfect little angels, showing no signs of anything but love for their daddy. They had no idea at all what was happening except that daddy might win a trophy and that tomorrow they were going to Disneyland.

Mic bowled four strikes in a row, but those would be the last strikes of this tournament. He had no excuses afterwards, he just couldn't release the bowling ball properly, whether it was the oil on the lanes or the lanes had broken down; he had no idea. He knew that he'd given it his best, and he had nothing to be ashamed of. He ended up in third place, received a check for $9,300.00, and walked out of the bowling alley in Los Angeles, California a happy and contented husband, daddy and professional member.

It was the last time Mic Collins would ever bowl in a PBA tournament.

Chapter Fifty-Three

$\mathcal{J}$ill Casey picked up the telephone on Friday of the second week of her trip and dialed Jennifer Collins. It has been weeks since they had spoken, and Jill needed to chat with her. Jen picked up the telephone on the third ring and was surprised to hear Jill's voice. Jill assured her that nothing was wrong; she was just curious as to how Jen was doing, how her workouts were going, how the boys were doing and if she had heard anymore from the Paralympic Committee?

"Actually, Jill," she said. "Mic and I and the boys just got home from a two-week trip to California."

She shared some of their vacation experiences with Jill and told her that, no, she wouldn't compete again until spring, and she hoped at that point she would do well enough to make the US Team. Yes, she was still square dancing and playing basketball, but since they had been gone for a while, she'd get back on schedule the next week. Jill mentioned that she was in Maine visiting her mother and wondered if after her return, she and Lucas could get together one evening with her and Mic?

"I really want to see you more often, Jen, and I know you're terribly busy with your family, but I would love for you all to meet Lucas and for him to get an idea of what it's like to be a woman in a wheelchair with a family. Am I imposing on you, Jen? "She asked.

Jen assured her that, no, she wished to help out in any way she could and for her to call when she returned to Colorado, and they'd set a date. Jill thanked her, asked after the little guys again and hung up.

Jill liked Jen a lot and had learned a lot from her. She had a suspicion that Lucas would soon be asking her to marry him, and although they had talked about having children a few times, she was certain he had a number of questions to ask her about her disability and childbirth. She knew she couldn't answer all of his questions, as she didn't know the answers herself, but she thought perhaps Jen and Mic Collins could.

Jill wanted to be married again, and she wanted desperately to have a child. She knew Lucas would make a wonderful father, and if he did ask her to marry him in the near future, she wanted to make sure, she was physically and mentally ready to have a baby. Her doctors had assured her that she could get pregnant, and she would have little or no labor or delivery pain. However, there could always be complications for a pregnant woman with a spinal cord injury. She knew that Jen had lost a baby during childbirth, and that bit of information had scared her. She would talk with Jen about it more when she returned to Colorado.

Jill spent the remainder of the week sailing with her mom and Joe Spencer. Loren had her assistant manager run the diner on Saturday and Sunday, and they sailed in and around the harbor, eating, drinking, and talking about old times. She could see that her mother was also in love, and she hoped that Joe wouldn't hurt her, like her father had done. On Monday prior to her leaving for the Portland airport, Jill and Loren had talked openly about Joe and Lucas, and Jill left Maine feeling so good about her and her mother's futures.

Chapter Fifty-Four

Mic had three days of vacation left, and he spent it at home with his family. He set up plastic bowling pins in the hallway, and played bowling with the two older boys. At times, Ronnie would crawl down the hallway and knock over all the pins, much to the dismay of Lennie and Mickey. He took them to the park where they swung on the swings, played in the sand box, and even waded in the creek, of course, without telling Jen. One evening, Jen's parents came to watch the boys, and Mic and Jen enjoyed a date night with dinner and a movie.

Mic had been back on the night shift at the brewery just three weeks when Jen's telephone rang during the middle of the night. She rolled over, turned on a light and answered the telephone on the fourth ring. It was Norm, Mic's supervisor. There had been an accident, Mic was injured, and he was being taken by ambulance to the nearest hospital. Still groggy from sleep, Jen asked for the information once again, hung up and dialed her parents.

As soon as her parents arrived, Jen drove to the hospital. Upon her arrival, she was told that Mic was being looked after, and that she could go into the emergency room as soon as the doctor came out of Mic's room. The nurse assured her that Mic was doing well, that it was a hand injury of some kind and for her not to worry.

It was some kind of hand injury all right. Mic had caught his hand in a piece of machinery, the safety hadn't come down in time, and his hand had been severed. When she saw him for the first time, his hand was in a huge blood-soaked bandage and he was being prepped for surgery. Her heart seemingly sank to the bottom of her stomach—it was his right hand, his bowling hand.

She rolled up to his hospital bed, and although groggy, he recognized her, asked her who was with the kids and drifted off into a drug-induced sleep.

After a four-hour surgery, and three more hours in recovery, the hand surgeon informed Jen that Mic would need lots of luck if his hand were to be saved. He had repaired what he could and saved what nerves he could, but there was more severe nerve damage, and most likely, he would only ever have 30-40% use of his hand again. If indeed she believed in prayer, she should pray now, not only for healing but for no infection.

Jill prayed like she had never prayed before. She spent an hour in the hospital's chapel, talked to the priest on call, then after contacting her parents, she called her own pastor, who came to the hospital within the hour. For hours, she and her pastor, Mic's parents, and more and more friends stayed and prayed with her. Twenty-four hours after the surgery and while in intensive care, Mic's fever spiked to 105 degrees. He was rushed back into surgery where the wounds were cleaned out again, but infection had already set in. The doctor was not optimistic, but within another twenty-four hours, his fever broke, the antibiotics were doing their job, and the infection was slowly leaving his body.

By this time, the entire church was praying for Mic and his family. Church friends brought in meals; friends took turns staying with the boys, and finally two weeks after the accident, Mic came home. The boys had seen him only twice in the hospital, and were glad to have their daddy home. They asked all kinds of questions about the big bandage, and why did he have to hang his arm on a wire above his head, and why did he have stitches, and "could they seen his ouchie"?

During the third week post surgery, the doctor removed the bandages and the stitches, but Mic's hand was frozen in position. It would take five months of rehabilitation and therapy to get his hand back to 50% usage, and another year to get it back to 90% usage, a percentage that the doctor marveled at—Jen and Mic knew it was an answer to prayer.

Mic missed almost a year of work, and after a short court case where he was awarded a small settlement, and after Jen had opened up a day care center in their home to make extra money, he went back to work part time. His hand, although only working 90%, was a miracle of faith and prayer, and although Mic tried bowling left handed, he was never the same again. His PBA days were over, and he mourned.

Chapter Fifty-Five

Jen spent very little time working out, square dancing or playing basketball. Her life now centered around taking care of her husband and babysitting for three other children besides her own. She had no choice—they needed the money while Mic was on leave. They had lived fairly comfortably when Mic worked so many overtime hours, but now they were just barely getting by on his part time pay and their savings. She didn't mind watching the other children, but by bedtime she was exhausted. Mic couldn't drive, so even though he watched the children on occasion, most of the household duties, shopping and doctor appointments were hers and hers alone.

Mic was a fairly good-natured patient. He suffered a lot of pain during therapy and slept a lot afterwards, but when he could, he watched and played with the boys, and after a few months started to vacuum and clean the house with one hand. He even cooked and baked for Jen with one hand. He missed bowling, Jen suspected, but he never mentioned it or complained about it.

After seven months of therapy, his right hand was working well enough to go back to work fulltime. He hated the desk job, but at least he was able to take care of his family, and he was hopeful of getting his old job back soon.

Jen knew that unless she started to work out again, she wouldn't be in good enough physical condition to compete in the wheelchair games in the spring. Granted, she could play basketball during the winter months, and try to work out some at home with weights, etc., but she began to worry about making the Paralympic Team. As Mic improved, she spent more and more time pushing through the neighborhood, swimming at the YWCA twice a week, and playing basketball again. By the end of summer, she had lost a few pounds, improved more muscle tone and also regained some of her confidence.

Jill Casey had called in the early part of August, but Jen had told her their situation, and sadly, the two young women hadn't gotten together at all. Jen felt guilty, but at the time, her family had to come first, and besides, she really couldn't handle anybody else's needs right then. She promised herself that she would call Jill within the next few days.

Jill returned to her home in Littleton after two wonderful weeks in Maine. She said goodbye to her mom and Joe Spencer, and this time Loren shed no tears. She was so proud of her daughter and realized how far Jill had come since her accident and divorce. She knew there was no need to worry about Jill any longer. She was also quite certain that the next time she saw her daughter again it would be at her wedding.

Lucas picked Jill up at the airport, spent the night with her in Littleton, and said that on Tuesday after his ten days of night shifts were over, they would spend more time together. He also told her that he had put in a request to work the day shift from now on. He hoped the request would be approved, as working days would be so much better for them both.

Lucas had all the plans in place for his big surprise cruise to the Caribbean for Jill and him. All he had to do now was wait to tell her about his plans. He'd paid for and picked up her ring a week earlier, and this week he planned to tell her about the cruise at dinner. He was like a kid waiting for Christmas Eve. As Tuesday drew near, he called Jill and told her that he would like her to come to the Springs on Wednesday afternoon, that he had a surprise for her, including dinner at a lovely bistro—a favorite place of his. She of course said yes, that she would drive down, and he reminded her to bring whatever she needed to spend the night at his place.

Lucas had spoken with Loren earlier in the week and, although she was cautious with him at first, she wasn't surprised at his request to marry her daughter. Yes, she had said immediately. Jill, she thought, was expecting him to propose and would be surprised at the cruise and the way he planned to propose. She and Joe approved of all of it.

On Wednesday, three weeks before classes started, Jill drove to the Springs and met Lucas at his home. He helped her out of the car, and while he dressed, she drank a wine spritzer and pumped him for answers to her questions.

"It's a surprise, Jill, baby," he said. "You have to be patient. Just wait a little longer, and you'll get your surprise."

The hostess at the bistro took them immediately to their table where wine and cheese were laid out. There was also a beautiful bouquet of yellow roses in the center of the table and a beautifully wrapped gift box at her place.

She was smiling when the hostess pulled out the chair from the table, and Jen rolled her wheelchair into place at the table.

The waiter first filled their glasses with water and then poured each of them a glass of wine. He served Jill the cheese first, then offered Lucas the plate and immediately left their table.

Jill said very little. She was so surprised at Lucas' beautiful gesture and wondered what might be coming next.

They each drank a second glass of wine, and the waiter brought the menus. He also explained the specials, which were written on a lovely silver trimmed black board, and after placing their order, Lucas smiled and asked her to open the gift.

Jill carefully untied the ribbons, then gently took off the wrappings, and began to open the gold colored envelope lying neatly inside of the box. She gasped when she saw the two airline tickets to Miami and started to tear up when she saw the colorful photo of the Caribbean and the two cruise tickets in their names.

"I don't know what to say, Lucas," she stuttered. "I...what...I am just speechless. What is the occasion?"

He took her hand in his, and explained that he loved her and wanted to show her how much, by taking her on a romantic cruise. He explained how he'd never been on a cruise, and he knew that, except for working on the cruise ships, she'd never been on a romantic cruise, and he wanted this trip to be special for them both.

Lucas was right. She'd never been on a cruise for her own enjoyment or with someone so special. It had always been a job for her. She was elated and found herself asking if he thought she could handle the cruise from a wheelchair? He said that yes, he had checked it all out, and she had five days to get ready.

The next morning, Jill called her mother in Maine, and Loren acted surprised and congratulated her on finding such an awesome young man. They chatted for a few more minutes, and Jill hung up, thinking she was the luckiest woman alive.

She spent the next two days shopping for new clothes. She even purchased a new bathing suit, something she hadn't done since before her accident. This time, however, it was not a bikini—**that** had always been Tom's request.

She was ready to go five days later. Lucas picked her up, and they drove to the airport. They left their car in the parking garage and walked towards security checkpoint. It irritated him when Jill was asked to remove her shoes for security reasons and irritated him even more when they asked her to transfer to a regular, hard, straight back chair, so they could check out her wheelchair cushion. Jill didn't seem to mind, however, it was just part of life now.

They boarded the plane first, stored their carry-on luggage, and Jill transferred from the aisle chair to her seat. Once seated, she watched as the men took her wheelchair to the cargo area. She hoped it would arrive in one piece, as she had heard nightmare stories of wheelchair and airline travel. She had been lucky on her trip to Maine; she hoped the same would be true for this trip.

She, Lucas, and her wheelchair arrived in Miami with no glitches. They took a cab to their hotel, which was right on the water front, had lunch at a quaint little seafood restaurant and after lunch took a leisurely hand-in-hand stroll around the harbor. She loved the water so much, and Lucas enjoyed watching her eyes light up with every seagull or sailboat she spotted. The two talked about her life in Maine, and Lucas shared stories about his life in Colorado and with the Highway Patrol. There was still so much to learn about each other, and this seemed to be the right time and the right place to share many of those stories. They spent the evening hours sitting out on the patio of their hotel, sipping colorful and tasty drinks and watching the full moon rise in the sky. They turned in early, knowing that they probably wouldn't sleep much although their arrival time wasn't scheduled until 2:30 pm.

In the morning they were both anxious to go on this cruise—Lucas more so than Jill, knowing that the best part of the surprise was yet to come. They arrived at the loading area with plenty of time to spare and after they'd checked in, had their complimentary photo taken, they were shown to their stateroom. Their room included a large wheelchair accessible bathroom, a queen size bed, and plenty of storage room. There was also champagne on ice and a basket of yummy looking fruits and chocolates. Jill wheeled around the room feeling like a princess, stopping her wheelchair at least twice to grab Lucas' hand and dance around the room with him. He stopped her wheelchair took her face in his hands and gently kissed her.

"I love you, Jill Casey," he said, kissing her again. "I love you more than you'll ever know."

She kissed him back passionately, told him she felt the same, and if it hadn't been for a knock on the door, they would've never made it on deck, when the ship left the Miami harbor.

Chapter Fifty-Six

Mic Collins continued in physical therapy for another three months. The therapist, along with his specialist, agreed that 90% usage was all he would get back. Everyone was pleased that he had made it back that far. Work was no problem at all. He went back to the graveyard shift, and once again worked many weekends, and when he was at home, he fell back into the 8-10 hours a day sleeping habit. Jen was pleased to have her husband back, but not pleased to having him sleep so much and missing out on family times.

The boys had all celebrated birthdays throughout the summer months, and Lennie would start kindergarten in the fall. He had physically caught up with other boys his age, was filling out nicely, but, due to his premature birth, his testicles still hadn't dropped, and the pediatrician had scheduled another surgery to try to drop the scrotum, stitch it to the inside of his legs for ten days, and hope they didn't draw back up once the bag was released.

Once again, the surgery was unsuccessful. The doctor promised that perhaps one more surgery when he turned six would be successful, but that surgery was unsuccessful as well. Her handsome little boy would most likely be sterile. Jen cried for him, and for many months she blamed herself for his sterility—had she not been disabled, had she not given birth to him too early, had she taken better care of herself during her pregnancy? Then, maybe, her son would not have been sterile.

Again, Jen's priority was to take care of her son and her family, and once again, she went for over a month without working out or playing basketball. She began to worry, or at least ask the question—why? Why were all these things happening to their family? Was she not supposed to be a Paralympian? Did God have other plans for her? She tried talking with Mic about it, but he was always tired or working. She tried talking it over with her best friend, but Belinda was not an athlete, and she couldn't understand why Jen wanted to be a Paralympian so badly. She wasn't much help, but at least she listened. Jen even spoke with her pastor, and as he always did—told her to pray about it—and she did.

Jen asked God for one thing and one thing only—to become a Paralympian and win one, just one, gold medal for Him, for her country and for herself. She hoped that wasn't asking too much.

As the sun shone brightly through the Collins' kitchen window one Friday morning, Jen took a break from her morning house cleaning chores to just peer out the window. Yes, the sun was absolutely brilliant, with sunbeams bouncing around everywhere, and it seemed to Jen that the Father, Son and Holy Spirit were shining on her directly—just her, Jen Collins, and no one else. Heaven seemed to calling out to her.

She felt a real calling at that particular moment to do something good for someone else, to stop thinking of herself, her family, her Paralympic dreams, and to concentrate on someone else's needs. As Jen folded her hands in prayer at the kitchen table, it was as though the Spirit of God entered her already spirit-filled heart and told her exactly what to do—she needed to call Jill Casey. Something was happening to Jill at that very moment. She could feel it in her heart and in her soul—Jill Casey needed prayer at that very moment. Jen had no idea why, but she accepted God's calling for her to stop what she was doing and to pray for Jill. She had no idea if Jill was a Christian, or whether her boyfriend was saved. She had no idea where Jill was at the current time, if she was in trouble, or if she was okay. Jen just knew that God had requested this of her, and she would answer His call.

Jen looked up Jill's telephone number, dialed it and waited for an answer, but there was none. She hung up, dialed the number again, and again there was no answer, so Jen left her a short message.

"Hi, Jill, it's Jennifer. I really wanted to talk with you and apologize for not getting back to you sooner. Since Mic's accident, I've been so busy with his care and with the boys, but," she hesitated and continued, "but that's no excuse; I should've gotten back to you much sooner. I hope you're okay, and if you have time, call me back."

Jen hung up, somewhat disappointed, but certain that she was still supposed to contact Jill. Jen asked God to please give her a sign.

Jen continued on with her house keeping chores, picked up Lennie at noon from kindergarten, and took the three boys to the park for a picnic and play time. When she returned home around 2:30 pm, her landline telephone was ringing, and as she rolled into the kitchen to pick it up, she noticed it was from Jill. She took a few seconds before answering, asking God for a sign as to what exactly it was that she was supposed do for Jill, and said hello.

Chapter Fifty-Seven

*J*ill and Lucas were just being seated at the Captain's Ball, when she heard her telephone ringing. She ignored it. She and Lucas were ordering their drinks and Lucas was telling her how absolutely stunning she was in her gold, sequined evening gown. He had not seen Jill in this gown before, and was amazed at how beautiful she looked. She told him that she had purchased the dress in the 'five' days he had given her to prepare for this trip, and she chuckled stating she always did what she was told.

Again, her telephone rang, and this time she noticed it was Jennifer Collins, and once again she didn't answer it. It couldn't be anything to pressing, and Jill figured she could call her back the next day.

Jill and Lucas enjoyed a wonderful dinner starting with a Shrimp Cocktail Supreme appetizer, Slow Roasted Prime Rib, and Strawberry Cheese Cake. They topped off the meal with brandy and coffee, and Jill didn't think the evening could go any better.

As the orchestra softly played Love Is A Many Splendored Thing, the Captain stood up and told the guests that there was a very special event about to take place, and he asked if everyone would stand and draw their attention to table number sixteen. A spotlight immediately shown down on the table where Jill and Lucas were seated. The other couples seated at their table also stood up, and as Jill looked inquisitively at Lucas, he also stood up, moved his chair away from the table, and asked her to back her wheelchair away from the table. He got down on his knee, took her left hand in his, and told her that he loved her more than anything else in the world, that he wanted to spend the rest of his life with her, and would she be his wife? Jill had no time to respond before Lucas took the beautiful diamond and pearl ring out of the case, and slipped it onto her finger.

Jill was speechless. She figured that some time in the near future this would've happened, but not here, not in front of all these people, not in the middle of the ocean! She was at a loss for words—but just for a moment.

"Yes. Yes. Yes." Jill said as tears streaked down her cheeks. "Yes, Lucas, yes. I will marry you."

The Captain's guests all cheered and as they did, Lucas kissed his fiancée passionately while the Captain asked that everyone please be seated once again, and that the dancing would commence. He asked that everyone remain seated until Jill Casey and Lucas Lopez enjoyed their first dance. Lucas led Jill onto the immense dance floor, and as they had practiced, Lucas sat down on her lap, put his arms around her, as Jill pushed her wheelchair to the music. Once again the crowd gathered for dinner and dancing at the Captain's Ball, cheered.

Lucas and Jill danced until the last song ended. He would dance with her as before, then he would switch pick her up and set her down on his lap in her wheelchair and dance the opposite way. When they fast danced, he would swing her around, or just dance and sway with her, no touch needed. This, he thought, has to be one of the best nights of my life.

As they left the Captain's Ball, one person after another stopped to congratulate the young couple. Jill held on to Lucas' arm as one by one they thanked everyone for their best wishes. When the Captain came by their table, he too, congratulated them, kissed Jill on the cheek, and shook Lucas' hand. He then handed them an envelope with a gift certificate for the ship's gift shop. He hoped something they saw in the shop might always remind them of this exciting evening on board his cruise lines.

The two lovers strolled along the deck until 2:00 am in the morning. They were tired but knew they wouldn't be able to sleep. Around 5:30 am, after first watching the moon and stars and then the sun come up over the horizon, they made it back to their stateroom. Lucas helped Jill out of her gorgeous ball gown, and lifted her into bed. Lying naked together, they fell asleep in each other's arms. There would be plenty of time in the future to show their love for one another. Tonight was just for holding each other and talking of the future.

Chapter Fifty-Eight

Lucas and Jill spent several days just sitting on deck, reading, drinking Mai Tai's, and relaxing. The days were sunny, with only a little breeze, and every now and then they would spot another cruise ship in the distance. A few small children had run up to Jill and asked her about her wheelchair, and she'd told them sweetly why she was disabled. Jill, it seemed to Lucas, had a wonderful way with children, especially the younger ones. He hoped and prayed that she'd be able to conceive and give birth to their children, but, first things first he was reminded, and then whatever God had in His plan.

One topic that had not been discussed in the past several months was one of religion. Jill knew that Lucas enjoyed church, that he had spent a lot of time with a pastor and a counselor after his wife's untimely death, but the two of them had not gone to church together, nor had they talked much about his faith or denomination, nor hers. She knew that Lucas had a family Bible in his bedroom, but she'd never seen him read it. He had also mentioned in passing the note that Erica had written to him when she feared she was going to die. It was in that Bible. If Jill recalled correctly, the note had included writings of her new found faith, her love for Jesus and an admission of no fear of dying.

Jill thought as she remembered the note that she had enjoyed Sunday school as a child, but in her later years church had not been a priority. She saw a pastor at the center a few times during her hospitalization and rehab, and he was some comfort to her, but she really never took faith or the lack of it seriously. She always figured that a strong will and a good attitude, along with a great team of medical professionals, had all been a part of her recovery process. Jill made a mental note to talk to Lucas about his spirituality in a few days. She was interested in every aspect of this man's life—yes, she decided, she would bring up the subject soon because she was not only curious about his faith, but her own.

The subject came up sooner than she had expected. After a wonderful lunch of shrimp scampi, fried oysters and crab, they were about to leave their table when an older man a few seats across from them grabbed his throat and fell from his chair onto the floor. From experience as a Highway Patrol Officer and EMT, Lucas immediately stood up and rushed to assist the man and his frantic wife.

"He's choking, he's choking!" His frantic wife screamed.

Lucas assisted the choking man from off the floor and set him quickly back onto a chair. He began a maneuver to clear the man's throat and within only seconds, a small piece of meat popped out from the man's throat.

The wife, although still distraught, came closer to touch her husbands face, and as she did so, she uttered words of thanksgiving to God and made the sign of the cross across her chest. She then began to cry, and as ship personnel gathered around the woman and her husband, Lucas too, while still on bended knee, gave thanks to the Lord Almighty for saving the man's life. He also immediately thanked his Maker for giving him the knowledge to save the man's life. As Lucas stood up, allowing the medical personnel to take over, he looked over to where Jill was still seated at the table. Her hands were covering her mouth, and a tear gently fell from her eye. She had just witnessed Lucas save a man's life, and the first thing he'd done afterward was to thank God. He took no credit; he asked for nothing in return. He had faith in his Maker and had faith in himself and faith in what had been taught him.

She needed to find out more about that kind of faith.

Chapter Fifty-Nine

A week after Jen's telephone message, Jill returned the call. Jen was pleased to hear from her and asked how she was doing.

Jill explained with great jubilation that she had been on a cruise, that her boyfriend had proposed, and she was sorry she hadn't gotten back to Jen before now.

"I want to tell you all about the cruise and my wonderful husband-to-be and my beautiful ring and, oh, Jen, I want to talk to you about so many things," Jill continued, "I am so excited, Jen, pardon me if I'm rambling, but I haven't been this happy in years!"

Jen congratulated her and told her a little about Mic's accident and rehab, and that they needed to get together soon, and all the while she was waiting for that sign from God as to why He wanted Jen in Jill's life.

Jill knew that classes would be starting in a week, and asked if she had time to meet before then? Jen, said, yes, she would make time, and they set a lunch date for the following Thursday. Jen knew she would have to get a sitter and someone to pick Lennie up from school, but she promised she could get it done.

They planned to meet around 11:30 am at Fratelli's Italian restaurant in Englewood CO. Jen appreciated the fact that Jill had selected a place closer to Jen's home than hers. She would have to be home in time to fix dinner and get Mic up to spend time with the boys.

Jen daily asked God for a sign as to why she should spend more time with Jill Casey? She knew very little about Jill except that she had been in a tragic accident, and her husband had left her because of it. She had come to really enjoy Jill's telephone calls, and once in awhile her company, but she had a feeling that she needed to get to Jill on a more personal basis.

On Tuesday afternoon, Jen received a telephone call from the assistant pastor at their Lutheran church.

"Hi, Jen, it's Pastor Mark Coleman," he said cheerfully. "I hope you and your family are doing well."

Jen assured him that they were, thanked him for asking, and said what a surprise it was to hear from him.

"Is everything all right?" she asked.

"Yes, Jen, everything is fine. I have a dilemma however, and I was hoping that you could help me out.

Pastor Mark continued to tell her that the guest speaker scheduled to speak at the Lutheran's Women's Retreat banquet on Thursday evening had cancelled due to a family crisis. There were over a hundred women scheduled to attend the dinner and he was wondering if she would be available and willing, to speak at the banquet?

"Oh my," Jen said somewhat surprised. "You want me to speak. Mark, I've only spoken a few times and always to kids, I'm not sure I could do a good job for you. Are you sure?"

The pastor assured her that they wanted her to speak on Thursday evening.

"You have an awesome way of telling your faith story, Jen," he continued. "You have a great story to tell regarding your disability, being a wife and mother, and most of all your Christianity shines through you all the time. You would be great. Dinner is on us, and please pray about it will you, and get back to me right away."

She agreed to pray about it, but only after checking with Mic and getting his parents to babysit. She presumed that she would be back home by 10:00 pm, but wanted to make sure, and Mic would need to sleep.

But more important than the prayer, getting Mic's approval and getting a babysitter, she realized, was that God had just given her the sign she was waiting for. She would call Jill and invite her to the retreat dinner—her treat and let her know that she would be sharing a lot about her life with a hundred other women and this would be a good way for Jill to get information from Jen and also an opportunity for Jen to share her faith in God with Jill in the audience.

She called the pastor to let him know that she would speak to the women and thanked him for the opportunity to do so. She then hung up and thanked God once again for the sign.

"Thank you dear God," she said, her eyes closed. "Thank you for this sign and for your love for me and for Jill Casey".

She then picked up the telephone and dialed Jill's number. She prayed that Jill would say yes to her invitation.

Chapter Sixty

Lucas and Jill had dinner together on Monday evening in Littleton, and along with talks of school starting and Lucas' events of the day, Jill told him that she was going to spend Thursday with Jennifer Collins. She told him about their lunch plans and that Jen was going to speak at a women's church retreat dinner, and Jen had invited her to attend.

"I really want to get to know Jennifer a lot better, Lucas," she said, smiling. "I think I could learn a lot from her. She's been a wheelchair user for such a long time, is a wife and a mom, and has such a great outlook on everything. I'm looking forward to speaking with her and hearing her speak at the retreat."

Lucas looked at her lovingly and mentioned that he knew someone else who had a great outlook on life. Jill chuckled, kissed him across the table, and the conversation continued.

"What is she going to speak about at the retreat?" he asked. "Is it for a church group?"

Jill shared with him the little that she knew—that Jennifer and her family belonged to a Lutheran church, and that she was filling in at the last minute for another speaker who had to cancel because of a family situation. She figured Jennifer would speak about her disability, being a wheelchair mother, athlete, and how she adapts to life.

Lucas decided that this was a good time to talk to Jill about his faith, and his struggles when Erica had died in the airplane crash, and his church. He and Jill had spoken a little in the past few months—the note Erica had left him, and the fact that he had been to a shrink, but the two of them had not talked about Jill's religious background, or her faith, or starting to go to church together on his weekend's off. He knew that he had put it off, in part because he didn't want to lose Jill, and if she didn't believe in God or didn't want to go to church with him, well, he hadn't wanted to bring it up before. She had accepted his ring and agreed to become his wife, so now the next step. Maybe he should have talked to her about God before he proposed, but he felt God was with him and approving of everything he had done to this point, so it was time.

They stayed at the restaurant until almost 9:00 pm. They lingered over coffee, ate delicious peach cobbler, and began and ended the evening in a deep conversation about God, faith, life's challenges, and was there a hereafter? Anything at all that came up about religion, they discussed it.

Lucas need not have worried about Jill's faith or background. Although she had really never accepted Jesus into her life, she did believe in God and believed there had been a higher power in charge when she had her accident, otherwise, she probably would have died. She said, she wasn't sure what God expected of her, but since she was a fairly new injury, and she was learning so many new things about life as a wheelchair user, she was certain there was a plan for her.

"Maybe he has me going into counseling the disabled, or working with newly injured women, or new mothers. I don't know Lucas, but I do know that my injury happened for a reason. I also know that my marriage to Tom was meant to fail so that I could meet and marry you. Perhaps God has a plan for the both of us, together, to do something extraordinary."

The two newly engaged lovers talked until the restaurant manager said they were closing. When they returned to Jill's home, Lucas thought of driving back to the Springs, but decided instead to stay the night with his beloved Jill and leave early in the morning for work.

On this night, as they snuggled in bed, Lucas told her that the weekend after next, he would have a three-day weekend. He would love for her to attend church with him, meet some of his friends who also attended, and join in the Singles Club Luncheon afterwards. He laughed when she jabbed him and said it was time for him to leave the singles group and get ready to join the married couples group. With that said, he also asked her when she would like to get married. Did she want to wait a while or get married soon?

"You know what I would like, Lucas?" she asked.

Without giving him a chance to answer, she said she would love to get married at Christmas.

"The Colorado mountains are so beautiful all the time but especially in the winter," she said smiling at him and leaning on one arm. "Do you think we could find a place in the mountains at Christmas? Maybe a ski resort or a mountain hotel?"

Lucas kissed her gently and told her there was no reason why they couldn't get married in the mountains, but there was always the chance of a blizzard, and then what?

She laughed, kissed him back more passionately, and the conversation went no further. Lucas took her to himself, making love to her as only a man in love could do. They would talk more about a mountain wedding tomorrow.

Chapter Sixty-One

$\mathcal{J}$ill drove to the restaurant and met Jennifer a little past 11:30 am. They drank iced tea for the first hour, and finally after the waitress had stopped by three times to take their order, they both ordered the soup and salad special. As they ate their lunch, Jill asked Jennifer a multitude of questions about her polio, her hospital stay, rehabilitation, her parents, her school days, anything at all that she could relate too.

Jennifer shared how her parents had played such an important role in her childhood and acceptance of her disability. They had never treated her as special; they pushed her ever so lightly to be independent and only assisted her when she asked for help. She had graduated from Chamberville Christian High School, where she was the only disabled student. She had been deterred from attending college by her peers, saying that if "her legs didn't work, then her brain must not work either." She also shared how much that statement hurt, but how she regrouped, went to a community college for one year, and was enjoying a great career; at least she would enjoy it when she went back to work

"My boys are taking up my whole being right now, Jill", she commented. "But when they're all in school, I plan to go back to work at least part time. We really could use the extra money."

Jennifer, after Jill hesitantly asked, explained how sex was between her and Mic, that she had never been with another man, and how they made it fulfilling for the both of them, and what it had been like giving birth to a stillborn child.

The two women could have talked for several more hours, but Jennifer realized that it would soon be time to leave.

"Why don't you just follow me home, Jill?" she said. "We can chat some more, and you can meet the boys on the home front and see what being a mother is really all about. It's not just the pregnancy and giving birth that's difficult, it's raising them!"

Jill said she'd follow her home and asked if she was dressed appropriately for the evening event. Jen assured her that she looked very nice, and asked if from, now on would she please call her Jen? Everyone else did.

The two women paid the check, left the restaurant, and as they approached their vehicles, Jen told Jill how glad she was to have finally spent some quality time with her.

"I think we have a lot more to talk about Jill," Jen said. "I hope after tonight's event, you will have even more of your questions answered. I'm so glad you are joining me tonight at the women's retreat."

As they loaded into their separate vehicles, Jen added that she and Mic were also anxious to meet Lucas. Perhaps they could meet in the next few weeks.

Neither Jill nor Jennifer had any idea, that they already knew Lucas—Officer Lucas Lopez of the Highway Patrol.

Chapter Sixty-Two

Jill was impressed with Jen and Mic's home, which was decorated in a lot of antiques and Early American décor. She was even more impressed with the three little boys, how well behaved they were and how much they adored their mother. Jill held Ronnie on her lap, got the feeling of how to keep him there, without letting him fall, and she was asked immediately to read Mickey a story, and Lennie, wishing not to be left out, asked if she wanted to play dominos with him? She also watched as Jen took Ronnie from her, gently nursed him for a few minutes and then changed him on her lap.

"I won't be able to change him on my lap much longer." Jen said, smiling. "He's getting so big, but changing him this way has been so easy. I just put a pad with a blanket over my lap and that keeps him from falling through my legs." She laughed, and shared with Jill that her legs had separated once or twice, and he had fallen through.

The time spent at Jen's home went by quickly, and soon it was time to leave for the church. Jen's in-laws had come by to babysit, and had also brought Kentucky Fried Chicken and promised to wake Mic up to eat with them. Jen thanked them, kissed the boys goodbye, and opened the door. Once again, the two women planned to drive separate vehicles. This way, Jill could head home immediately after the event.

Mic's parents, watching the two women wheelchair users head down the wheelchair ramp to their cars, were again amazed how their daughter-in-law handled her life. They also wondered what the story was on Jill—Jennifer's new friend—why was she using a wheelchair?

The parking lot was full when Jen and Jill drove in and parked, but as always there were several handicapped parking places, and they pulled right in, parked and headed for the main entrance. There was a young woman waiting for them at the front door, and as she said hello, Jen introduced Jill to Maggie Rush and pushed the automatic access button to open the door. Their instructions were simple, to access the elevator at the end of the hallway and join everyone in the basement fellowship hall.

After an opening prayer and welcome, everyone enjoyed a wonderful dinner of pecan crusted salmon and broiled chicken breast, twice baked potatoes, corn with red peppers, and chocolate raspberry filled cake. Towards the end of dessert, the mistress of ceremonies introduced Jeri Mansfield who played a beautiful rendition of Jesus, Joy of Loving Hearts on the harp. After another round of applause, she introduced Jennifer.

To fervent applause, Jennifer rolled up the accessible ramp onto the stage, accepted the microphone from the MC, and before starting her speech, took the time to introduce Jill and thanked everyone for being there and for the invitation to speak.

Jen was stunning in a long brown and pink flowered skirt with matching brown blouse and a similar colored scarf draped at her neck. Women of all ages had their eyes on Jen even before she began her hour-long talk.

She began by telling the women in the audience about polio and what having the disease had meant to all those around her—the quarantine, how she barely missed being in an iron lung and that during her six-month hospital stay she could only have visitors every other day for only one hour at a time. She shared how her daddy would sneak in after hours to see her, as he worked late, and her little brother could not come into the hospital ward, so the nurses would roll her bed up to the window so she could wave at him. She had only been eight years old—a child who just took each day as it came along—even the day she fell out of the hospital bed, cracked her head open as she hit the floor, and laid there for over three hours before a nurse came in to check on her. There had been 8 stitches sewn into her head that day and railings installed on the hospital bed from then on.

She talked about the two goldfish and turtles that kept her company for the six months she spent at Children's Hospital—Sparkle, Marvel Fred and Buck, and how on the first night after her release, they were left on the patio and all froze. She talked about what it was like not to swallow, and how she was fed through tubes into her stomach and lines into her veins, and that on the first day she was able to swallow again, she drank forty pints of chocolate milk, and then chucked it all up. She shared about the hundreds of get-well cards and gifts she received, and how painful the therapy had been, and then, how one day she realized—she would never walk again.

She talked about her education, how mean and thoughtless people were and how now she wanted to fight for the rights of all people with disabilities because of those few people. She shared her current employment status, talked about her wonderful, good-looking husband, her three children, and her dream of becoming a Paralympian. Then she began to speak on the topic most of the women had come to hear—how and why she had such a tremendous faith in God.

Jen looked down at Jill several times while she spoke. Jill seemed to be taking in every word that came out of Jen's mouth. Jen began her faith testimony hoping that if no one else in the room except for Jill Casey, was blessed by what she had to say, then God had intended for her to be here, and she silently asked God to bless the words she was about to speak—for Jill Casey's sake.

Chapter Sixty-Three

Jen began her testimony stating that she had a dream—a dream to become a Paralympic' gold medalist. She had asked God for one thing, and one thing only—that if she be allowed to compete, that He allow her to win a gold medal, and one gold medal only, and she would use that medal for His honor and glory. She continued by sharing information on the Paralympics because most of the women in the audience had no idea what the Paralympics were all about—competition exactly the same as the able-bodied Olympics, except all Paralympians had a disability. She then read a short scripture, and began:

"I have a dream and have had this dream since I was a small child! I want to win a gold medal in the Olympic games. Along with dreams I also know that God has a purpose for everyone." Jen began, as she waved her hand around the entire room filled with women. "And He has a plan and a purpose for you. He also had and still has a plan and a purpose for me and for my life, and I want to share part of that story with you now.

His first plan was to see that I was born into a loving, God-fearing family. I have an awesome mother and dad, a loving brother (well, most of the time), and had a little sister, although for only a couple of years, before God took her home to live in Heaven—yes, that too was a part of His plan.

I'm sure it was heart-breaking when my parents were told that their 8-year-old daughter would never walk again, that because of it, their lives would change forever, but God was in control, and I never heard them complain. I'm sure it was even more heart-breaking when they were told that their 2 1/2-year-old daughter had leukemia, and that it was so far advanced, there was little the doctors could do for her, and she died. People said, why should so much heartbreak come upon one family, but my parents positively thanked God for the short time they had little Lilly and never complained because they believed God was in control. Did they cry? Of course they did. Did they ask God, why? I'm certain they did, but I never heard them. They knew that God had a plan and a purpose, and losing Lilly was part of it.

God gave me a quiet, loving heart, a somewhat intelligent mind (on any given day I sometimes wonder and so does my husband!), a positive outlook and an outgoing personality. I have used all of these qualities to constantly better myself, constantly work at being a good wife and mother, and hopefully, to make this world a better place for all persons with disabilities. That, I believe, is what God has planned for me, and that is His purpose for my life."

Jen continued to talk about her faith, how she read her Bible daily, and somehow God showed her daily the passage of scripture she needed, each and every day, to be a good wife, a good mom, a good listener, a good friend, and most of all how to stay positive, stay healthy and never be afraid to ask God for help. She also admitted, however, that she was incredibly independent, maybe too independent, and she had a hard time asking anyone for help or accepting help when it was offered. She found throughout her life that almost all post polio survivors had a hard time accepting assistance—they were all taught to be seriously independent from the very first onset of the paralysis; maybe it was the era, no one could really ever answer that question of why.

Jen shared the last fifteen minutes of her talk about her will, her drive and her dream to be a Paralympian. She told about workouts—that she pushed her wheelchair through her neighborhood at least 100 miles a week, that she lifted weights, that she had lost almost 50 pounds of pregnancy weight gain, and all this while trying to be the best wife and mother in the world. She also admitted that it was definitely not easy, and that it was working because God was on her side.

"I know it's hard for us to believe in something we can't see," she said, smiling. "There are a lot of unbelievable things in this world, and all of us, at one time or another, are doubting, just like Thomas in the Bible, but one thing is for certain, the Word of God is true, scientifically proven true, and if we believe in what we read, that the Bible is the true Word of God, then you can believe in anything. So, therefore ladies, I believe that God is with me at all times, even if I can't see Him, because the Bible says so. I see Him in the world around me, in the blue skies, the sunflowers, my baby's smile, and yes, I see Him in my disability. He allowed me to use this wheelchair, to have a debilitating disease, and because of it or in spite of it, I believe that God's plan is for me to win an Olympic Gold Medal, and use that win to spread His good news—that all men and women are created equal, that we are all made in His image, that just because we have a disability, or wear glasses or have a wart on our nose, we are not special, we are EQUAL!"

Jen ended her talk with a bit of humor, stating that the reason she had been successful in life so far was that she had "a great attitude and had great insurance!" She, of course, told the audience that the biggest and greatest reason for her success was that she had an awesome faith in the One and Only God, Ruler of the Universe and Creator of All Things Good. She knew she might have and already had been given trials and challenges in her life, and she knew there would be more to come, but with God as her protector and Jesus as her Savior, she would roll on, one day, one week, one month at a time and take whatever God gave her. She would persevere, she would conquer, and all while she was trying to win that gold medal.

Jen thanked the women's group once again for inviting her, for being a great audience, and that she would be happy to answer a few questions at the end of the evening. She rolled off the stage and down the ramp to a standing ovation.

Jill had tears in her eyes, and for the first time in a long while, she actually wished that she, too, could stand up and cheer for this lovely woman—this woman with such an amazing faith—a woman who would become and remain her best friend for years to come. She couldn't stand up and cheer, but Jill clapped, then whistled, and rolled over to wait her turn to thank Jen for being such a big part of her life—tonight.

Chapter Sixty-Four

*J*ill and Jen finally managed a weekend when both Lucas and Mic were off work at the same time and they set a time to meet. The women agreed that they would spend a Saturday afternoon and evening together with dinner, maybe cards or board games, and spend it at Jen and Mic's home. This way, the newly engaged couple could spend time with the entire family and the boys could still go to bed on time. Jen knew how important it was for Jill to spend time with children and have Lucas see how she handled a family environment. Having children seemed to be a priority for Jill, and she could understand wanting Lucas to see her in "action".

Jen cleaned the house, planned a nice dinner, and asked their guests to arrive around 3:00 pm. When Lennie noticed Jill's blue Mustang pulling into the driveway, he immediately ran out the front door to welcome his mommy's new friend.

"Jill, Jill," he yelled. "Jill, Jill, are you here to play with me?"

Jill opened the car door and said, sure she would play with him, but first he needed to meet her friend, Lucas. Jill was barely out of the car when Mickey came out of the house, too. Both boys gave Jill a hug and said hi to Lucas.

Jen called the two boys to come back in the house, and as Jill and Lucas were coming up the ramp, she recognized Lucas, even without his Patrol uniform and hat. But it took a minute or two for her to remember from where?

"My goodness, Jill," she said, surprised. "I know who this fine looking gentleman is! He stopped us on our wedding night and searched our car. Officer, ummm, I know it's Lucas, because Jill told me, but I'm sorry I can't remember your last name."

Lucas was speechless. A woman who remembered him from so many years ago and was now a friend of his wife-to-be, it just didn't seem possible. He held out his hand to shake her outstretched hand, and politely told her his last name, and as she invited them both into her home, she called for Mic to come in from the garage.

"Mic, Mic, you aren't going to believe this. You know who Jill's fiancé is? It's the officer who stopped us outside of Crested City on our way to Buffalo Springs on our honeymoon. Can you believe this?"

Mic shook Lucas' hand, said how nice it was to meet him again, and that he was so sorry, but his memory, evidently, wasn't as good as his wife's.

The four young people laughed, hugged, and, as the three little ones scampered around to get some of the attention, they all managed to sit around the kitchen table while Jen poured everyone iced tea. Ronnie crawled up on Jen's lap, and Lucas watched as she helped him onto her lap.

"My goodness," Lucas said. "What a small world. I do remember stopping you two, because I remember seeing your wheelchair in the back seat of your classic car, uh, what was it Mic, a Chevy, blue if I remember correctly?"

The four talked for over an hour, drinking their iced drinks, discussing highlights of the past several years. It was during this conversation that Lucas told the Collins that his wife had been killed in a plane crash and that he'd also been the lead officer at Jill's accident sight, and that was how they'd met.

"I watched the medical team get her off Cinnamon Ridge and escorted them to the hospital, and then visited her once or twice while she was in rehab," Lucas said. "I was pretty shook-up for a few years after my wife's death. I didn't go out much, but we saw each other several months ago, just by chance, in a Chamberville restaurant, and then again about four months ago in Crested City. From that point on, we have been seeing each other non-stop," and reaching out for Jill's hand, he continued. "I just asked Jill to marry me last week. I know it seems fast, but we both agree that we love each other very much, and don't want to wait much longer to get married."

Once again, congratulations abounding, Jen said she needed to put Ronnie down for his nap, and the guys should keep chatting, but she needed to get dinner started. Lucas and Mic stepped into the garage for some guy talk, and after Ronnie was in his crib, Jill and Jen began dinner preparations. It was a little tight for two wheelchairs in the pretty blue and yellow kitchen, but the two women managed. Jen gave Jill a cutting board, which she placed on her lap, and she cut up salad greens, onion, tomatoes and cucumbers, while Jen began to fry the chicken. She had made potato salad earlier that morning, would add warm rolls to the menu and ice cream for dessert.

Jen congratulated Jill once again on her engagement, and asked if they had set a date for the wedding. Jill said, no, but they were hoping to get married around Christmastime with just a few friends and family members present. Jen said anything at all she could do to help, she would be there for Jill.

Lucas and Jill were enthralled with how well three little boys not only behaved themselves, but how Lennie had said a child's blessing and Mickey had chimed in with the amen. Jill had to choke back a chuckle as little Ronnie also put in his two-cents worth. The older boys had hardy appetites, and Jen commented that she very seldom had leftovers. Ronnie still had serious problems with food allergies, but he was gaining. Lucas asked a few questions about Ronnie, and then dinner was over.

The boys, all tucked into bed by 9:00 pm, gave the new friends a time for an after dinner brandy and coffee and time to talk like adults. Jill and Lucas talked about wedding plans, and Jen and Mic talked about raising a family and keeping their marriage happy and contented. Mic and Jen both agreed that it took a lot of work, especially with Mic's graveyard shift at the brewery. They admitted that they had tried to have at least one night a week put aside as a "date night", but it usually ended up being one night a month. Jen also talked about her dream of being a Paralympian and that she planned to start working out even harder before winter set in.

At around 11:00 pm, the happy couples said their goodbyes, agreeing that they would get together again soon. The Collins wished them God speed, and safe travels, and an added good luck message with their wedding plans.

"Jen offered to help me with the wedding plans,' Jill said as she headed down the ramp to her Mustang. "We'll be seeing each other often I think."

Jen and Mic went back into the house, hand in hand, and Mic kissed her gently as she began rolling into the bedroom.

"I hope I can keep my promise to Jill to help her with her wedding," she said, yawning. "If she wants to get married at Christmastime, I had better start working out really hard at the gym if I'm going to be in shape by March for wheelchair games tryouts and help plan a wedding."

Mic just shook his head, knowing full well that if anyone could handle a multitude of tasks at one time, it was his wife.

Chapter Sixty-Five

$\mathcal{J}$ill kept busy teaching and holding tryouts for the Drama Club's production, while Lucas kept busy pulling two shifts. His friend and co-officer, Doug Pole had succumbed to the cancer, and Lucas grieved once again. He couldn't decide which was worse—losing someone unexpectedly like Erica, or watching someone steadily fade away and then die. Either way, Lucas grieved once again for his wife and for Doug's family.

He was in hopes that another officer would be hired soon, but in the meantime, he worked hard and put extra money away for him and Jill. She had suggested just a small, intimate wedding this time, but as time went on and the two made wedding plans, the invitation list grew larger as did the expense account. They had found the perfect little mountain church, completely accessible, in beautiful Evergreen Colorado, and had set their wedding date for the 22nd of December. Jill had been out with Jen twice, looking for a gown, and she couldn't decide what color or what style she wanted. Her first wedding had been a huge affair—beautiful, but very expensive—and she wanted something much simpler and more intimate this time. However, as the date got closer and closer, she still hadn't selected a gown. She had selected poinsettias, carnations, red roses and holly for the altar, and she would have a lap bouquet of red roses with sprigs of holly leaves, bound with white ribbons. The cake had been ordered, as were all other essentials for a simple reception to be held at the church.

Jill had asked her mother, Loren, to be her maid of honor, and Ken Porter agreed, readily, to stand up with Lucas. Since her mom and Joe Spencer were now engaged as well, she had asked Joe to give her away, and since Joe loved her like his own daughter, he had immediately said yes.

By November, they had met with the minister, had a few pre-marital counseling sessions, and had spent at least three more evenings with Jen and Mic talking about an able-bodied/disabled couple's life. The four young people were so completely open with one another, that each time

Lucas and Jill left the Collins' home—a home filled with not only love for one another and their boys but a sincere love of God and church—they knew, with their deep love for one another, they too would have a blessed marriage.

Jill had attended church with Lucas in Buffalo Springs every free Sunday, and the two realized that this distance between the two cities was too far to continue commuting. Lucas lived and worked in the Springs but drove to Crested City and back several times a day. Jill lived in Littleton, but worked in Crested City and had a new home, so, after only a few serious talks, the dilemma was resolved. They would sell Lucas' house, and live in Littleton. Lucas would still have to drive back and forth to the Springs but would apply for a transfer to the Chamberville offices of the Highway Patrol. It could've been a hard move for Lucas, as he had been in the Springs area for so many years, but Jill was his motivation, his love and his life, and he had no qualms about the transfer.

As Jill planned her wedding, Jennifer Collins continued to work out at the gym, swim at the YWCA, play basketball and she and Mic square danced. She had lost all of her extra weight and was down to a slim 130 pounds. Her coaches were very happy with her workouts, and by the time the holidays arrived, she was in the best shape of her married life.

The Collins' planned a surprise couples bridal shower for Lucas and Jill for the 13th of November. Around fifteen of Jill and Lucas' friends from Crested City High School, the Patrol, and a few of Jen and Mic's friends had been invited. Around 5:00 pm, pleading a last minute babysitting need, as an excuse to get them over, Jill and Lucas arrived at their home to the surprise of their lives. Jen had contacted Ken Porter, who in turn contacted the Patrol, to make sure Lucas was off duty that night, and all went as expected. There was a wine tasting followed by a lovely dinner, and of course, beautiful gifts, as well as humorous wedding night attire. Jill and Lucas were so thankful to have found Mic and Jen and couldn't thank them enough for this delightful and unforgettable evening.

Chapter Sixty-Six

$\mathcal{J}$ill was a beautiful, breathtaking bride. She rolled slowly down the red-ribbon adorned aisle, one arm intertwined with Joe's, in an ankle length, off-white, chiffon gown, with an A-line-princess waist. It had fit perfectly on the first fitting—that being only two weeks ago! She added a shoulder length veil, held in place with pearl and chiffon flowers and around her throat, a single pearl on a white gold chain—a gift from her beloved Lucas. Joe was looking so sharp in his black tuxedo, and for the first time, ever she had seen tears in his eyes. Jill chuckled as Lucas took her by the hand, thinking that the groom looked much more delicious in his tuxedo than Joe Spencer looked in his.

After Joe and Loren had given their approval for this marriage, Lucas sat on a chiffon-covered chair directly across from his beautiful bride. Facing one another with loving eyes and while holding each other's hands, the two promised to love, to honor and to obey, for as long as God would allow. They exchanged matching white-gold wedding bands with the inscription, "Forever In Love", and enjoyed a passionate first kiss as man and wife.

After a reception of cake and punch and what seemed like hundreds of photographs, the bride and groom left the Evergreen Methodist church in Jill's Mustang—all decorated out in green and red crepe paper. The words JUST MARRIED were written in shaving cream across the back window. They were off to an undisclosed location, as Lucas knew what some of his Patrol officers were capable of and was taking no chances.

They arrived in Estes Park, Colorado a little under two hours later. A soft, gentle snow was just beginning to fall as the newlyweds pulled into the valet parking at the famous Stanley Hotel. The hotel was decorated in gorgeous red, white and green twinkling lights, with enormous matching bows. The biggest Christmas tree Jill had ever seen lit up the entire front lobby, while carols played throughout. Lucas had made reservations over two months ago, for three days. They wanted to spend as much time as they could doing nothing but talking, making love, talking some more, and making more love, and hopefully by the time their honeymoon was over, they would make a baby. The timing should be perfect, Dr. Patterson had said.

It was their third night at the historic Stanley Hotel. Snow was falling lightly across the majestic Rocky Mountains, while inside their historic bridal suite, and after an earlier decision to use no more protection, that Cameron Joseph and Christina Joy Lopez were conceived.

Jen spent the entire months of January and February working out, lifting weights, swimming, pushing inside the gym on nice days and outside on the track when the weather permitted. The first part of March she applied for the Rocky Mountain Wheelchair Games as well as the California, New York and Illinois Wheelchair Games. She knew to have a chance at making the Para Games, she would have to do well in at least three state meets, so her coach made preparations for her to attend four meets. If she did well, she might also compete in Hawaii.

She and Mic made arrangements for the boys to have a sitter for the New York and Illinois Games, but planned to take them along to the California games. Mic had asked for his vacation early, and his supervisors, once knowing the situation, gave him three weeks off. He would fly with Jen and the team to New York, Illinois and possibly Hawaii, and they would drive to California. Her first meet would be at home in Colorado.

In the middle of March, the Rocky Mountain Wheelchair Games were held at the Metro State College in Chamberville. Jen's class of female athletes had only a few competitors, and she easily won gold medals in track, field, table tennis and swimming. There was no women's basketball competition. She and Mic flew with the team a week later to Illinois, where the first actual wheelchair games had begun in the 1970's, and again she won gold in track and field, and silver in swimming and table tennis. She had her first taste of playing basketball with an all-women's team. She had always played with the men's team prior to these games, as there was no women's team in Chamberville. It was much easier playing with all women, and she hoped that someday Chamberville would have a women's team.

After driving to California, checking into their hotel and watching Jen practice for a few hours, the Collins family drove to the meet on the San Diego College Campus. There was a large field, a track, and a playing area for the boys, and a beautiful indoor pool. Jen won easily in field events, but struggled in track, when a wheel on her racing chair lost a bearing. She finished the race, but didn't qualify in that event. She had qualified at an earlier meet, but worried a little about not qualifying in California. At the same time Jen was competing, Mic was involved with a few of the coaches and players, going over stats, etc, and after Jen finished for the day, she asked Mic where the boys were? He pointed to where Lennie and another six-year-old were playing, and to Ronnie, who was playing with several other children at the swings.

"Where's Mickey?" Jen asked.

"He's over there with Ronnie." Mic said pointing. "Well, he was just there, Jen. I'll go over and check."

Jen watched as Mic briskly walked over to the area where Mickey was supposed to be playing. She watched him walk around and around the area, and then watched as he spoke with several other athletes and coaches.

"He's not there, Jen," Mic said, a concern in his voice. "I'll start walking around the campus; he couldn't have gone far."

Jen wasn't too sure. She knew her son had a curious streak in his little body and could be anywhere. She pushed over to a few of her friends and asked them if they had seen Mickey, and when they said no but offered to help look for him, they all headed in different directions.

When Mic finally found him, about an hour later, Mickey was having a grand time. He had found an unused high-jump pit and was busy playing "army" in the sand with all of his soldiers and horses. He couldn't understand why everyone was so worried about him. "I knowed where I am," he said nonchalantly. "I'm right here, daddy."

Jen left California with several medals and the Outstanding Woman Athlete of the Games trophy. She was thrilled. She had worked hard, but she also knew that this honor would help a long way in getting her a position on the Paralympic Team. Next stop, New York. If she could win at least five gold medals in New York, she would have an awesome chance of making the Para Games. She prayed about it and worked out even harder. "Time will tell," she thought to herself on the flight to New York. "I'm getting older, and if I don't make it this year, I may not ever make it." Adrenaline was running high when she rolled off the airplane in New York's JFK airport.

Chapter Sixty-Seven

*J*ill knew she was pregnant by the second month after missing her period. She just had a feeling—a motherly feeling. She hadn't been sick or hadn't craved any certain foods—she just had a feeling. Lucas was elated at the possibility of a baby in the family and showed Jill his feelings by babying her on a daily basis. He brought her flowers once a week, took her out to dinner at least that many times, kissed her and hugged her more often (if that was possible), and went with her to her first OB/GYN appointment.

Jen had recommended her gynecologist to Jill, and she had appreciated Dr Patterson immediately. She had seen him prior to her marriage to Lucas, and now here she was again, hoping and praying that she was pregnant.

In the "olden days" she would have been told that the rabbit died!

Lucas was elated. Jill was ecstatic, and the doctor was amazed that she had conceived so quickly, until Jill informed him that she had stopped taking the pill over a month before their wedding. Dr. Patterson began a regiment of vitamins for her, talked to her about more frequent voiding, possible discomfort, and that she should make appointments for each month until the seventh month, then he wanted to see her more often.

"Please call immediately if you have any concerns, spotting, or anything else unusual," he said happily. "I'm sure you will do fine, Jill, but you are a first timer, and you are a spinal cord injury with no sensation. We will talk more as the months go by, okay?"

Jill made the first call to Loren. Loren screamed with happiness into the telephone. Jill laughed, and after a few more minutes, hung up and called Jen. Jen had just left for the gym the babysitter informed her, but would give her the message to call Jill back.

Jen was as excited for Jill as anyone. The two women talked for fifteen minutes, when Jen excused herself to put the little boys to bed and to help Lennie with his homework. She promised to call Jill later, and they could talk more.

September 18th was marked in big bold letters on Jill's kitchen calendar. This was her due date, or at least the doctor hoped it was. He wasn't exactly sure when she had conceived, but by the third month, he was pretty sure this baby would be born in September. He assured Jill that teaching would not be a problem, as she would be finished with school the first of June, and would have a few more months to prepare for motherhood. She went shopping a few times, purchased a few cute baby items, and she and Lucas went together one evening in May and purchased a crib and matching dresser at Sears. Around the 15th of May, just as Jen was preparing for the National Wheelchair Games in New Jersey, Jill received some unexpected news at her monthly doctor's visit. She had been gaining more weight than the doctor thought appropriate, so when she came in for her monthly visit, he shared the news with her.

"I really feel like there may have two babies, Jill," Dr Patterson said. "I want to do another exam, and see if I'm right, and then we want to do an ultrasound and see for sure."

Jill was speechless. She knew there had been movement, as she could feel something, but she had no idea there might be two babies. She didn't know what to say or what to do. She just sat in her wheelchair in bewilderment.

"Two. Two babies? Are you sure?" Jill asked.

"No, that's why we are going to do the exam and an ultrasound, Jill. I'll step out while you get undressed. Do you need help getting onto the exam table? Jill said, yes, that it was starting to be more difficult to transfer.

Dr. Patterson said upon examining her, that he was almost positive there were two babies. "One baby is turned, and one is straight up, but I'm positive we have two babies. Let's do an ultrasound to make sure. I'll see if we can schedule it right now. You may have to wait a few minutes, is that okay?"

Jill, still in shock, said sure, and in the meantime she tried calling Lucas on his cell. The telephone rang seven times before Lucas picked up.

"Hi, babe. What's up? Aren't you at the doctor's office?" Then beginning to panic a little, he added. "Jill, are you okay? Is there something wrong with the baby?"

Jill said no, that she was fine and that the babies were fine too. At first, there was just silence, then finally Lucas replied. "Did you say babies, Jill, babies?"

Jill couldn't decide if she should laugh or cry. Two babies. How in the world would she, a wheelchair user, take care of twins? The ultra sound showed exactly what Dr. Patterson had predicted—there were two babies. He was very happy for Jill and shared his excitement with her.

"I've delivered many sets of twins during my practice," he said. "I will be proud to deliver yours. Also, I think there is one boy, see here, as he pointed to the baby's tiny penis, but I can't tell the sex of the second baby because of the way the baby is turned. Time should tell us when the baby turns some more."

The doctor and patient talked for another twenty minutes. He told the soon-to-be mom of two that he wanted to watch her more closely now, and she would need to see him twice a month. He didn't expect any problems but wanted to be sure.

Jill left the doctor's office still in amazement and still a little bewildered. She transferred and loaded her wheelchair into the back seat of her car, took a deep breath, and called her mother.

Chapter Sixty-Eight

*J*en competed like her life was on the line in New York, and it was. She had tough competition, something she hadn't completely prepared herself for. In the last games, she had sailed right through almost all of the events due to little or no competition, but here, a woman who almost looked Amazonic in comparison to Jen would give her a run for her money.

Claudia Jamison, an athlete from Georgia, looked to be about Jen's age, maybe a year or two younger, but she would be at least 5'11" if she were standing. "Thank goodness!" Jill said to herself, "She will be sitting! Competing against her sitting down is going to be hard enough. Just look at her shoulders; they're massive!"

After classification check-in and a two-hour practice session with her coaches, she returned to the college dormitory where they were staying, took a shower and later met Mic at the cafeteria for dinner. As she took her plate from the stack on the line, she saw Claudia again. She felt the need to introduce herself, and get a little more acquainted with the competition. She filled her plate, followed Mic to the table where he was already seated, and told him she would be back directly. She pushed over to where Claudia was just pulling up to a table and politely introduced herself.

"Hi, Claudia, is it?" she asked smiling now."

"Yes, I'm Claudia Jamison," she replied.

Jen extended her right hand, and Claudia accepted it readily. Jen told her who she was, where she was from, and that they evidently were in the same Class – Class 4, and she just wanted to say hello before the games began.

Claudia seemed surprised that a competitor would want to get friendly before they met on the playing field, but she smiled back, saying, that, yes, she was a Class 4 also, and then asked Jen what events she was competing in.

Jen swallowed hard, wondering just how tough this woman was going to be over the next few days, but then politely answered.

"I'm in track and field," Jen said. "I'm also swimming with my Colorado relay team, and I sort of play table tennis for fun. How about you?"

Claudia responded that, she, too was in field events and that the javelin was her favorite event, but she would also compete in discus and shot put, but she didn't race or swim.

Jen sighed a small sigh of relief, and pointing towards where Mic was seated, told her that her husband was waiting for her, how nice it was to have met her, and she would most likely see her a lot over the next few days.

Over dinner, which wasn't the best she had ever tasted, she and Mic talked about her strategy in track events and how to get herself psyched up for the field events. She shared with him that Claudia Jamison was better at javelin than the shot-put, which was Jen's best event, but she was still a tid-bit worried.

"Don't be silly, Jen," her loving husband said. "You know where your heart and mind are at all times when you're competing, and how you love the stress of the competition. Just let God be with you, and let those implements fly when it's your turn. No worries about Claudia Jamison."

Jen knew he was right. She was getting herself all worked up for nothing. Tomorrow would be a brand new day, and a gold medal was calling her name. She felt in her heart that this was the meet that would grant her a spot on the Paralympic Team.

On the first day of competition, Jen qualified in the first round of the 60 and 100-meter track events, and her team also qualified in the swimming relays. She swam last and swam the backstroke. She had never been very good at swimming the breast or free stroke due to her paralysis of her throat and breathing problem, so backstroke it was.

During the evening hours, she and other teammates watched some of the other competition but went to sleep early. After telephone calls home to speak with her little guys, she and Mic slept like babies and were ready to go again when the alarm clock sounded at 6:00 am. They first had devotions and prayer together and then Jen would sign in for her appropriate events for the day.

Jen competed well, qualifying in every event, so she knew she would make it to the semi-final and, hopefully, the final rounds of competition. She hadn't kept track of what Claudia Jamison was doing or what her distances were in field events. She only concentrated on herself during the events.

She almost lost in the qualifying round of the shot put, her best event, when the straps holding her wheelchair in place broke loose. Knowing that she was allowed three tries, the volunteers strapped her in place once again, but this time the strap not only broke loose, but her foot also slipped off of her wheelchair footplates and dropped outside of the circle—another foul. Jen always put the shot put out with such power and vigor, that prior to the third and final throw, she asked if her coach could sit on the ground behind her wheelchair? He sat on the ground, placed his feet under her wheelchair on her small front casters and pulled back on her push handles. This way, hopefully, along with the strapping, she would not break free when she put out the shot put. This time it worked. She not only qualified, but the shot put landed within an inch of the national record.

Jen was elated. If she put it out there once, close to the record, she could do it again. She went back to the dormitory that night, convinced that tomorrow she would break the national record in the shot put and have a spot on the Paralympics team. God was good, as always He was right on track, and Jen thanked Him.

Chapter Sixty-Nine

*J*ill wondered how her friend, Jen, was doing in New York at the national competition, but didn't feel she should call her. She wanted her to concentrate on the games and not worry about Jill. Jill had called her to tell her about the twins, and they had gotten together before Mic and Jen left for New York. Jen had been almost as excited as Jill. Having had two boys a year apart had almost been like having twins—two sets of diapers, two who needed help eating, nursing one, potty training two at a time but most of all she had two bundles of joy. Jill would just get her babies at the exact same time and share herself with two tiny babies at once.

Jen did worry a little about Jill's capability of caring for two tiny babies. Even though Mickey wasn't walking when Ronnie was born, at least he was crawling, and he could entertain himself at times. Wheelchair mothers are very capable, Jen thought, smiling, but two babies at a time, whoa!! She wondered how Jill would do it? She'll have to have help, I'm sure, Jen thought to herself. Maybe, her mother will come from out East for a while or Lucas will take some time off of work.

In the first part of May, Jill and Lucas decided to start shopping for their two babies. Jill was feeling great, the babies were doing fine the doctor said, and so with credit card in hand, they spent a Saturday purchasing another crib at Sears, a twin stroller for Lucas, as Jill would most likely carry the babies on her lap—one at a time or two at a time—time and practice would dictate that, a changing table that could be lowered, and a multitude of diapers, nighties, undershirts, and blankets. Jen had promised to have a baby shower for Jill later on into summer, and hopefully the young mother would be showered with everything two little ones might need.

Jill planned to teach until the end of the year. She had put on one drama production already and was about to have tryouts for the last play of the school year—**The Sound of Music**. She had a talented group of seniors this year, and she wanted their last presentation to be their best. It was. For three nights in a row, the school auditorium was filled with families, friends and students, who gave a standing ovation to the senior class and to Jill Lopez. Everyone knew that Jill was going to take a leave of absence due to her pregnancy, but she had just recently shared with her principal that she was having twins. At the end of the last night's play, Jill was asked to stay on stage while her students and two of her co-workers presented her with red roses and a gift card for $500.00, to be used for her new babies. The entire staff had chipped in. There were hugs and tears, and Jill could barely speak. When she did, she thanked everyone, especially her principal, for giving her the opportunity to teach at Crested City High School, and she hoped and prayed she would be able to return one day. She shared how much she loved her students, and then the tears began again. In the back of the room, a tall, good-looking daddy-to-be in a cop's uniform was also wiping tears from his eyes.

Jen woke up on the last day of competition at the New York Wheelchair Games with a bright outlook, a smile on her face, hoping, no expecting, that this would be the day to bring home the gold. There were eight women in Class 4 competing for that same goal—one being Claudia Jamison. From viewing the leader board, Jen saw that Claudia had qualified in all three field events, but her distances weren't as good as Jen's. She was hopeful and prayerful as she pushed over to the competition area.

Jen, looking good in her Colorado uniform, signed in for her 10:00 am event and waited. She didn't always watch her competition, but today she would. She felt so confident, that no matter what distance any of the other women threw their implements, she knew hers would be better. She didn't feel egotistical, just confident.

After the first three women threw the javelin, Jen was strapped down to throw. All three of her throws were good, but she ended up with a bronze medal. Later in the afternoon, she threw the discus, and this time she did not place. She wasn't disappointed, as discus was not one of her better events. However, when her name was called for the shot put, she was ready.

All three puts were the best of any she'd ever done, and one, the last put, broke the national and international record in the Paralympics. Jen was beside herself. She didn't know whether to laugh or cry, so she did both. Her Colorado teammates applauded her efforts, as did several other competitors, including Claudia.

"Congratulations Jen," Claudia said. "We each got a gold medal, yours in shot put, and I got the gold in javelin. Perhaps we will meet again in England."

"England. England," Jen repeated over and over again. "I'm finally going to the Para Games."

However, it was going to take a little more effort and fight for Jen to actually make the Paralympic Team going to England in August. At the annual awards banquet, Jen's name never came up when the team selection was announced. She and everyone at her table were amazed, no surprised, no shocked, that Jen had not been picked. After the banquet ended, Mic took it upon himself to approach the director of the Paralympic Games. He introduced himself, said he was representing Jennifer Collins, and why, with her incredible games here at the nationals, was she not selected? Mr. Ben Larson, Director, admitted that he had no idea, that there may have been a mistake, and he would look into the matter immediately. It wasn't until after she had flown back to Chamberville, spent three nervous days sitting by the telephone that the call finally came. There had been an oversight, and Jen was definitely on the team. She would be competing of course in the shot put, plus the other field events, four track events, table tennis, swimming backstroke with the USA women's swim team relay event, and would be playing basketball.

The dream was finally coming to fruition. Jen's life-long dream of being a Paralympian had come true. She hung up the telephone, bowed her head and thanked her Lord and Savior. He had been her support system through all these years, giving her strength, both physical and spiritual. "Thank you, dear Jesus," Jen said, crying openly now. "Thank You. I pray that I can be of service to you in the coming months, and that I never, ever forget that you gave me the strength, the integrity and the will to compete." And then, at the last minute, she added. "And thank you for allowing me to have this disability."

Chapter Seventy

$\mathcal{J}$ill ended the school year with mixed emotions. She had thoroughly enjoyed her few years at Douglas County High, but now her life had taken on a completely different meaning—being a wife and future mother. She was anxious to be a mom but also very scared. She had been spending more and more time in prayer, asking the God whom she had really never known personally, to now be her best friend. He was. She and Lucas had been attending church on his days off, and since he had put in a transfer to Chamberville, they hoped to join a Methodist church in the Littleton area soon. He had already sold his place in the Springs, and they had moved all of his belongings into her home shortly after their wedding, but they enjoyed the Springs Methodist church so much that they attended when they could.

She planned to spend the first few months of summer working on her own life, her newly found spirituality, her marriage and her babies. She was steadily getting larger and had gained almost thirty pounds. It was getting more and more difficult to transfer into the Mustang, so Lucas did most of the shopping, running errands and taking her to her OB/GYN appointments.

Jill had never been a seamstress or learned to knit or crochet, but now she found that teaching herself came quite easily. She was knitting two sets of baby sweaters and booties, a matching baby blanket for each crib, and although she still had no idea the sex of the second baby, she was sure it was a girl. But just in case, she made both blankets pink, white and blue. She had always loved to draw and paint, so she was working on two wall hangings for the nursery, also in pink, white and blue. Her greatest feat however, was embroidering an 11x14 hanging of the baby prayer – NOW I LAY ME DOWN TO SLEEP. Her mother had sent her the kit, and she was enjoying this project more than anything. She would embroider in the evenings when she and Lucas watched television or listened to music together.

Jill had talked with Jen after her incredible week in New York, but they hadn't seen each other. Jen was so busy with her family and working out, and Jill was getting so large that she traveled very little, but they promised to see each other within the next two weeks. Jen also had to raise part of her entry fee for the Para Games and all of the money for Mic to attend. Mic approached his supervisors at the brewery, and they willingly worked to get the brewery owners to pay Jen's fee, and between parents and friends, Mic's expenses were also covered.

A challenge arose a few weeks after Jen's selection to the USA team. Mr. Larson called to say that Mic would not be flying on the same airplane with Jen. All team members, coaches and directors would be on one flight, and all family members would be on another flight. Mic was furious! Jen had never seen him like this before. He was even more furious when he found out that he would stay in a hotel in Stokes-Mandeville, England, and Jen would stay in the dormitories on the campus, ten miles away, with women from various countries. He had always been protective of Jen, but he had never been jealous or spiteful like this. He wanted to be with her on the trip and with no one else. He was adamant about it until, after speaking with his parents, Jen's parents and the pastor he calmed down, realized that rules and regulations were there for him and the other families to follow.

The Collins made arrangements for the boys to stay with one of the coaches who had not been selected for the Para Games. The boys were used to Mary and John and looked forward to staying with the older couple. Ten days was a long time, and Jen worried just a little about Ronnie, but she shouldn't have because all three boys did fine, only missing their parents every now and then.

A week before the team gathered in New York for the flight to Heathrow Airport in England, Jen's USA uniforms came in the mail. There were sweat suits, blouses, blazers and slacks, scarves, sweaters and more. The reality finally hit her. She was a USA Paralympian, and in seven days time, she would fly to England, meet with hundreds of other athletes and prepare to win her first Paralympic gold medal. The time had come. Jen was on her way. Her childhood dream was coming true. Once again she thanked the one responsible.

Chapter Seventy-One

$\mathcal{J}$ill and Lucas saw the Collins family two weeks prior to their departure. Jill had given Jen a beautiful silver cross necklace, along with a meaningful card and letter. The writings stated how much she loved Jen and her family and how much she appreciated her friendship and her help with her wedding, her pregnancy and, most of all, how much she appreciated her love for God and how she shared it so willingly with everyone she met.

Jen and Mic wished her and Lucas the best in the weeks to come, as well. Together, the four young people and the three boys, prayed for safe travels for Jen and Mic, and that if it was God's will, Jen should bring home the gold. In turn, they also prayed that Lucas and Jill's babies would be healthy and that Jill would go full term. After amen was said, Mickey wanted to know "why Jill's tummy was so big, and why were there two babies in there?"

Mic tried his best to explain about Jill's big tummy and that he had been a baby inside mommy once, and he seemed to be happy with the explanation. Jill and Lucas laughed and gave Mickey and all the boys a hug before leaving for home.

Jen promised that they would call Jen's parents when, not if, but when, she won the gold, and they in turn would call Lucas and Jill to share the news. Again the women hugged, said their goodbyes and went their separate ways.

On a Thursday in mid-August when Flight #2351 was leaving New York's JFK Airport with forty-six USA athletes, seven coaches and two directors on board, Lucas Lopez was assisting his wife into the Mustang for an unscheduled trip to Lutheran Medical Center, five weeks early. Jill was in labor.

Jen was having an incredibly good time on board Flight 2351. She and Mic had kissed and hugged goodbye at Chamberville International

Airport four hours earlier, and now she was bound for England. It would be an interesting flight. The coaches had three aisle chairs on board, so when athletes, who were unable to stand or walk needed bathroom facilities, they would transfer to aisle chairs, use the facilities, and get assistance back to their seats. Some athletes using catheter bags would empty them into containers at their seats, and the coaches would take them, empty them, clean them and return them to the athletes. This flight was just not about forty-six athletes vying for medals, but their personal needs and wishes as well. There were medicines to take, water and drinks to share, hot meals to serve, pillows and blankets to hand out, and with so many wheelchair users on board, the coaches happily helped out the flight attendants. The captain welcomed them all on board, the co-pilot handed out wings to everyone and Jen stashed her wings away, after asking for two more for her little guys back home. There were jokes told, songs sung, and after seven hours on board, silence reigned, as most tried to sleep. Eight hours after take-off from JFK, the USA team landed at Heathrow.

To make things easier, representatives from customs boarded the flight to check passports. After all were cleared, wheelchairs were brought up from the cargo area, athletes transferred to aisle chairs and then to their own wheelchairs. Racing wheelchairs, luggage, implements and other essentials were loaded directly onto semi trucks, and athletes, coaches and directors loaded into three school busses for the trip to Stokes Mandeville.

The USA team arrived two hours later at the site. However, after a serious mechanical problem on Fight 2384, Mic and the rest of the USA teams' families on board were just taking off from JFK. Mic wondered how Jen was holding up. Was she nervous? Was she worried about the competition? Was she missing him?

Chapter Seventy-Two

Jill tried hard to stay calm. She'd lost a lot of fluid, but had no idea if one or both of the babies' sacs had broken. All she could think of was the story of Jen losing little Timothy. Lucas spoke to her calmly as he drove cautiously but slightly over the speed limit to the hospital.

"The babies are only five weeks from being born," he assured her. "They'll be just fine, sweetheart, if they come now, and you'll be fine too."

Upon their arrival, a nurse immediately took Jill to the OB/GYN floor, helped her undress, took her vitals, listened for the babies' heart beats, and with assistance from another nurse, helped her onto the examining table. Jill was assured the doctor would be there soon. Lucas had called Dr. Patterson prior to leaving home, and his nurse informed Lucas that the doctor was already at the hospital delivering another baby.

"Jill will be fine, Mr. Lopez," she said. "Don't worry; I'll call Lutheran and a nurse will meet you, and the doctor on-call will see her right away. Dr. Patterson will be in to see Mrs. Lopez as soon as he can."

Within minutes of her arrival, the on call doctor examined her, asked her if she could feel the contractions, when did her water break, and told her that she was dilated to a three, and there was most likely no way to stop her premature babies from being born.

"These babies are ready to be born," he said. "I know they're early, and I know that you're worried, but, Jill, don't be, these babies are both over four pounds, and, although they will need some assistance for a few days, they will be fine."

He asked Jill if she could feel anything at all, and she said just a little discomfort every once in a while and some pressure with what she presumed were the contractions. The doctor assured her they would assist her in every way possible, and that she'd be told when to "push", since she couldn't feel the contractions, when the time came.

"We're here for you, Jen," he said, taking her hand in his. "Dr. Patterson has asked another of his associates to help with the delivery. Each of these little ones will have the best of care, and so will you. I have called for your pediatrician also to be in the delivery room. Now we just wait."

He asked if she needed anything and asked where her husband was. Was she comfortable, considering the situation?

Jill said she was fine, that Lucas was getting her admitted, and, yes, she was really okay. She lied. She was a complete wreck. She was worried about her babies, worried about how she would handle this delivery, and most of all she worried about Lucas. Neither she, nor her husband could handle any more "bad" in their lives, or at least she thought they couldn't. Jill took a deep breath, prayed a short prayer, and wished that her mother were here.

Lucas filled out all of the proper paper work and took the elevator to the 4th floor. As he walked to the nurse's station, he couldn't help but notice all of the darling baby photos lining the hallway walls. He smiled, then checked in at the nurses' station where he was told that Jill was doing fine and was being monitored closely, as were the babies. Dr. Patterson was still in delivery, but an associate had been in to see his wife. The nurse assured him that all was going well.

Lucas opened the door slowly to the pre-delivery room where Jill was lying. She reached out her hand to him as he came closer to the bed and began to cry.

"Come on, Jill, please sweetheart, don't cry," Lucas said, hugging her. "Everything's going to be just fine. These babies are just ready to be born, that's all. Don't worry Jill. Honest, I know everything is going to be okay. Please, don't cry."

Another contraction came and went, and an hour went by, then another and another. Around 1:30 am, the contractions finally started coming just a few minutes apart. Dr. Patterson had been in to check on her twice, and around 2:00 am, he told Jill that it was time. He wanted her in delivery and that her babies would be born soon. He also had the nurse start an IV, just in case the babies would have to be born by C-section. He assured her that one could be born naturally, and if there were any problems at all with the second baby, he could do a C-Section right away. If worse came to worse, he would take both babies by Caesarean, but he doubted that would have to happen.

As two surgery nurses wearing green scrubs came into the room, Dr. Patterson told Jill he would meet her in the delivery room, and Lucas was welcome to be there as well. Lucas had planned to be with his wife all along, but was pleased by the personal invitation.

Chapter Seventy-Three

$\mathcal{M}$ ic drove the short distance to Stokes Mandeville every morning around 7:00 am to be with Jill for a few minutes before the team meeting and before her first rounds of competition. He still wasn't happy about her being away from him, but he was trying to accept it. They'd been together the day before when the opening ceremonies had taken place. Prince Charles had officially opened the Games, and Jen had taken a lot of photos and also asked for and received his autograph. She was meeting so many great athletic women from around the world, and even some awesome athletic men. She knew that Mic was just a little bit jealous, but she assured him that he needn't worry. They'd been able to eat dinner together the first night and then separated, Lucas going to the hotel, and she back to the dormitories. The food was greasy and tasteless but at least they ate a meal together.

Jen had been told to pack cleaning products for the bathrooms at the dorms, as the seventeen women on her floor would have access to only two bathrooms and cleaning personnel were not an option. Each athlete took care of her own cleaning. The second day in England, she showered in a stall that definitely had not been cleaned earlier and was so thankful for the "heads-up" to bring cleaning products in her suitcase. She had scrubbed and disinfected everything before she rolled into the shower.

Meals were not a highlight, but she enjoyed the heavy cream on top of clear glasses of steaming, hot coffee each morning, and there was always Corn Flakes or Rice Krispies and toast, and some days fruit. Lunch consisted of cheeses, meats and breads, and maybe fruit. For the evening meal, there was always Fish-n-Chips or was that for **every** evening meal there was always Fish-n-Chips? There was no variety, just greasy Fish-n-Chips. On several occasions, Mic would bring her healthy food from town, or when Jen's daily competition was over, they would drive into town and eat a decent meal. The worst part of all was that there was no cold milk, nor was there ice for sodas or juice. Jen learned to adapt. She needed good food for energy, as her main consideration was doing her best in the shot put, her one, and her best chance for winning gold. She ate the food for energy, but definitely not for nutritional value.

On the third day in England and her first day of competition, Jill won a silver medal in table tennis and was rewarded with her silver medal on the platform alongside the gold medalist from China and the bronze medalist from the Netherlands.

"My first Paralympic medal, Mic," she had said, proudly displaying it. "My very first Paralympic medal."

On the days Jen did not compete, she watched all of her USA teammates. Several gold medals were already noticeable around teammates' necks and the women's basketball team had won two games and had four games to go. No one expected the USA women's basketball team to win gold. After winning one more game, then losing the next two, the women did win the bronze medal in basketball. Jen had played sparsely, but long enough to be knocked out of her wheelchair onto the floor once, and she had shot and made three baskets. She was proud of herself and very proud of her bronze medal. She loved being up there on that platform with the rest of her teammates.

Now, she just had to win gold.

On the sixth day of competition, having made the final qualifying rounds in javelin and shot put, Jen was fourth up in the final round. She anticipated not doing well in the discus throw., as she didn't like the discus throw, nor did she excel at it. Her coaches had been the ones to insist that she do all three field events in England. After her final three throws, she proved herself correct. She did not medal. But the shot put would be her final competition other than the swimming relay, and this event, she could count on. Shot put was her implement, her best event, and her best chance at winning gold.

After being strapped down to the steel plate in the ground, and as the pouring rain beat down upon her, she readied herself for her first put. She first closed her eyes and thanked God for allowing her to be here. She looked ahead of her, saw the small orange flag blowing freely at the international record placement marker (the record had not been broken in eight years), and was handed the shot put. She placed it in her right hand, grabbed the back of her wheelchair push handle with her left hand, looked up to the sky and with a grunt and a pull she let the shot put fly. The shot put hit the international record marker. She knew that if nothing else, she had tied the record. Her second throw was not as good, falling short of the record marker. When asked if she needed a few minutes before her final throw, Jen shook her head no, and said she was ready. Realizing what had happened in New York, however, she asked her coach to sit behind her (a legal request), push his feet against her wheelchair's front casters, and pull back against himself with his hands on her wheelchair push handles. Once again, Jen mentally, readied herself, said a prayer of thanksgiving, and let the shot put fly. As she pulled on the back of her chair, counting one…two…three…she noticed a small red bird flying high in the black rain-filled sky. She placed her eyes on the bird and with a grunt let the shot put out, as if to hit the free flying bird. The shot put soared like that bird and landed three inches past the international record placement marker. She had done it. She may not win the gold. There were still competitors waiting their turns, but she had broken the record set eight years earlier.

Three more athletes put out the shot put after Jen's world breaking put. Claudia came close to breaking the record, but the other two women were far from hitting her mark. Jennifer Collins had won the gold. Her teammates mobbed her, her coaches high-fived and congratulated her, and her husband kissed her, hugged her, and later brought her English style pink roses. She had done it. After years of dreaming about it, after years of working out and after years of praying and asking God for His guidance, His love and His signs, she had done it. She had first accomplished the greatest feat of all times—having a family, then, she had competed and accomplished what she thought was the second greatest feat of all times—winning a Paralympic gold medal.

At that very moment, she thought of her mom and dad, her brother, and her baby sister who'd died. She saw Mic and waved at him, then blew him a kiss, and as he ran over to hug her and congratulate her, she thought of Jill and Lucas. Something or someone told her—maybe it was God—that she needed to share her good news with Jill. Right now, this very minute, she needed to call Jill Lopez. Something was happening, something more important than her winning gold. Jen needed to make a call to the United States.

Chapter Seventy-Four

$\mathcal{L}$ucas sat with his wife until Dr. Patterson said it was time for Jill to move to the delivery room. Jill was taken to the delivery room where a C-section could also be performed if necessary. Jill wanted to try to have the babies naturally, but Dr. Patterson had mentioned earlier that one baby was face down and headed in the right direction, but the other might have to be manipulated into turning. In case of any problems, he would immediately do a C-Section.

Lucas was draped in a hospital gown and mask, and with video camera in hand, he waited for permission to stand at the far end of the delivery table, close enough to take videos, but far enough away not to be in the way of the medical personnel. The young couple earlier on, had decided they wanted a video of the birth of their children, vowing to keep it private and only sharing with their parents if they wanted to witness their grandbabies' births.

With no sensation, but being told when to push, Jill gave birth easily to a 4 pound 3 ounce boy. After cutting the umbilical cord and whisking the baby away, the medical staff prepared for the second birth. Keeping very close watch and making sure her cervix was not closing, the doctor carefully manipulated the baby girl so that she turned just enough to come, not face down, but face up into the birth canal. Jill asked if this baby was going to be okay and Dr. Patterson answered with, "no worries Jill".

After three more hard pushes and four minutes after the first birth, the second baby was born, a girl, weighing in at 4 pounds 7 ounces. The same process completed, the baby was immediately taken to the neonatal unit to join her brother. They were placed in incubators to keep them warm, and, Dr. Patterson, having finished stitching Jen up and watching her vitals closely, informed her that her babies were healthy, crying fiercely in the neonatal unit and waiting to see their mother.

"You did great, Jill," Dr. Patterson said. "You'll be able to see your babies soon, but first, let's make sure you're doing okay. I don't see any problems, but without sensation and with quite a few stitches, you'll need to refrain from sitting much for a few days. The nurse will give you instructions on sitz baths, and I think it's in your best interest to stay in the hospital a few days. Also, I think you'll be able to nurse those babies in a few days. You might want to consider pumping your breasts, and saving up milk for them. They may not be able to suckle for a few days without assistance of an artificial nipple over your breast nipple, but talk to the nurse about this, and pumping and saving your breast milk too."

Jill was exhausted but Lucas was floating on Cloud 9. He had finished videotaping when the baby girl was born, had sat himself down in the delivery room for a few more minutes, then left, tossed his gown and mask into a hamper, and went to find a long overdue cup of coffee. He waited about fifteen minutes, then headed in the direction of the neonatal unit. He held up a card with the name Lopez written in big bold letters at the nursery window and immediately a nurse pointed to the door, motioning him to come on in. She informed him, at the door, that the babies were still being weighed and measured, and he should wait a few more minutes to see them.

An hour went by, and Lucas was invited into the nursery. He was amazed at how many premature babies were in the neonatal ward. He walked by three incubators before coming to the two where his little ones were being tended to. It upset him at first to see how tiny they really were and lying only in a diaper. The nurse assured the new daddy that the babies were doing well, and that they were getting oxygen as a precaution and they were nice and warm. She also said that if the babies continued to do this well, their mommy could maybe hold them later that day.

"As soon as Mrs. Lopez is ready, her nurse will bring her here in a wheelchair to see the babies." She said, unaware of the fact that their mommy used a wheelchair for everyday life. "That will be after she's out of delivery and cleared to be up and about."

"Thank you, thank you very much," Lucas told the Neonatal nurse, and then asked, proudly. "Is it okay if I stay for just a few more minutes?"

The nurse said it was fine for him to stay and encouraged him to put his hand through the open side of the incubator and touch the babies' hands and fingers. Lucas did as was suggested, and a tear fell from his eye as he touched his little boy for the first time.

Lucas did the same with his beautiful baby daughter, told her softly that he was her daddy and that her mommy would be in to see her as soon as she was feeling better. Lucas left the neonatal ward and walked briskly to see if his loving and miraculous wife was in her room.

Chapter Seventy-Five

Jen, Mic and the entire USA team, coaches and families celebrated the next three days by touring London and seeing all of the surrounding sights. They visited Westminster Abbey, Buckingham Palace and on the final day, Mic carried Jen on his back, down seemingly hundreds of steps, in the Tower of London to see the Crown Jewels. Other than winning the gold medal, it was the highlight of their trip. They learned everything there was to know about the Symbols of the Monarch, and why they were so important to the British people. They picked up souvenirs, took more photos, and as Jen and Mic parted ways at Heathrow Airport for separate flights, Jen had her wallet, along with her passport and travelers' checks stolen out of her backpack. She had unzipped her pack, leaned over the back of her wheelchair to take out some cash, and before she could zip it back up, a lady brushed her slightly, said excuse me and in that instance the wallet and the thief were gone. Luckily, she was with an American Team and had no problem getting out of England. Her empty billfold was returned to her eight months later

As she waited to load onto the airplane for home, Jen thought about her boys. She and Mic had called them three times during their ten days away and had tried to explain to them about mommy's gold medal. Lennie was the only one who really understood what it all meant. They were anxious to see them.

Jen had tried calling Jill two days after winning gold, but there had been no answer. She'd left her a message sharing her good news. Looking at her watch, she realized that, although there was a time change, it wasn't too early to try Jill again. Once again, there was no answer. Jen wondered why Jill had her cell turned off, and since she didn't have Lucas' cell number, she left her another message.

"Jill, it's Jen," she said cheerfully. "I hope you're doing okay. I'm a little worried about you and those babies. We're leaving England in an hour, but call me when you have time."

She knew there would be little or no cell service on the flight, but as she boarded the airplane, she said a little prayer for Jill and Lucas. She'd had a strange feeling about her close friend for a couple of days, and although she presumed Jill was just away from her telephone, she still had a premonition that something was happening back home, and she prayed it was all good.

Jen needn't have worried. Jill Casey Lopez had everything under control.

Chapter Seventy-Six

At 3:00 pm, after sleeping a few hours, Jill cautiously transferred into her wheelchair for the trip to the neonatal ward. Lucas had told her how absolutely beautiful the babies were, but warned her how tiny they were, and about the oxygen, but for her not to worry; they were doing well. He also told her about the pink and blue blankets, and how he had touched them both, and how he had cried.

"I cried because I'm so happy, Jill." he said touching her shoulder as he pushed her wheelchair with the other hand. "And I cried because I'm so proud—so proud of you, and so proud of those two beautiful babies. God is amazing, isn't he?"

Jill made no comment as she touched her husband's hand on her shoulder, as she was choking back tears herself.

As Lucas held up the card at the neonatal ward window, a nurse motioned them to come in and met them at the door. She introduced herself and said she would be the babies' nurse for the next three days.

"You can come in to the ward anytime, Mrs. Lopez. Day or night, whenever you want to see them. In fact, I believe that Dr. Martins, your pediatrician, left orders that you can hold your baby girl, but should wait a day to hold your baby boy."

Jill looked worried for just a moment, but was assured that her son was fine, just a little jaundiced, and he needed to stay in the incubator for several more hours.

Jill admitted that she was scared. What if she dropped her, what if she made her cry, what if, what if, what if? Lucas gave her shoulder a gentle touch, and after the nurse draped her in a sterile gown and handed one to Lucas, she gently lifted the baby girl out of the warm incubator and placed her in Jill's arms.

Jill touched her sweet face, played with all ten of her tiny fingers, unwrapping the blanket to make sure there were ten toes, and when the baby started to cry, Jill gently laid her across her shoulder, patted her gently and soothed her as only a mother can.

Lucas walked the few steps to where their son lay, opened the incubator door, and after putting his arm through the opening, took his baby boy's fingers in his. He grinned widely as the baby gripped his daddy's finger. Lucas talked to him, told him about his mommy and his baby sister, and as he looked over to where his wife held their tiny daughter, he once again praised his Maker for his miraculous works.

Jill and Lucas spent twenty minutes with their new family, and after returning to Jill's hospital room and getting Jill back into bed, the young parents discussed baby names. They'd chosen two boys and two girls names prior to the delivery, but now they were sure the names would be Cameron Joseph and Christina Joy. A few hours later, when again they visited their babies, the names they'd chosen seemed to fit their children perfectly.

Jill had just finished her bathroom duties and was back in bed, when she checked the messages on her cell phone. There were eleven messages—one from her mother, one from her best friend at Douglas County High, and along with several other messages, there were two from Jen. Lucas had called her mother immediately after the births, but hadn't taken the time to call Jen and Mic. He knew they were in England, but still, he should've called them.

"What time is it in England," Jill asked Lucas, looking at the clock on the wall. "I really need to let Jen and Lucas know about the babies. You didn't call them did you?"

He apologized and said no, he was sorry he hadn't, and Jill said no worries. "You had other things on your mind today, daddy!"

Lucas chuckled and said that he wasn't sure how many hours difference there was in the time zones, but why didn't she try and get in touch with Jen, and he would take another quick run to the nursery to see their babies.

Jill laughed as she watched Lucas quickly leave her room, and as she hit Jen's number on the speed dial of her phone, she thought he would make a wonderful daddy. He had wanted children his entire life, and now he had them—two at once.

The telephone rang and rang, and when Jen finally answered, Jill was certain she had awakened her.

"Jen, it's Jill," she said happily. "Did I wake you up? I'm not sure where you are or what time it is. Are you still in England?"

Jen, said yes, they **were** asleep but that was okay. They had gotten into CIA earlier in the morning after having had little or no sleep on the planes all night, and then with the time change and three bouncing boys anxious to see there parents, they had gone to bed early and exhausted.

"I've been thinking of you, Jill," she said, now fully awake. "How are you? Are you feeling okay? I wanted to call you all week but things were hectic in England, hectic but exciting. I'll tell you all about it, but how are you and Lucas? How fat are you?"

Jen continued. "I'm kidding, Jill, but seriously, have you gained any more weight since I saw you last?"

Jill was so excited to tell Jen the news she could barely get it out, but Jen wouldn't stop talking.

"No more weight gain, Jen," she laughed. "In fact, I lost a bunch of weight today. We have two beautiful babies, Jen. A boy, Cameron, and a girl, Christina."

Before Jill could say anything more, she could hear Jen hollering at Mic to wake up, and now sitting on the edge of the bed, Jen said, "What did you say? Babies? You already had them?"

Jill told Jen, that Cameron and Christina were born prematurely at 2:37 and 2:41 am, told her their weights, how she had managed, how healthy they were, how Lucas was doing, and that everyone was doing great. When they hung up, both mothers had sworn to catch up more the next day when they'd both had some rest.

Jen was as excited, or maybe more excited than when she had her own babies. She was so happy for Jill that she started to cry. When Mic finally calmed her down and they'd talked for a while, he finally convinced her they needed sleep and **please** could they talk about this tomorrow? "Women. Women," he thought, smiling to himself.

Jen lay back on their bed, and although Mic was almost asleep, they thanked God for his love and grace, his power and his wonder. Two babies, Jen thought to herself. It seemed to her that winning a gold medal was nothing in comparison to the two new lives born today. God was good. His love was all empowering and all surrounding. How blessed Jill and Lucas were to now have a family. She fell asleep, anxious to hear more and maybe to see Jill tomorrow.

Chapter Seventy-Seven

Jill's mother came for three weeks. Mic's mother helped out whenever she could, and neighbors and friends brought in food, helped clean the house and ran errands so Jill could get some rest while taking care of her beautiful babies. Jen came over when she thought Jill needed a shoulder, gave her motherly advice now and again, and all in all, the Lopez family did incredibly well. Jill tired easily and no wonder, nursing and handling two babies was a large task, and doing it from a wheelchair was an even more difficult task, but like Jen, she managed.

When the babies were three months old, Jill and Lucas set a date to have them baptized at their Methodist church. They had visited the church several times, and prior to their wedding, they'd both joined. Now, they wished to have their babies baptized there. Lucas had been baptized as a child, but Jill had never been, so she planned to be baptized on the same Sunday as the children—it would be a celebration of life. They asked Mic and Jen to be godparents to their son and daughter, and Jill also asked Jen to be her sponsor. Jen shared her experience on how she had accepted Jesus into her life as a teenager, but since she had been baptized as a child, of course she didn't remember that time of her life. She just knew that her parents had dedicated her to God, had her baptized, and because of that she knew that she had always been, and would always be, a child of God. It only became real to her as a teenager.

"Even after my acceptance, Jen. I still struggled. I struggle with things in my life all the time, I just try to let God handle them, instead of trying to handle them myself."

Jen and Jill spent a lot of time together—Jen giving Jill assistance with taking care of her children, and Jill asking Jen for assistance with her Bible study and up-coming baptism. Jen shared scripture, her favorite verses with Jill, and camaraderie like no other began to knit these two women together for a lifetime: two women with husbands and children, but two completely different types of disabilities.

Upon Jen and Mic's return to the United States and after spending many days assisting Jill with her babies, her life changed drastically. As a gold medalist, she was in the limelight a lot, being interviewed by the news media, writing articles on the Paralympics for local, church and school newspapers, and speaking at least five times a month. She loved the limelight, and although she loved speaking, she realized that her family was suffering because of it. The boys were with baby sitters too much, she and Mic barely saw each other, and when they did, it was only to discuss family or financial issues. Something had to change.

After speaking at a local civic organization one evening, a guest approached her during the coffee break and made a sexual advance towards her. He told her how lovely she was, how much he enjoyed her speaking, but wondered if she could tell him more about her sexuality. He came right out, while taking her hand, and asked her what sex was like when you were disabled. Somewhat taken aback, and although she'd been asked these types of questions before from women, she realized she had never been approached in this manner by a man before! She pulled her hand out of his, answering that this was not the time or place to discuss this type of a question and moved to join in a conversation with another group of people.

As she drove home that night, she wondered if she might be coming across wrong, maybe she was appearing too "sexy", maybe she was the one asking for this type of questioning. Maybe her audiences wondered the same thing, and wanted to ask her the same type of questions but were afraid to ask. She knew she couldn't ask Mic about it. He would just get upset and tell her to quit speaking and then go on and on about their personal sex life, which of late was almost non-existent.

She called Jill the next day, and asked if she had some free time (crazy as that sounded), and wanted to come over.

"I'll bring lunch, Jill." she had offered over the phone. "I really need some girl talk time."

For over four hours, between diaper changes, nursing two babies, the telephone ringing and eating a little of their submarine sandwiches, the girls got their talks in. Not only did Jen get advice from Jill on her situation, but also Jill got advice from Jen on her problems. It seemed, several years before, a man had approached Jill too, just as the one had approached Jen the night before.

"One night, Jen," Jill began. "I went for drinks at a bar close to the center. There were five of us. This good-looking guy (as if that made a difference), came up to me, said I was cute and asked if I could have sex?

He added, that if I could have sex, he would like to take me out on a date. Before, I could answer him, I had a leg spasm, and since he was sitting directly in front of me, my foot hit him right in his privates!"

The girls roared with laughter. Jen asked her what the guy did next?

"Grabbed his "you-know-what" and left to tryout his charms on someone else I guess," Jill said, laughing so hard tears were running down her face.

Jen and Jill both agreed that some people, especially men, tended to believe that women who are attractive and use a wheelchair can't or don't have sex, and therefore their curiosity gets the best of them, and they just **have** to ask that question. No sex. No date.

They continued to talk about sex, or the lack of it in Jen's case, and as their time together ended, Jen realized that she and Mic had to make more time for each other, and the friends agreed to take turns, once a month, babysitting for each other's children. This way the couples could each have a "night out", away from their children—something, they both agreed was necessary.

It wasn't an easy task, with Mic's hours at the brewery, Jen's speaking career and taking care of her boys, and Jill nursing twins, but they made it a goal each month, and it worked. Jen wished, after a night out and lovemaking with her husband, lover and best friend, that all women in wheelchairs could have the lives that she and Jill had. No one, absolutely no one, had the incredible husbands that she and Jill had. The two friends were incredibly blessed with wonderful husbands who were also great daddies to their children.

Jen continued to do speaking engagements over the next several years, just cutting down on the number per month. She continued to play basketball and she stayed in shape. Four years after winning her first Paralympic gold medal, Jen was again, selected to the USA team, and she won another gold medal in her second and final Paralympic Games.

She had asked God for one gold medal, and he had allowed her to win two. She had run her race, she had kept the faith, and she had seen her dream come true. Truly, God was good.

On a beautiful, sunny Sunday morning in Littleton, Colorado, Jill Lopez received the gift of baptism, along with her one smiling and one crying baby. Loren, now Mrs. Joe Spencer, had flown in for the spiritual event with her husband and planned to stay for a week. Mic's parents were there, gifts in tow, and even Lucas' 89-year-old grandfather, wheeled in by a nurse from the nursing center where he lived, came to witness the event.

As the minister read the scriptures, prayed the prayers, and sprinkled the water onto each child (Cameron held by Mic, and Jen holding Christina), he re-read the scriptures and sprinkled the water onto Jill's forehead. There wasn't a dry eye in the church. Sunbeams shone through the church's' painted glass windows depicting Christ's resurrection and ascension into heaven, and those gathered surely felt the Holy Spirit entering their hearts.

A reception was held in the fellowship hall where the Lopez babies were passed around from friend to friend and grandparent to grandparent and finally as the day came to an end, Jen, Mic, Jill, Lucas, with their families sat down to reminisce. Jill, nursing Cameron while Lucas bottle fed Christina, shared her love for Jesus with her husband and best friends and told them all how truly grateful she was for having not only found the love of her life and her best friend in Lucas, but for finding Mic and Jen, too.

"It was a glorious day when I fell off of that mountain," she said quietly while her baby boy slept in her arms. "I would never have married Lucas or ever given my heart to Jesus. I also would've never—taking Jen's hand now in her own—never found my best friend."

Chapter Seventy-Eight

Jen returned home the afternoon of the baptisms, realizing once again how wonderful her life was. She recalled times when she had been doubtful, doubtful about what God wanted from her, and even doubtful at times about her marriage to Mic. He was such a wonderful man, but sometimes she wondered if there was more to a marriage than just a ring on your finger and a signed piece of white paper. She loved him and she loved her boys, but sometimes she wondered if she hadn't missed out on a part of her life by marrying Mic, by not dating more, by not "burning the bridges", as it were.

With Mic in bed for a few hours sleep before his shift, and after the boys were all bathed and settled for the night, she pushed into the kitchen, took a glass down from the cupboard, opened the door to the refrigerator and poured herself a glass of cold lemonade. She retrieved a pad of paper and pencil from off the kitchen table, rolled into the living room where, after setting her tea on the end table, she transferred from her wheelchair to the big red recliner. She loved this time of night when she could just "let down", although it didn't happen very often. She took a sip of the cold drink and began to write.

Earlier in the week, she had driven down a street in south Chamberville, and while stopped for a red light, she'd noticed a dilapidated old house with a rusty old fence around it. There were weeds and tall grass in the yard, and a rickety old wooden chair, but beautiful white and yellow daisies had bloomed and seemed to stand tall here and there among the weeds and tall grass. A few butterflies flittered and fluttered around, and as she watched, a thunder boomer hit, and raindrops immediately began hitting the windshield of her car. As she looked up onto the roof of the old house, a small bird flew over and then perched itself under the protective ledge. That scene had stayed with her the entire week, for what reason, she didn't know. But today, after the baptisms and just now after her thoughts about Mic and her marriage, that picture, lodged in her memory, came back again, and she knew she had to do something with it—something that would give her answers or some sense of calm and wellbeing for her life. Right now, at this very minute, she needed to write about it.

Jen took another sip of tea. She heard Ronnie cry out but just in case he fell back to sleep, she didn't move from the recliner, instead she continued to think and then write. She closed her eyes, picturing the iron fence and rusty old gate as the braces that kept her legs intact, legs that were useless but still an intricate part of her body, and braces that, if she could, she would tear from her body and run, run like the wind through all of those weeds, through the tall grass, and through the daisies. She would try to catch the butterflies and when it rained, she would throw her head back and catch raindrops in her mouth.

There was only silence in Jill's home. Ronnie must've had a bad dream for he was quiet, and the clock on the wall showed she had another hour before Mic had to go to work.

Her eyes closed, she once again thought, and then wrote down those thoughts.

She remembered a pastor telling her years ago that God had a calling for her, and that some day, when she least expected it, God would tell her or show her a sign, and she would know what that calling was. As Jen pondered that message over in her head and then pondered the memory of the dilapidated old house in her head, she continued writing and realized, that, although she could always wish to be a "normal" person, God wanted her to be disabled, that was His plan for her, and without it, she would never be the person she was now and would continue to be. No matter how hard she tried to be non-disabled, she would always be disabled—it was God's plan—that's what He wanted for her life. She could tell the remarkable story of her life, and the story of Christ in her life at the same time.

Jen continued to write and when she finished, she realized for the first time in her life, that God intended for her to be a wife, a mother, and an advocate for the disabled. She was a wife, she was a mother, and having worked with and counseled Jill in so many ways, she knew that her life as an advocate was just beginning. She would always need Mic in her life, the boys would always need him as their daddy, and together, they would somehow live the Word of Christ in their own lives, and Jen would spread the word of Christ as she advocated for others.

Her doubts, her fears, her life as of an hour ago were now changed—changed forever.

Jen laid the paper and pen on the floor beside the red recliner. She slid down to the floor, turned, and as she pulled herself up on the seat of the recliner, she balanced herself on her knees and began to pray. She thanked God for His goodness and thanked Him for His Son, Jesus the Son of God. She thanked Him for Mic and for her boys, and she thanked Him for showing her the way of life—the way she was to go from now on with Him guiding her the entire way. She had always known the Savior, but now believing had a whole new meaning, and she thanked Him and praised Him again for her disability. "Sure," she thought, "if I had the chance, I'd like to walk again, but, that's not in the Maker's plan, so I no longer need to push so hard to prove that it's okay to be disabled. I am who I am."

As her back grew tired and her balance gave way, she sat herself down on the floor and finished her prayer, choking back tears of happiness and joy.

"Father, God, I ask that you'll be with me from this moment on, that I'll be able to share your word and your love with a whole new meaning. That I'll be able to share what you have done for me with the entire disabled and able-bodied nation, for without you, I'm just another disabled person, disabled without a purpose. I know that I'll not always be ready and that I'll not always say the right things, so please, be with me every step of the way."

With her prayer complete, Jen pulled herself back into the recliner, sat for a few minutes longer, and then, noticing the time, transferred into her wheelchair, checked on the boys and woke Mic up for his shift.

Mic opened his eyes immediately, smiled at her, and noticing her red eyes, asked if she'd been crying.

"I have been crying," she said, kissing Mic on the lips. "I've been crying tears of joy, and I'll explain it all to you after you call in and tell your supervisor you have a bad cold."

"You're not going in tonight, Mic Collins," she said smiling. "Mrs. Collins needs you at home."

Epilogue

The bride, dressed in white satin, walked down the aisle on her father's arm to meet her husband-to-be—Mic and Jennifer Collins' third son, Ronnie. Lennie and Mickey were already married to wonderful young women and Mickey and his wife had blessed Mic and Jen with three beautiful grandchildren, and sadly, Jen knew that Lennie and his wife would never be able to have a child. She hoped that perhaps they would adopt, but that would be theirs and the Lord's decision to make.

Jen took her eyes off of the bride for just a second and looked at Mic, sitting next to her in the church pew. It seemed like only yesterday that they had repeated their wedding vows. She reached over, took his hand, and saw the proud look on his face.

"So many things have occurred in the past thirty years," she thought. "A few memories, of course I'll put aside, but so, many good memories to remember."

Mic continued to work for the brewery and coach children's bowling and soccer leagues and she couldn't recall how many middle school and high school sporting events they had attended, as all three boys had been athletic. Mickey still was. The three boys had also played musical instruments in their high school bands and had been active in the church. Together, Jen and Mic had taught Sunday school classes and had cooked for the church's Wednesday night youth club for over fifteen years.

Two of the boys had attended college and received their degrees. Mickey's degree was in Business Administration and Ronnie's in Graphic Art and Design. They both had good positions in local corporations. Lennie had struggled due to his premature birth, and suffered from ADHD, but with medication, he managed to control the disease, get his certificate of completion from a Diesel and Mechanic's School.

Jen was still employed by the local public school system, as a bookkeeper for the county's trade school. She loved her position and loved working with the teenage students. She had continued to speak about her Paralympic days and her faith and had run with the Olympic Torch when it came through Chamberville on its way to the Olympics in Atlanta, Georgia. She continually wrote articles for newspapers and had five poems published. She had been crowned Ms, Wheelchair Colorado and later became the state coordinator. She had convinced Jill to also enter the pageant, and she too had been crowned. They had both toured the state of Colorado doing speaking engagements, riding in parades, meeting with professional athletes and politicians—proving to both women that politics would never be in their areas of expertise. Jen would continue her fight for the rights of the disabled but never wanted to run for a political office.

Mic and Jen, both being avid sports enthusiasts, enjoyed the Denver Broncos and were season ticket holders. They attended all home games, rain or shine and during the really cold temperatures, Jen would bring a heating pad along to the games and plug into an electric outlet at their seats to keep her legs and feet warm. Several years after becoming season ticket holders, Jen wrote her first book, a history of the Broncos football club as seen through the eyes of the fan. It sold over 5000 copies, and she donated all of the profits to the local wheelchair sports team.

Mic and Jen had saved as much money as possible over the years and had sold their classic Chevrolet to purchase a station wagon for their large family. Later on they purchased a 1968 Chevrolet Corvette and restored it to its natural state. They enjoyed participating in car shows and traveling across Colorado with their Corvette Club.

As Jen watched her handsome son take his bride's hand in his own, she thought of how much she enjoyed being a mother. Granted, there were some tough times, especially with Lennie's seizures and ADHD and Ronnie's serious childhood allergies. As she moved her eyes from one son to another, she took an extra special and longer look at Mickey. Mickey had survived a horrible accident in his sophomore year of high school— an accident that could've or should've killed him. God had prevailed once again and Mickey was saved. He had been on a three-wheeler and had hit a tree head-on, breaking all the bones in his face several of his teeth were broken or missing and he had broken one arm and one leg. He had been airlifted to the local hospital and after many weeks and months in the hospital, rehabilitation and being home schooled, he returned to a normal life. God had indeed been good—again!

Jill and her family seated in the family-of-the-bride section of the church, not only had their eyes on the groom, but especially had eyes on the bride. Their daughter Christina Lopez was marrying Ronnie Collins.

The children had grown up together and although the Collins boys were a few years older than Jill's son and daughter, they had spent a good amount of time together growing up. They spent summers together hiking, fishing and camping in Mic's huge twelve-man tent and winters skiing in the Rocky Mountains. They bowled together and participated in different church events together. As the years went by the parents were certain they were seeing a growing closeness between Christina and Ronnie—not just the casual friendship they'd seen over the years. The parents were right. The two began dating when Ronnie was a senior and Christina was a freshman, and although a few changes had come about after Ronnie's graduation and they'd spent several years apart, they'd found each other once again.

Jill continued to teach English at a high school in the area and Lucas was still a highway patrol officer. They square danced with the same dance team as Mic and Jen and although Jen begged and pleaded with Jill to play basketball, Jill never did play the game after her accident.

Together, they had raised their two children in the ways of God and the church and hoped that their children's lives would be as blessed as theirs had been.

As the minister pronounced the young couple man and wife and the newlyweds walked hand-in-hand down the center aisle of the church, Jen glanced over at Jill, smiled and bowed her head to pray. She prayed for the new bride and groom, thanking God for his mercy, his kindness and love to them and to all of them. The families had been friends for over twenty-five years having first met on their honeymoons. Now here, in this beautiful House of God where they watched Jen's son and Jill's daughter take their vows and begin their own journey as husband and wife, the two families were together again.

As a tear slipped down Jen's cheek, she looked over once again at her best friend. Jill was also wiping away a tear. The two looked at each other and laughed.

As the two best friends exited the center aisle of the church, each on their husband's arms they asked themselves where life's journey might take them next. Only God knew. He had been in control all these years, guiding them to their husbands and guiding them to each other. There was really no need to ask where the journey might lead them. They would be contented to go wherever God sent them.

About the Author

$\mathcal{B}$arbara Roose Cramer moved to Denver, Colorado, from Iowa in 1951. She is married to Bill, her husband of 50 years, has three sons and seven grandchildren. She is a paraplegic due to polio and has used a wheelchair for 64 years. She is a paralympian gold medalist, a retired bookkeeper, an avid quilter and she and her husband are assistant managers at the Wilderness on Wheels outdoor disability center in Grant, Colorado. Barbara writes for magazines and newsletters, has several pieces of poetry in print and Child of Dreams is her third book.

CPSIA information can be obtained at www.ICGtesting.com
Printed in the USA
LVOW11s1958040814

397462LV00003B/5/P